SPRIT

D0452439

Please return / renew by date shown.
You can renew it at:
norlink.norfolk.gov.uk   6/14
or by telephone: 0344 800 8006
Please have your library card & PIN ready

NORFOLK LIBRARY
AND INFORMATION SERVICE

AMY & MATTHEW

CAMMIE McGOVERN

AMY & MATTHEW

MACMILLAN

First published 2014 by Macmillan Children's Books
a division of Macmillan Publishers Limited
20 New Wharf Road, London N1 9RR
Basingstoke and Oxford
Associated companies throughout the world
www.panmacmillan.com

ISBN 978-1-4472-3900-0

1 3 5 7 9 8 6 4 2

A CIP catalogue record for this book is available from
the British Library.

Printed and bound by CPI Group (UK) Ltd, Croydon CR0 4YY

For Mom and Dad

Who have, in their fifty-four years of marriage,
exemplified my belief that the truest love stories
start with being best friends . . .

UNSENT MESSAGE FOUND ON AMY'S COMPUTER
IN THE HOSPITAL:

You want the whole story, but you don't realize – it's impossible to tell the whole story. You probably think it was all about sex, but that's where you're wrong. It was about love. And you. Mostly you. Other people would look at me and think sex was impossible but love was not. Then it turns out, both are possible and also impossible.

CHAPTER ONE

Amy's emails started in late July and kept coming all summer.
Each one made Matthew a little more nervous:

To: mstheword@gmail.com
From: aimhigh@comcast.net
Subject: I'm happy!

I just slipped into my mother's office to look at the names
of my new peer helpers, and I'm so happy! Your name
is on the list! I thought maybe I'd scared you by coming
right out and asking you to apply. I realize it's an unusual
set-up, but try not to think of it as my parents offering
to pay people to be my friend. I know there's something
unsettling and prideless in that. I prefer to think of it this
way: my parents are paying people to *pretend* to be my
friend. This will be much closer to the truth, I suspect,
and I have no problem with this. I'm guessing that a lot
of people in high school are only pretending to be friends,
right? It'll be a start, I figure.

The note made him anxious, but still he wrote back to her:

To: aimhigh@comcast.net
From: mstheword@gmail.com
Re: I'm happy!

I don't mind, Amy. It's a good job, plus your mother says we might get community service credit. Best, Matthew

To: mstheword@gmail.com
From: aimhigh@comcast.net
Re: I'm happy!

Community service credit? For a paid job? I'm trying not to take this personally, Matthew, but does the job sound so onerous you should get both money and volunteer credit for doing it?

To: aimhigh@comcast.net
From: mstheword@gmail.com
Re: I'm happy!

Sorry, you're right. No, I didn't mean that. The truth is I'm very glad to do this job. I don't have a lot of friends at school, so I'm happy I'll get to know you and the other people working with you. Matthew

PS Maybe I shouldn't have said that thing about community service but, come to think of it, maybe your mother shouldn't have suggested it, either. I think we all got a little confused.

Already Matthew had a feeling this wasn't going to work out. The more he thought about it, the more certain he was it wouldn't. He'd known Amy since second grade, but he didn't *know* her. They weren't friends. He remembered her, sure, but he remembered a lot of people from elementary school that he wasn't friends with now.

To: mstheword@gmail.com
From: aimhigh@comcast.net
Re: I'm happy!

Why don't you have many friends? You seem pretty normal, right? I remember you having friends in elementary school.

To: aimhigh@comcast.net
From: mstheword@gmail.com
Re: I'm happy!

I have some friends, I guess. I was never all that good when it started to be about sleepovers. Those things made me nervous.

He wasn't sure why he'd written that. Being too honest was always a mistake — especially with someone like Amy, he was afraid. He had no idea what he'd say if she asked him why he had trouble with sleepovers.

To: mstheword@gmail.com
From: aimhigh@comcast.net
Re: I'm happy!

Why do you have trouble with sleepovers?

He didn't answer her question. He couldn't because here was the real question: why did she keep writing to him? He wasn't sure what she was doing this summer, but he assumed she was taking some college-level summer classes. He heard a rumour once that Amy took courses through UCLA Extension every summer, and had enough credits to start college a year from now as a second-semester sophomore. It probably wasn't true, but that's what he'd heard. There were a few stories like that about her.

After a week, he felt guilty for not responding and wrote this:

To: aimhigh@comcast.net
From: mstheword@gmail.com
Re: I'm happy!

Sorry I couldn't write back for a while. I got really busy. Can you believe school is about to start? I'm looking forward to the training sessions for this job. That should be interesting. Do you attend too? Your mother didn't say in her letter.

He sounded like a dork. Oh well. At least he'd written her back.

To: mstheword@gmail.com
From: aimhigh@comcast.net
Re: I'm happy!

No, I won't go to the training sessions. Why do sleepovers make you nervous?

To: mstheword@gmail.com
From: aimhigh@comcast.net
Re: I'm happy!

How did it go? My mother said you were there but you were pretty quiet the whole time and then you left early, which makes me nervous that maybe you've changed your mind. Please don't change your mind, Matthew.

To: mstheword@gmail.com
From: aimhigh@comcast.net
Re: I'm happy!

Matthew? Are you there? Please write back. My mom said you came to the training session today but she can't tell whether you're really interested in this job. She has her doubts. I told her to give you a chance. Everyone else is doing this to round out their college application. With you, it's different, I think. Maybe I'm wrong about that. But please don't quit.

She was right about this much: he wanted to quit. One 'training session' with Nicole, Amy's mother, talking about choking hazards and seizure risks was enough to make him feel like there was no way he could do this. *Seizure risk?* Just hearing that phrase made him start to sweat and wonder if he was having one.

At the end of the session Nicole made it clear: 'We're replacing adult aides with peers because this is Amy's last year of high school and she wants to learn about making friends before she goes off to college. This is her number-one goal for the year and we're hoping you all can help her achieve it.'

To: aimhigh@comcast.net
From: mstheword@gmail.com
Re: I'm happy!

Your mom has pretty high goals for your peer helpers. I'm not sure I'm cut out for this.

To: mstheword@gmail.com
From: aimhigh@comcast.net
Re: I'm happy!

What goals?

To: aimhigh@comcast.net
From: mstheword@gmail.com
Re: I'm happy!

She wants each of us to introduce you to five new people
a week. Does that seem like a high number? It does to
me, but then, as you know, I don't have a ton of friends,
so I'm not sure.

To: mstheword@gmail.com
From: aimhigh@comcast.net
Re: I'm happy!

PLEASE don't worry about it.

He *was* worried about it. Very worried. Now that he'd told
his mom about the job, though, he wasn't sure if she'd let him
back out.

'Wait a minute,' his mom said, after he told her he might
be working as Amy's aide one day a week. 'Do I remember
this girl? From sixth-grade chorus? Did she sit in a chair up
front and sing louder than everyone else?'

'Yes,' he said, embarrassed by the memory.

'And she waved her hands the whole time, like she

9

was conducting the audience?'

'Yes,' he said. This conversation made him think of a line Amy had written in one of her first emails to him. *I want you to tell me when I'm doing stuff wrong.* That request alone was enough to worry him: Where would he begin?

His mother clapped her hands and threw her head back, laughing like she hardly ever did any more. 'I *loved* that girl. I always wondered what ever happened to her.'

To: aimhigh@comcast.net
From: mstheword@gmail.com
Re: I'm happy!

Okay. See you at school. I'm not scheduled to work until Friday, which pretty much confirms that your mom thinks of me as the least promising of your peer helpers. I'm fairly sure she isn't saving the best for last. I think she's hoping someone else will show up between now and then. If that doesn't happen, I'll see you on Friday, I guess. . .

To: mstheword@gmail.com
From: aimhigh@comcast.net
Re: I'm happy!

Sorry to harp on this but why don't you like sleepovers?

CHAPTER TWO

The night before school started, Matthew lay awake in bed and tried to picture himself doing this job – walking beside Amy between classes, carrying her books as he'd only seen adults do in the past. Maybe it would work out okay, but it didn't seem likely. Because of her walker, Amy couldn't really walk and talk at the same time. There would be silences that could be excruciating. Until this summer when she'd emailed him, he'd never known she was funny and easy to talk to. But what good would that do if they couldn't talk? Not much.

Then there was Amy's mother, who had high expectations and obvious doubts about him. All through the training sessions Nicole kept saying, 'If you don't feel comfortable with any aspect of this job, please let me know,' looking straight at him as if she could tell he felt uncomfortable with pretty much all of it.

He'd only applied because Amy had written to him in July and asked him to. And that was such a surprise he couldn't think of any reason to say no, though he probably should have.

They didn't know each other, really. They'd only had that one conversation that he still thought of as horrible and awkward, though apparently Amy didn't.

Maybe it wasn't right to say he didn't know her at all. He still remembered the first time he saw her in second grade, and the speech the teacher made before she arrived, about how Amy might 'look different on the outside but inside she's exactly like everyone else'. Because the teacher didn't explain what she meant by 'look different', Matthew imagined a girl covered in fur, or wrinkly skin with bug eyes like Yoda. That year, Matthew had discovered the Human Freak section in the *Guinness Book of World Records*, and used to stare at pictures of the men covered in warts and the women with heavy beards. When Amy appeared just before lunch, inching into the classroom with her wheeled walker in front of her and an adult on either side, he was disappointed.

Mostly she *did* look like other girls. She had curly blonde hair that hung down her back and she wore a flowered pink dress. Sure, she couldn't walk without her contraption, but beyond that she had no particularly freakish qualities. Yes, her mouth hung open. Yes, she drooled enough to wear a bib most days – which was embarrassing, maybe – but she wasn't a *true freak* like he'd hoped. She was most interesting when she tried to talk at morning meeting, where everyone else sat on a carpet square – except Amy, who sat in a low, blue plastic rocking chair she sometimes fell out of. She never raised her hand to speak. Instead she rocked in her chair and squawked like something was caught in her throat.

'Oh my goodness,' the teacher said the first time Amy did this. She looked at Amy's aide. 'Is she *all right*?'

'She has something she wants to say,' the aide said.

They all waited while Amy's mouth opened and closed. No sound came out. A minute ticked by and finally the teacher couldn't wait any more. 'We'll let Amy gather her thoughts and come back.'

The next year they moved up to third grade, where the teacher, Mrs Dunphy, talked about Amy when she was out of the room. 'The doctors predicted that Amy would be a vegetable for the rest of her life, and look how far she's come! The most important thing for you all to know is that she's extremely bright with a very high IQ.'

This was news to Matthew, who was in the highest reading and math group. For the rest of third grade, Matthew waited for Amy to do or say something extremely smart. Maybe she did. Mrs Dunphy called on her regularly but the problem was, no one – including Mrs Dunphy – understood anything Amy said.

She spoke in a language that used no consonants, only a long string of vowels. Matthew tried to imitate it once, and sounded like he did when a doctor asked him questions with a tongue depressor in his mouth. Amy's aide understood a few words: *Bathroom. I need a break.* Some girls *pretended* to understand secrets Amy whispered in their ear at recess. They went up one by one, held their ear to Amy's mouth, and ran off to giggle on the bench. The joke was ended by a recess monitor who wasn't sure, but thought the game might be hurting Amy's feelings. Matthew overheard the conversation between two teachers. 'I thought Amy liked it,' one of them said. 'It's better than sitting by herself the whole recess, isn't it?'

'No,' the other woman said. 'They're making fun of her and she knows it.'

Matthew noticed that neither one of them *asked Amy*, which he supposed made sense. They all knew by then Amy wouldn't have answered with a simple yes or no. She never did. She had long, complicated answers for every question she was asked, answers no one ever understood. Sometimes Matthew watched adults pretend to understand Amy — laugh at one of her 'jokes' or nod at a comment — and he thought: *They look like the freak, not her.*

In fourth grade Amy started using a talking computer, programmed with phrases that required pushing only a few buttons for Amy to 'say' them. There was also a keyboard with a word-prediction program. At recess, all the kids gathered around and tried to get Amy's new computer to swear. Which made Amy laugh for ten minutes, then start to cry. 'PLEASE STOP,' she typed. 'NO. NO. NO.'

The talking computer changed how everyone saw Amy. She still drooled and was messy when she ate. Sometimes she got too excited in class and choked on her own spit. But now she sat with other kids in reading and math groups. They figured out that Mrs Dunphy was right the year before — Amy could read and spell, better than most of them. She wasn't the best math student in the class, but she was in the top three.

She had good control of the one hand she typed with, but the other went spastic at times and knocked over messy things like hot coffee and boxes of pencils. When she made messes, though, she wasn't punished like other kids, because she wasn't like other kids. Her clothes were different. So were the books she read and the shows she watched. So was the fact that she always had an adult beside her.

She's not really a kid, Matthew decided by sixth grade.

He watched her less by that point because he had his own problems by then. New ones that had cropped up out of nowhere and scared him a little. A voice in his head telling him to do things. Wash his hands twice before lunch, up to his elbows. Wash them again after lunch. His new fears were related – slightly – to his old fascination with bearded ladies and wart-covered men. Freakishness could happen to anyone at any time, he'd learned. Kenny Robinson lost half a finger in an accident with a boat-engine propeller. Now he pointed with his stump, which scared Matthew because lots of things scared him these days. A month before sixth grade started, his parents told him they were getting divorced, but he shouldn't worry because it was a friendly divorce and what everyone wanted.

It wasn't what *he* wanted, but he felt too scared to point that out, afraid if he did it wouldn't matter anyway.

In seventh grade, he and Amy had English together and once she asked him to help her print an essay. Because he was curious, he sent two copies to the printer and secretly kept one. It was a personal essay in response to the question: *What worries you most about the future?*

It was a terrible topic for someone like Matthew, who already worried too much. They'd spent the last two days in class reading one another's essays and offering 'feedback', which meant everyone wrote, 'Good job. I like your honesty,' on the bottom of everyone else's essay. Reading other essays, Matthew had learned that some people were too honest: 'What I worry most about in the future is getting fat.' Or else they tried too hard: 'I'm most worried about air and water pollution.'

Matthew, whose parents had got divorced the year before, thought of saying he worried most about his mother, who didn't do anything besides work, come home and watch TV. He didn't write about that because if he were honest and his mother read it she might get even more depressed than she already was. In the end, he wrote the only thing he could think of: 'I worry most about worrying too much.' After such an honest first sentence, he drifted into safe generalizations: 'We have grades to maintain, along with family responsibilities. Someday we'll have to worry about college applications and how we'll pay for college, if we can get in. After that, I worry about jobs and what the cost of energy will be.'

It went on like that for a few more paragraphs. At the bottom, most people wrote: 'Good job, but you might want to get more specific.' He wanted to see what Amy, who had more to worry about than the rest of them, wrote. Was it mean to think this? He wasn't sure.

Then he read Amy's essay:

I'm not sure I do worry about the future.

I don't know what lies ahead but I know I'm not scared of it. I'm in no rush to be an adult, but I suspect when I get there I'll discover it's easier than being a kid. There won't be so many ups and downs. Or crises that get talked about as if they're the end of the world. I think we'll all come to understand that there isn't any one big test or way to validate ourselves in the world. There's just a long, quiet process of finding our place in it. Where we're meant to be. Who we're meant to be with. I picture it settling like snow when it happens. Soft and easy to fall in if you're dressed right. I think the future will be like that.

Oh come on, Matthew thought. Was she *serious*? Was this a joke? Or – he had to admit this felt like a possibility – was she *completely crazy*? She could barely walk, she couldn't talk at all, and she wasn't worried about the future? It made no *sense*. It made him *mad*. Amy, who couldn't walk in snow, imagined a future that felt like falling into it?

Later, when the best essays got pinned to the board of the classroom, he read the comments she got: 'Oh my God, this is so amazing!'

'You are an awesome writer!'

Matthew felt small and stupid.

And then last year, at the end of eleventh grade, the whole school got to read one of Amy's essays when it was printed in *Kaleidoscope*, the school literary journal. Hers was the piece everyone talked about:

Lucky
By Amy Van Dorn, grade 11
When people first see me, they may not believe this, but most days I don't feel particularly disabled. In the ways that matter most, I believe I am more blessed by good luck than I am saddled by misfortune. My eyes are good, as are my ears. I've been raised by parents who love me as I am, which means that even though I can't walk or talk well I'm reasonably well adjusted.

I know that for a teenage girl in America, this is saying a lot. I don't want to be thinner than I am, or taller. I don't look at my body parts and wish they were bigger or smaller. In fact – and this will surprise many people – I don't wish I was fine. I don't pine for working legs or a cooperative tongue. It would be nice not to drool and warp the best pages of my favourite books, but I'm old enough to know a little drool isn't going to ruin anyone's life. I don't know what it would feel like to be beautiful, but I can guess that it makes demands on your time. I watch pretty girls my age and I see how hard they work at it. I imagine it introduces fears I will never experience: What if I lose this? Why am I not happier when I have this?

Instead of beauty, I have a face no one envies and a body no one would choose to live in. These two factors alone have freed up my days to pursue what other girls my age might also do if their strong legs weren't carrying them to dances and parties and places that feed a lot of insecurities. Living in a body that limits my choices means I am not a victim of fashion or cultural pressures, because there is no place for me in the culture I see. In having fewer options, I am freer than any other teenager I know. I have more time, more choices, more ways I can be. I feel blessed and – yes – I feel lucky.

Reading it the first time, Matthew felt angry all over again. Surely she didn't *really* feel this way? He thought about her seventh-grade essay where she said she wasn't worried about the future. Here she was again – the unluckiest person he could imagine – saying she felt *lucky*? It had to be an act.

But he wanted to know: Why did she work so hard at it?

In English, Ms Fiorina, famous for wasting class time discussing issues that were never on any test, asked what people thought of Amy's essay. Because Amy wasn't in their class, they were honest. One girl raised her hand. 'It made me want to cry. If I had her problems, I'd probably kill myself.'

'Maybe that's a little extreme, Paula, but that's her point, right? When you're a teenager, being different – if it's not

18

by choice – seems like the worst thing imaginable. But is it really?'

'But she's not just different. She can't *talk*.'

'I saw her choke once,' Ben Robedeaux said without raising his hand. 'It was really weird. She fell out of her chair and had like this seizure.'

Matthew was surprised. He'd never heard that story.

A few minutes later Matthew raised his hand. Usually he didn't participate in these discussions, but this time he had something he wanted to say. 'I've known her a long time and I don't think she really feels this way. She wants everyone to have this image of her as happy and well adjusted. I just don't think it's true.'

'*Interesting*,' Ms Fiorina said, looking up like what he'd said really *was* interesting. 'But is that a bad thing? She's a person with a disability conveying the message, *Hey, my life isn't all tragedy*. Do we hear that message enough?'

'But it *is* a tragedy,' a girl in the back row said. 'I mean, I'm sorry, but it *is*.'

'Explain what you mean, Stacey.'

'She can't *talk*.'

'But she communicates, right? She writes beautifully and some of you have had classes with her. You know her pretty well. Matthew says he doesn't think she's telling the truth. Maybe he knows something the rest of us don't.'

Matthew felt terrible. He didn't know, of course. He only knew Amy after years of watching her from a distance. That year he sat behind her in biology and had discovered a few new quirks to her body. The left side was more disabled than the right. Her floppy head made her look worse than she was. He learned to interpret the sounds she made. He knew she loved the cell unit, because she squealed every time the overhead projector with 'Parts of the Cell' came up on the screen. She also liked genetics, but not physiology. On frog-dissection day, they both let their partners hold the knife — Amy for obvious reasons, Matthew for less obvious ones.

The next day in biology, Amy surprised him by turning round at the end. 'COULD I TALK TO YOU AFTER CLASS?' her computer said.

He'd heard her automated voice often enough in class discussions, but it still scared him. 'Okay,' he said, looking down at the floor.

When they got out to the hallway, Amy pushed a single button to play a preprogrammed question. 'WHY DID YOU TELL PEOPLE MY ESSAY WASN'T TRUE?'

'I don't know,' he said, breaking out in a sweat. 'Because I don't believe it. I don't believe anyone could be so well adjusted.'

She typed. 'WHY NOT?'

'You said you look at your friends' lives and feel like your own is better, which is fine, except that you don't have any friends.'

'HOW DO YOU KNOW THAT?'

'I sit behind you. I notice things.'

'WHAT KIND OF THINGS?'

'It's not your fault that you don't have any friends. You always have an aide with you. No one is going to be themselves when there's a teacher standing right there. Plus, you talked about parties and dances, but I don't think you've even been to any, so how would you know what you're not sorry to be missing?'

He kept going. He started saying too much, telling her all the things he'd noticed – that she never said hi to other kids, that she never answered questions when people asked her things before class. 'I'm not pretending I'm Mr Popularity or anything. I'm just saying you've got this whole message that doesn't seem believable. To me, anyway.'

'I CAN'T BELIEVE YOU'RE SAYING THIS.'

Her facial expressions were impossible to read. He couldn't tell how mad she was. Probably pretty mad. 'I'm sorry. You're right. I shouldn't have said anything. It's none of my business. Like, none *at all*. I don't know why I just said all that. I had this theory that you're trying to be a certain kind of person, and that must be hard. But, God, I'm hardly one to talk. So let's forget the whole thing. Please. I'm sorry.'

It startled him when her machine blurted out a single word. 'NO!'

'No what?'

'DON'T BE SORRY. YOU'RE RIGHT. MY GOSH, I CAN'T BELIEVE HOW RIGHT YOU ARE.'

CHAPTER THREE

Everything changed for Amy after that conversation with Matthew.

For most of her school life, Amy had felt a little like Rapunzel, locked in the tower her walker created when she walked down hallways. In eleven years, no one had ever called up to her window or asked for her hair. No one had ever tried to be her friend.

Impossible, you might say. *Everyone has* some *friends*.

No, Amy would have to say. *Not everyone*. It *was* possible to spend a decade with the same children – from kindergarten through eleventh grade – and never receive a phone call once, though your number was listed every year in the directory. It was possible to have a mother who tried for years to schedule play dates with other children of mothers who never called her back or did so with apologies and talk of impossibly busy schedules. It was possible to be partnered on a school project and watch others build a Pueblo Mesa out of brown-painted mini marshmallows, a project you were never, in two weeks, allowed to touch.

Most surprising of all: it was also possible – for eleven years! – not to see this as a problem.

Or to put it another way: it was possible to believe that the adults who loved her – the teachers, therapists and aides who laughed at everything Amy said – counted as friends. It was possible to feel their love so strongly that she lived in oblivious happiness for over a decade.

Then Matthew came along and pointed out the holes in her thinking. He stood in front of her and told her he'd come not to climb her tower but to shatter it. In his clumsy way, he was like a prince who arrived with sweaty armpits and bad hair. *At least I'm here*, he might have said. *That's better than nothing.* And it was.

The very same day that she talked to Matthew, she went home and made some decisions: it was too late to do anything about it that year. But next year – her senior year – would be different. She would make friends before she graduated. She would look at her life with a more critical eye.

When he'd insisted that she couldn't be as happy as she pretended to be in her essays, he'd said something she'd never considered. *You don't have any real friends because no one acts like themselves around you. You're always with an adult.* For years Amy had blamed her lack of peer friendships on any number of factors: typing was slow. She'd try for a joke that came out five comments too late to be funny. She was too clumsy to play at recess, too messy to eat lunch with, too slow to keep up. Until Matthew pointed it out, though, this idea never occurred to her: *Being with you means being with a teacher.*

It was so obvious, she wanted to laugh. *Get rid of the adult and you might make some friends.*

That conversation opened up electrifying possibilities in her mind. Just because she'd never had friends didn't mean she wasn't interested in her classmates. Since she'd started middle school, she'd developed a habit every year of picking a different handful of peers to spy on and keep track of. Usually she picked one surly type (a troublemaker to see how much trouble they got in); a do-gooder (to see if their phoney persona broke down); a boy she might have had a crush on in a different life; and a shy girl like herself (or the person she would have been if she could walk and talk). She memorized their schedules and their lockers. If they were in a play, she went for the uninterrupted two hours she could spend watching them. So far as Amy knew, no one she'd kept tabs on knew what she was doing. Of course, she'd never talked to any of them, so she couldn't be sure. Which was why that conversation with Matthew floored her.

The shock wasn't his saying such unpleasant truths out loud. The shock was his saying, *I've watched you over the years.* She couldn't help it; she blushed.

Then he kept going: *You don't even try to talk to people. You walk past them without saying hi. You don't answer questions. You laugh when no one is making a joke.* He pointed out every social failing she had. Ten years without practice had left her with plenty. It didn't embarrass her to hear it; it thrilled her.

He's just like me, she thought. *He does the same thing.*

Matthew had never been one of her chosen people before, but he could have been. He was, for the remainder of their junior year. Until she decided she wanted more for next year. She wanted to make some friends. She wanted to get to know Matthew.

The law mandated every child with a disability have equal access to the same education all children had, meaning that — to some extent anyway — an aide had to do whatever Amy needed. They bubbled her answers on Scantron tests, changed her sanitary pads, helped her get in and out of the bathroom with a minimum of fuss. But that conversation with Matthew helped Amy say something she wanted to tell her mother for months. '*I DON'T NEED SOMEONE ALL THE TIME.*' Amy took class notes herself and kept her own schedule. She needed someone in between classes to carry her books and charge her battery pack, but, in class, not so much.

Her idea had a beautiful simplicity at first. She approached her mother a week after school ended. 'WHY DON'T WE HIRE STUDENTS TO WALK ME IN BETWEEN CLASSES?' They could get trained on charging her battery and other details. Girls could help her with the bathroom; they had in the past. Boys couldn't, of course, but that wouldn't matter. She could drink less on those days and improvise more. Having had the idea, she wanted to make it clear to her mother: boys should be hired too. 'WE'LL SET A SCHEDULE AND ROTATE. MAYBE WE'LL MAKE EATING LUNCH PART OF IT SO I'LL MAKE SOME NEW FRIENDS.'

For years Amy had eaten her yogurt-and-hummus lunches in the Sp-Ed teacher's resource room. Fine for the dribbling girl who had to wear bibs because she still dropped food all over herself, but now she was better. She could eat simple things in front of other people. Her stomach danced at the thought. She could eat in the cafeteria! All they had to do was pay people to sit with her!

Her mother hated the idea at first. 'You don't know how self-absorbed teenagers can be. They'd have a test one day or break up with their boyfriend and forget all about you.'

'WE COULD HAVE A SUBSTITUTE LIST. WE'LL

TRAIN LOTS OF PEOPLE. AND PAY THEM MORE THAN THEY MAKE AT McDONALD'S.' Amy had once overheard two girls talking about how much they hated their jobs at McDonald's, with the terrible uniforms and the rude customers.

'You don't *pay* people to be your friend, Amy. I don't like what that suggests.'

Amy pressed harder. 'KIDS NEED JOBS. I HAVE ONE THEY CAN DO.'

As it turned out, nothing was as easy as Amy imagined. The school said they would only pay for a 'trained paraprofessional', but if her parents were willing to cover the salaries and sign a waiver they would try the idea as an experiment.

Over the summer, Amy drew up a schedule where people worked a total of two hours a day, three if she stayed after school to join a club.

'A *club*?' her mother groaned.

'THAT'S MY GOAL. I WANT TO JOIN A CLUB AND MAKE TEN FRIENDS.'

Nicole loved goals. She loved evidence-supported theories and data-driven techniques. Say the word *goal*, Amy knew, and her mother would be looking to check it off.

At least this used to be true. This time, though, her mother surprised her. A shiny line of tears appeared in Nicole's eyes. She shook her head. 'Did we make some terrible mistake? Did we not prioritize socialization enough?'

Yes, Amy wanted to type. *We never prioritized it at all*. Not when academic successes came so easily. Why bother with friends when there were As to earn and state-mandated tests to ace?

Why bother with movie outings when Amy had such a knack for languages that her French teacher once joked that she'd be non-verbal, but fluent in three languages before she graduated? Amy filled every summer with extra courses and reading because it never occurred to her she had any other options. 'YES, MOM. I NEED TO MAKE THIS A PRIORITY.'

She thought about Matthew, a little taller than her, with freckles and curly, dark brown hair that fell in his face, sweating as he argued his point: *You're not really lucky. Get out more and you'll see. It's a hard life out here.* She almost laughed out loud remembering it, and then had to catch herself. Her mother would hate this being another person's idea. *You're not like other children*, Nicole always said. *You don't need to act like them, so please don't.*

A far better argument, Amy knew, was this: 'IF I'M GOING TO GO TO COLLEGE, I NEED TO PRACTISE RELATING TO PEOPLE MY AGE.'

College had always been the number-one goal. Ivy-covered walls. Dorm mates. Nicole had talked about it since Amy was in elementary school. 'You might be right,' her mother said. 'This might be more important than I thought.'

Over the summer, a letter was mailed by her guidance counsellor to a small group of handpicked students, mature enough for such a job. When response was low, another letter went out to a wider group, including all student council members and everyone in the leadership society, meaning anyone with a B-plus average or better.

That was when Amy first wrote to Matthew and urged him to apply:

I promise you won't have to do anything embarrassing. I want you to apply because I want someone who will talk to me honestly about things. You're the only person who ever has. Maybe you don't know this, but when you're disabled almost no one tells you the truth. They feel too awkward because the truth seems too sad, I guess. You were very brave to walk up to the crippled girl and say, essentially, wipe that sunny expression off your face and look at reality. That's what I want you to do next year. Tell me the truth. That's all.

   Amy

CHAPTER FOUR

That whole first day of school, Matthew was grateful that Amy's mother hadn't liked him enough to put him on duty from the beginning. He saw Sarah Heffernan, one of Amy's other peer helpers, from a distance, standing outside the bathroom holding two backpacks and looking uncomfortable. The next day, he saw Sanjay Modhi, another peer helper, leave Amy alone for most of lunch period in the cafeteria. Matthew told himself he'd never do anything like *that*. He'd spent enough time miserable and alone in the cafeteria not to let that happen to Amy.

The problem (or *one* of them anyway) was expectations. Matthew couldn't figure out what to expect or, even worse, what Amy expected of him. When he read that first email she wrote him in July, he thought, *She's wrong again, about pretty much everything.*

He wasn't brave. He was the opposite, actually. He was afraid of everything and had been for years. The worst of his fears started in sixth grade and only got worse in middle school when everyone, seemingly overnight, changed. Boys grew four inches over the summer and girls came to school dressed like their older, slutty sisters. Matthew hated all of it. The talk about shaving, the visible bra straps. The voice in his head came back, louder this time and more insistent. *Wash your hands. Like a surgeon, to the elbows.* By then it made him check faucets too. *Make sure they're off. Just double check.*

Counting made him less nervous. Twenty-four steps from

the bathroom to math class. Thirty-six chair desks, four left-handed. Counting was a relief. Almost a pleasure. A way to measure and contain a world that otherwise spun too quickly for him. He thought of his brain as divided. One half understood that counting had no bearing on his parents or his life. The other half hoped maybe it did. Gradually, that first year in middle school, he began to understand – there were many ways to be a freak. Amy had no choice, but other people did. If you worked hard and concentrated, you could hide your freakish thoughts. You could keep the same handful of friends you'd had since third grade. You couldn't push those friendships too far or sleep over at anyone's house when there were night-time rituals to worry about, but you could look okay.

That's what he assumed.

In eighth grade that changed again. Steven, his best friend, moved away, leaving Matthew with no one to eat lunch with. Sitting alone beside the trash cans, his fears grew worse. He went to see a guidance counsellor and told her about his worries, though he didn't get specific or mention the voice. He also said nothing about the deals he made with his brain.

The counsellor reassured him by saying there were other students like him. 'You're just anxious, that's all.' She told him to think of his mind as a Worry Wheel with three parts – an anxious mind, anxious body and anxious actions. She said an anxious mind got the Worry Wheel spinning, and an anxious body kept it going until anxious actions made it spin out of control. She talked about breathing and visualizations and 'calm-body' tools. She told him some people squeezed their fists to release the tension from their body. 'Yo-Yo Ma does this,' she said. And some basketball players, whose names she couldn't remember, before they took free throws. 'Believe it or not, everyone gets anxious,' she said. Did that mean Yo-Yo Ma went to the bathroom six times a day to make sure he didn't have skid marks in his underwear? Did Shaquille O'Neal say *excuse me* seven times if he farted?

Amy might have called him brave in that email, but he was afraid of everything about Amy, especially her body, which had the terrible problem of being crippled *and* attractive. He wondered if other people noticed that too. In ninth grade, she grew her curly blonde hair long like some princess in a fairy tale, and she was pretty now, in a bent, crooked sort of way. That was also the year she grew boobs. Did other people notice that?

The other problem with expectations was that Amy's mother made it pretty clear what hers were. 'As long as we're prioritizing friendship building, I want to be scientific about it,' Nicole had said in their first training session. 'We're going to ask that each of you introduce Amy to three new people a week. Keep track of the names and give them to me so I can keep a central database. We'll also ask that each of you invite at least one other person to join you when you eat lunch with Amy.'

At that first training session, there were four peer helpers, all seniors, all people Matthew knew vaguely. Sarah Heffernan was a girl he'd had a crush on in ninth grade because her mother died around the same time Matthew's father remarried, which meant they were both sad and quiet most of that year. He'd never talked to Chloe McGlynn before, mostly because she hung out with a Goth crowd and wore motorcycle boots to school and he'd always been scared of her. Now, mysteriously, she wore a green Izod shirt and khaki shorts and seemed to have left her Goth days behind. He'd gone to preschool with Sanjay Modhi, though twelve years had passed and they hadn't spoken since then. Apparently Sanjay had worked at Hot Dog on a Stick over the summer, where the uniforms were striped polyester and included a mustard-coloured baseball cap. 'No surprise why I'm here,' Sanjay said when Ms Hynes, the guidance counsellor, asked them to introduce themselves and say why they were interested in this job.

Because Amy wasn't there, apparently they all felt free to be honest. Chloe said her boyfriend, Gary, had been arrested in July, and she was trying to turn her life around. 'Like, I pretty much have to change everything. My friends, my focus, everything. I guess I'm hoping doing this job with Amy will help.'

On her turn, Sarah said, 'I'm here because I loved that essay Amy wrote. It made me want to get to know her better and find out how she got to be such a good writer.'

Nicole smiled and nodded. 'That's wonderful. Thank you, Sarah.'

Matthew was the last to speak. He felt his throat close up before he could start, like his brain was spinning cotton and stuffing it in his mouth. He coughed a few times and counted the empty desks in the room. 'I don't know Amy,' he finally managed after a silence that felt excruciating. 'But I would like to.' *Good enough*, he thought, stopping before he did something horrible like throw up on his shoes.

They spent most of that first training session going over how Amy's talking computer worked. They learned about preprogramming what she might say in class if an idea was complicated or too long to type in while everybody waited. They learned about battery packs and which bathrooms were best for Amy to use in school. They learned how much weight she could safely carry herself (almost none) and how to read her body's signals of overexhaustion: facial twitches, spasming, louder vocalizations. But mostly Nicole talked about expanding Amy's 'friendship circles'.

'We know friendships don't happen because you've been introduced to a person or eaten one lunch together. We're looking for a start. For eleven years, kids have been unsure about talking to Amy. They see that walking is hard work for her and they don't want to interrupt. With all these introductions, we're hoping to convey the message: "Go ahead! Interrupt her! She wants to get to know you!"'

Chloe raised her hand. 'When we're making these introductions and giving you the names, should we make some distinction between who we think Amy *should* be friends with and who she shouldn't bother with? Like, should we put a star by people we know are jerks?'

Sanjay laughed so hard one of his flip-flops fell off.

Chloe shot him a look. 'Well, I'm sorry, Sanj, but we all know some of my friends aren't model citizens. I'm just being honest.'

'No, I appreciate that,' Nicole said. 'Chloe has a good point. We want Amy to find people she shares common interests with. But we also want Amy to get a little practice deciding for herself who the jerks are.'

Matthew was less worried about the quality of people he could introduce Amy to than how quickly he'd run out of names he knew. He imagined himself in any of a dozen awkward scenarios. With someone whose name he thought he knew but wasn't sure. ('Amy, this is Vic or Nick; I've never been sure.') Or someone whose name he knew perfectly well – an athlete or a cheerleader – who had no idea who Matthew was or why this introduction was taking place. It was a big high school, sixteen hundred students – every year Matthew got the exact numbers within the first week – which meant some people were well known and an equal number unknown – a beige, amorphous mass. Ever since the worst of his troubles had started, Matthew worked hard to be part of the latter group. Unnoticed. Unseen.

He rarely talked in class. So rarely, in fact, that his comment in English at the end of last year might have been the first thing he said all trimester. (Before that day, the room had made him too uncomfortable – with an odd number of everything – desks, ceiling tiles, blackboards, file cabinets. Usually he sat there counting things he knew would come out even. Feet! Hands! Windowpanes!) Amy's essay was an exception because it had been on his mind anyway. He'd been sitting there that day counting, quoting Amy, counting, quoting Amy, when he realized the subject actually *was* Amy. He'd raised his hand.

That was how he'd got here, readying himself for a job at which he was fairly sure he wouldn't last a full day.

CHAPTER FIVE

Amy had another reason for pushing the idea of hiring peer helpers for this year. In June, her parents had bought her the newest edition of the best communication device she'd ever had, a Pathway2000 that was infinitely faster than anything she'd ever used before. By the end of fourth grade, Amy had mastered Minspeak and, later, Unity, the code languages of speech devices that condensed the work of typing tenfold, but this new model was more flexible and faster than anything Amy had ever had before. It remembered her favourite expressions, learned the rhythm of her sentences and anticipated responses with amazing accuracy. It also had something she'd never found in a speech-output device before: an honest-to-God human-sounding voice. For years she'd never understood why these devices could include wireless capability, Bluetooth connection, 3G internet access, and still make a girl sound like Stephen Hawking. With her new Pathway, it was different. Programmable as the beautifully simple 'teenaged girl', she sounded exactly like – well, what she was. She wondered if this was what someone with a new sports car felt like: if they wanted to test-drive the power it had, to see if flashy things could really change your life.

For the first three days of school, Amy discovered the answer was, sadly, no.

Even with the beautiful new Pathway at her side, walking down halls with a peer helper turned out to be exhausting and awkward. With adult aides, Amy could be quiet; with a peer, she could not. She spent most of her class periods trying to think of things to say, and couldn't believe how quickly she ran out of ideas. She ended up complimenting arbitrary pieces of clothing. She told Chloe she liked her shirt twice.

The worst part turned out to be the one she was initially most excited about: eating in the cafeteria. After all these years of hiding away for lunch in resource rooms and teacher offices, she thought it would be so thrilling to sit in the cafeteria like everyone else. But the cafeteria was louder and more crowded than she expected. For her first lunch, she sat with Sarah at the end of a table full of girls who said hi when Sarah introduced her, then nothing more to Amy or Sarah for the rest of the meal. Mostly the girls complained about the trips their parents had forced them to take over the summer.

Afterwards, even Sarah felt bad. 'That's what those girls do. They complain about stuff the rest of us don't have. I don't know why I'm even friends with them.'

Her first day with Sanjay, Amy spent most of lunch period with her cooler from home, waiting at a table while he bought his lunch from the cafeteria. When he finally emerged with a tray, he sat down with other people as if he'd forgotten all about her. A few minutes later, he ran over. 'Amy, I'm so sorry. I'm over here. I have some people who want to meet you.'

Her foolish heart leapt. *They do? Really?* She walked over, thinking they might compliment her essay from *Kaleidoscope*, but no. They were the second tier of the football team, even less interested in Amy than Sarah's crowd had been.

At least Chloe hadn't bothered sitting with other friends.

'I pretty much hate everyone at this school,' Chloe said. 'I'm sorry, but I do.'

Thursday night, Amy came home shaking with exhaustion. Adult aides were easier. With them, she didn't have to feel nervous or wonder what they were thinking of her the whole time. She'd done all this so she could get to know Matthew, but by the time she got to Friday − Matthew's day − she wondered if it was worth it.

Friday morning, she waited outside the front vestibule for Matthew in the same spot she'd met her other peer helpers. She was nervous, and so tired at that point that she just wanted to make it through the day and get to the weekend. She watched him walk towards her, smiling a little, his arms stiff at his sides, his hair hanging in front of his face. Before she could say good morning, he spoke first.

'I like your shirt,' he said.

She looked at him. Was he trying to be funny? Did he know she'd been using this stupid compliment all week? She looked down at her shirt, an aqua–blue one that she'd saved to wear today with him.

'THANKS,' she said.

'My problem is I don't like talking in the hallway,' he said as they walked up the hall. He kept close to one wall, tapping lockers as he went, every other one. 'I just don't.'

'THAT'S OKAY.'

They walked down two corridors and stopped. He followed her into her classroom, opened her backpack, and pulled out her textbook. None of her other peer helpers had done this. 'See you after class,' he said, tapping the book.

'QUIET IS NICE,' she said at the start of their next passing period.

'Good. I think so too.'

By the time they got to lunch, Matthew had to be honest. 'I need to tell you that I don't have a lot of friends to introduce you to. The ones I do have, you probably don't want to know.'

'DON'T WORRY,' Amy typed. 'SANJAY INTRODUCED ME TO FORTY-SEVEN PEOPLE ON WEDNESDAY.'

Matthew smiled, then frowned, then looked away. This whole day had been confusing. Amy looked prettier than she had last spring, her face tan, her hair even longer and curlier than he remembered. It made him feel shy in spite of the emails they'd exchanged, her last two saying how happy she was that he'd be doing the job. He wasn't sure why she liked him so much. They'd only had the one conversation. He'd probably only disappoint her now.

'I DID HAVE ONE IDEA,' she typed.

He looked up. 'What's that?'

She typed for a moment. He liked the slowed-down rhythm of conversation with Amy. It gave him a chance to breathe and think. 'YOU COULD INTRODUCE ME TO THE CAFETERIA LADIES. THEY'RE ALL WEARING NAME TAGS.'

He laughed and thought, *Maybe I'll make it through the rest of the day.*

He did. Much to his surprise, it was easier than he expected. And more interesting too. He got the sense Amy didn't agree with her mother's approach.

'SHE'S A SCIENTIST,' Amy explained over lunch. 'SHE LIKES TO MAKE GOALS, THEN TRACK DATA TO PROVE IF SHE'S MET HER GOAL OR NOT.'

Matthew thought about this. 'Even if the goal is making new friends?'

'EXACTLY. IT'S A LITTLE HARD TO FIND MEASURABLE BENCHMARKS FOR POPULARITY. SHE THINKS PEOPLE SAYING HI SHOULD BE ONE.'

They were five days into the school year. 'How's that been so far?'

'WELL, YESTERDAY FORTY-SEVEN PEOPLE FELT OBLIGED TO SAY HI, SO GOOD, I GUESS.'

He laughed again. He could tell when she was joking even if the computer delivery was slightly off. He started eating his lunch, carefully, the way he always did, holding his sandwich still half wrapped in its baggie. He looked at her lunch, a single can of Boost. 'Don't you have more than that?' he asked.

'NO,' she said. 'JUST THIS.'

He remembered the old days in second grade when mothers brought in cupcakes for birthdays, and Amy ate hers like a baby painting itself with frosting. The problem wasn't her good hand that had freakish control over her talking board. It was her wavering head and mouth. Eating must still be a little like target practice.

Towards the end of the day, it occurred to him: the job was going better than he'd expected. The strangest thing of all: last night he worried for hours about hearing the voice while he was walking next to Amy. And then – surprise, surprise –

no voice at all! This whole day, it stayed silent. He would never understand why he got a break on certain days and not others, but he had to wonder if it helped having other things to think about: Amy's cooler, her books, the battery pack. He had his own schedule and hers, two sets of classrooms to walk quickly between. After seventh period, his legs were tired, but he'd never felt more energized. It was as if one half of his brain had taken an all-day vacation. He wished he didn't have to wait four days to be her peer helper again.

'SO I HOPE THIS WASN'T TOO AWFUL FOR YOU,' Amy said when they were outside, waiting for her mom in the parent pick-up circle. On the other side of the road, he saw Bus #12 – his own – pull away. He didn't care. Easy enough to walk the mile and a half home.

'Awful?' he said. 'Hardly. I've had a great time.' He laughed, though neither one of them had made a joke.

'YOU HAVE?'

Did he sound overeager? Was it wrong to like a job you were getting paid for?

'Yeah.' He swallowed. 'I mean, yeah. You're interesting, Amy. You always have been.'

Her head flopped from one side over to the other. Her ear looked like it was listening to a secret from her shoulder. 'HOW SO?'

He saw her mother's car pull in. 'Well, I can't tell you now; your mother's here.'

All at once he remembered his biggest failure of the day: he'd introduced her to no one.

Lie, the voice said. *Don't be stupid. Just lie.* It sounded angry.

40

As if it had been watching him all day, waiting to remind him of all his failures.

'Hi, Aims! Hi, Matthew! How did it go?' Nicole got out of her car to open the trunk.

'I don't have many friends,' he mumbled to Nicole as he loaded her walker and her backpack into the trunk of the car. 'None Amy would want to know. I'm sorry.'

Unable to look either one of them in the eye, he turned quickly and sprinted away.

That night after dinner, Matthew stood at the sink washing pots and pans. He'd told his mother very little about his day. It was fine, he'd said. Amy was nice. His mother told him a story from work as she sipped her wine. As he finished the dishes, his mom touched his shoulder and asked why he checked the faucet so often. 'It's off, honey. I promise.'

He tightened the faucet again. He couldn't help himself. 'I know.'

'So why do you keep checking?'

He couldn't look at her. She'd never asked him about the faucet thing before. She'd asked about other things, but not this one. 'No reason.'

She took a deep breath. 'I see you do these things that I never used to see you do. I worry that it's taking up so much of your time.'

He wanted to tell her the truth, he really did. *It's taking all my time, Mom. I don't understand. I hate it but there's nothing I can do.* He heard a noise – like water moving through pipes, only it was blood in his capillaries, rushing to his face, up the back of his neck.

'Can you tell me why?'

He should tell her. He wanted to. His throat grew tight. He couldn't speak. He feared for a minute that he couldn't breathe.

Don't tell her, the voice hissed. *It will make her cry and she's sad enough as it is.*

'A woman at work – Cheryl, you remember her? She has a sister she told me about. Apparently she has these – oh, I don't know – routines, she calls them. Where she checks on things before she can leave the house. The stove, the coffee, her hairdryer, all that. She has to go through the house over and over. Checking and rechecking. Some days it's so bad she leaves work at lunch and goes home to recheck.'

That wasn't his problem. He wanted to laugh and say, *She sounds* crazy, *Mom.*

'Is it a little like that for you?' she waited. 'Where you try to calm your worries with these routines?'

'*No*,' he said. 'It's *nothing* like that.'

It was, though. It was like that.

Don't tell her, the voice said. *Whatever you do, don't tell her the truth.*

'Because if it is, honey, you can get help. It's a treatable thing.'

'I just told you it's not.'

'All right, all right. You don't have to yell.'

'I don't want you to worry about me being too worried. That's not going to help.'

'Okay.'

CHAPTER SIX

Amy figured something out. Her mother – who had come round to the idea of peer helpers eventually – hated the actual people who'd signed up. At the end of the first week, Nicole came into Amy's darkened room and sat down on her bed. 'I can't help it,' she said. 'They all seem so ordinary and unworthy of you.'

'MOTHER –'

'That's how I feel.'

'THEY'RE MY FRIENDS NOW. YOU'RE NOT ALLOWED TO JUDGE THEM.'

'Fine, I won't. But I told Chloe that she's fired if she puts any make-up on you.'

'MOM. PEOPLE WEAR MAKE-UP.'

She shook her head like she was trying not to cry. 'I know they do.'

'I'M SEVENTEEN NOW.'

'I know.'

'THIS IS PART OF YOUR JOB. YOU'RE LETTING ME GO.'

'Will you promise to tell me if these people do or say anything that makes you uncomfortable?'

'PROBABLY NOT.'

'You must, Amy. You must tell me if anything doesn't feel right.'

'YES. OKAY, FINE. I WILL.'

No, I won't, she thought.

Amy surprised herself. Though the second week had gone marginally better than the first, it wasn't by much. It was still slightly agonizing to creep along beside someone who wanted to walk faster. And humiliating to watch Sanjay flirt with cheerleaders by saying, 'What I do is I'm kind of a babysitter for Amy. I love it! Best job I've ever had.'

And yet here she was – defending her friends. Yes, anyone could see that Chloe was overly devoted to a boyfriend who was in a juvenile detention centre instead of school. Sure, Sarah texted a lot during their time together, probably more than she should have, but what did Amy know? Sitting across from Sarah bent over her phone, Amy looked around the cafeteria and saw about a quarter of the people there doing the same thing. Her mother was right, in a way. Maybe they could have hired more responsible – or at least more polite – people. But, if they had, then the group wouldn't have been a real cross section of peers, and it wouldn't have included Matthew.

That was the important part. That was why Amy felt defensive of them all. Because she needed the others to get Matthew every fourth day.

With Matthew it wasn't painful or awkward. With Matthew, the silences felt okay. He didn't make nervous excuses about why he needed to be on the phone with someone else. He didn't grimace when she did something clumsy. He was just there. Happy to pick up the contents of her spilled backpack, happy to wipe her face and shirt, happy to get hair out of her jacket. With Matthew it felt both easy and real. She tried to think of the right word to describe him, and finally it occurred to her: he felt like a friend.

'Greetings,' Matthew said. It had been four weeks since the peer-helper programme had started, and he wasn't sure why, but he'd started goofing around more with Amy – bowing when she walked up, saying, 'At your service . . .' Now he held out his hand and said, 'May I carry your buff-coloured card for you?'

It was the last day of add-drop period and they were all carrying around schedule cards to collect teachers' initials. He took her backpack and plucked the card out of her hand. '*BIEN SUR*,' she typed. She was just getting out of French. She'd switched her Pathway out of foreign language mode so it sounded like she was saying, 'BEEN SEWER.'

'Charming.' He smiled. 'I've been a little sewer myself.'

Being with Amy continued to surprise Matthew. This was his fifth day, and each time it felt easier. Before the year had started, he'd wondered how he'd think of things to talk about over lunch, and was grateful for the list of Amy's interests Nicole gave them during their training session. 'Amy needs to find people she has things in common with,' Nicole had said. 'To help with that, I've come up with a list of Amy's favourite things.' She passed them out:

Impressionist art
Korean food
Diary of Anne Frank
Simon and Garfunkel
Movies from the forties, especially those with Bette Davis

The list went on, but even Matthew could see the problem with Nicole's thinking. High-school students don't sit around and talk about the diary of Anne Frank. No one broke open their lunch bags, saying, 'Who here loves Bette Davis?' Teenagers didn't talk about *subjects*. Teenagers made fun of one another or, failing that, made fun of their teachers.

Now, at lunch with Amy, Matthew mentioned the hobby/ interest list. He assumed she knew about it, but apparently not. Amy squawked in either a laugh or a gasp of horror. 'OH MY GOD. WHAT WAS ON IT?'

He told her the items that he could remember.

'*ANNE FRANK?* ARE YOU SERIOUS?'

'I thought maybe that sounded a little funny. Not that Anne Frank wasn't a great writer.'

'I WAS TEN WHEN I READ THAT!'

'*Really?*' For Matthew it was assigned two years ago. He liked the book, but it took him a long time to read and was harder than he expected. 'Were you really ten? That seems young. Were you a reading prodigy or something?'

'NO. I USED TO READ A LOT. NOT MUCH ELSE TO DO.'

She told him she didn't understand why her mother listed that book when there were so many others she'd read and loved more recently. It was like Nicole wanted people to be impressed with her fifth-grade accomplishment. 'IS THAT WEIRD? IMPRESSING PEOPLE WITH HOW SMART I *USED* TO BE?'

'I don't know.' Matthew shrugged. For the first time, he tried to imagine his own mother as involved in his life as Amy's

46

was. Since that faucet discussion a few weeks ago, she hadn't asked him many questions. She hadn't even asked what he was doing about college applications, which seemed strange since that was the only thing his classmates talked about these days. 'It sounds like you were pretty smart.'

'I STILL AM! WHAT ABOUT THE BOOKS I'M READING NOW?'

He couldn't tell if she was really upset or joking. Her head moved side to side and her hand pushed her Pathway to the edge of the table. 'Okay.' Matthew smiled and pushed the computer back near her hand. 'What books are you reading now?'

'I DON'T WANT TO TALK ABOUT IT.'

She *was* upset. She pushed her computer away again and stopped sipping from her can of Boost. He was pretty sure Amy was mad at her mother, not him, but still he wasn't sure how to get her out of this mood. 'I used to read a lot, but I don't any more,' he said. 'It makes me too anxious.'

The expression on Amy's face changed. 'WHY?'

Now that he'd said it, he realized he shouldn't have. However he explained himself, it wouldn't sound right. She waited. He had to say something: 'I get worried about reading things the wrong way. Sometimes I have to read the same page over and over. I keep thinking I've made a mistake.'

'HOW DO YOU GET THROUGH HOMEWORK?'

By taking forever, he almost said. *By not doing it.* He couldn't tell her this. Or that reading sometimes felt like a battle with the voice. 'Slowly, I guess. I don't always do all the reading. I can't.'

'WHY DO YOU READ THE SAME PAGE OVER AND OVER?'

He could hear the voice now. *You missed a word. Go back. If you don't go back nothing will make sense.* He'd made a mistake telling her. 'No reason. Just trying to be careful.'

When he got to chemistry, his first class after lunch, he opened his notebook and realized he hadn't given Amy her schedule card back. He laid both their cards side by side on his desk and noticed that her birthday was one day after his. His was April twenty-fifth, hers the twenty-sixth. Typed out on the line below – *Place of birth: Mercy Hospital.*

What a coincidence, he thought, and then he remembered Nicole telling them that Amy was fine at birth but had an aneurism the day after she was born. His heart began to pound against his chest. *You were there*, the voice said. *You were with her when it happened.* He waited for the inevitable: *It probably was your fault.*

He began to sweat. Was it possible? Were they infants lying beneath the same warming lights when it happened?

Suddenly the fear consumed him. What if he and Amy *were* infants lying together under a plastic oxygen tent? What if he rolled over and cut off her oxygen supply? It was possible, wasn't it? He'd been a ridiculously big baby, over ten pounds, all cheeks and rolls of fat, his mother used to say. He would go home and look it up, but he was pretty sure aneurisms meant the oxygen supply was cut off to the brain.

Maybe this explained his lifelong fascination with Amy and her body's quirks. Why would he feel so responsible otherwise?

CHAPTER SEVEN

Matthew was never sure if anyone noticed his rituals. He hoped not, of course. Occasionally people asked questions that made him wonder. *Why do you wash your hands up to your elbows? Why do you avoid the blue tiles on the floor? Why do you tap lockers?* He always gave short, panicky answers. 'I'm not!' he'd say. Or: 'I got something on my arms in bio lab.'

Amy was the first person he gave a real answer to.

A week after his revelation about their birthdays, they were on their way to lunch.

'Why do you sometimes walk on your toes?' Amy asked.

Matthew blushed. He hadn't realized he was doing it in public. 'I do things like that sometimes.'

'WHY?'

He told her the truth. 'Usually I walk on my toes when I'm happy.'

She laughed, then typed: 'YOU'RE HAPPY WITH ME?'

Because this wasn't about his rituals, it seemed safe to clarify. 'Yes, I am. Most of the time. Except when you ask me embarrassing questions.'

'WHY IS THIS EMBARRASSING?'

'Because people aren't supposed to walk on their toes after a certain age. I know that. I just like it. It's not the weirdest thing I do.'

'WHAT'S THE WEIRDEST THING YOU DO?'

By then he couldn't remember: had *he* brought this up? 'There're just things I do sometimes.'

They walked into the resource room where they'd started eating their lunch after Amy pointed out that neither one of them bought any food and technically they didn't need to eat in the cafeteria. She'd had enough of the cafeteria.

'The truth is I have problems like you do, only mine don't show,' he said as he unwrapped the sandwich he'd packed for himself, wrapped once in wax paper, then plastic, then tinfoil. 'I worry too much. Logically I understand that my fears aren't rational, but I can't stop myself from thinking about them. I go over them in my mind. All the time.'

'FEARS ABOUT WHAT?'

'Mostly I worry that I've hurt people unintentionally. Or ruined someone's life without meaning to.' It felt strange to say this out loud. He wasn't sure why he was telling her except that yesterday, at their monthly peer-helper meeting, Nicole had told them a story about Amy being a preemie. 'She was such a tiny thing. Less than three pounds. Nobody expected her to live. If she did, they said, she'd be a vegetable. Now I send those doctors a copy of her report card every year!'

Matthew raised his hand. 'Does that mean Amy was in an incubator by herself?' As soon as he asked it, he knew it was a strange question.

'Oh my, yes,' Nicole said, unfazed. 'She was in intensive care for close to two months. There weren't many other babies around. One or two others who weren't so lucky.'

Matthew was euphoric. Proof he hadn't caused Amy's problems! It made him chattier now.

'HOW WOULD YOU HAVE HURT OTHER PEOPLE?'

'It's easier than you think. Like the other day a can of Sprite spilled in my locker. It made a mess in there, but I kept worrying: What if it leaked into someone else's locker? What if I ruined some project they've been working on all semester? Or all their class notes for the year?'

'DID THAT HAPPEN?'

'I don't think so, but how can I be sure?'

'HOW MUCH SPRITE?'

'A quarter of a can.' He waited. Now he understood why he'd told her all this. He wanted her to reassure him.

'IT'S PROBABLY FINE.'

'But I can't be absolutely sure.'

'YOU CAN BE PRETTY SURE.'

'That's just it, though. Pretty sure isn't good enough. Pretty sure can keep me awake all night.' He was surprised at what a relief it was to tell someone about the Sprite. 'I give myself tasks – hard ones – to complete, and then hopefully nothing bad will happen because of what I've done. It's sort of a game I play in my mind. Except that it's not any fun and not really a game. It feels like terrible things will happen if I don't do everything right.'

'WHAT DO YOU HAVE TO DO?'

'Walk certain ways. Touch objects. Wash my hands. Different things. It varies.'

'LIKE OCD?'

He didn't know what that was. 'I don't think so.'

Four days later, Amy met him in the morning with something she wanted to say already typed out.

'I'VE DONE A LITTLE RESEARCH. YOU SHOULD

READ THIS BOOK CALLED *THE BOY WHO COULDN'T STOP WASHING*. IT'S ALL ABOUT OCD AND IT'S JUST LIKE WHAT YOU DESCRIBED.'

'I used to wash my hands a lot.' He felt a little self-conscious now. He didn't want to tell her he still did.

'WHAT'S A LOT?'

He wasn't sure if he should say. He didn't want to spend all day discussing it. 'Twelve times a day. I liked that number. It wasn't about the washing so much as the number.' Did that make it better?

'YEAH, YOU'VE GOT IT.'

'I don't think so.'

'TRUST ME.'

They walked in silence for a while as he thought about things he'd like to say to her: *Look, who made you a doctor anyway? What medical school did you go to? How would you like it if I started reading up on all your problems?* The trouble with this argument was that he already *had* read up on all her problems. He'd looked up cerebral palsy and had even rented *My Left Foot* and watched it twice. He wanted to ask Amy if she'd liked that movie too, but didn't know if he should.

'MAYBE I'M WRONG,' she finally said, outside her classroom door. When he came to pick her up, she kept talking as if an hour hadn't elapsed. 'I THINK YOU SHOULD READ THE BOOK, THAT'S ALL.'

He couldn't take it any more. 'Fine. I think you should watch *My Left Foot*.'

'WHY?'

'Because it's fun to be told what all your problems

are named, so you should try it too.'

'I ALREADY KNOW THE NAME OF MY PROBLEM. IT'S NOT A BIG SECRET.'

Later that afternoon, he went to the public town library and found the book. Then he had to wait an hour for a librarian he didn't recognize to be behind the checkout desk. By the time that happened his throat felt too tight for him to speak. When the librarian asked how he was doing, he nodded vaguely like a deaf person. That night, he had to read slowly but he got through most of the book. The people in it all seemed much worse than him. They were in hospitals spending twenty-four hours a day trying not to wash their hands.

The next day before school he went looking for Amy. She was waiting for Chloe, who was usually late.

'Those people were *crazy*,' he told her. 'I'm not crazy.'

'NO. BUT SOME THINGS ARE THE SAME. LIKE BLAMING YOURSELF FOR STUFF THAT ISN'T YOUR FAULT. THAT'S THE SAME.'

Did she know that he'd spent a week blaming himself for her condition? Was she saying all this because it probably *was* his fault? 'Look, I'll admit the book was interesting and it had some things I recognized, but I'm not anything like those people. I'm not about to start taking medication or go to some doctor and tell him all this stuff.'

'IF YOU DON'T WANT HELP, WHY DID YOU TELL ME?'

'Because I know you. And I like you.' He didn't say: *And I thought I was responsible for all your problems.*

'WHY DID YOU APPLY FOR THIS JOB?'

'Because I wanted it. I thought helping someone else might take me out of my own head for a while.'

Amy's head bent down as she typed for a minute. Then she rethought what she'd written, pushed delete, and typed something else. 'THAT'S EXACTLY HOW I FEEL.'

CHAPTER EIGHT

For Amy, being friends with Matthew felt like being on a roller coaster. He was so many things: handsome (far handsomer than he had any idea of, with beautiful blue eyes and a wonderful smile), smart, funny and surprisingly gallant. He was her only peer helper who stayed with her after school to wait for her mother's car to pull up. The only one who carried her backpack to the trunk and knew how to fold her walker flat with two moves. More often than not, he held open the car door, and recently he had begun a heart-stopping new flourish: buckling her seat belt round her. He'd done it twice now, which meant twice his curly hair was bent over her waist while one hand touched her hip in search of the buckle.

'There we go!' he'd said last time, smiling and a little breathless when the job was done.

He had no idea how wonderful he was. How his hands were so beautiful she could hardly look at them. How his truest smile was crooked and lifted higher on the left side than the right, which made her feel like he might understand her better, her hemiplegic face that was all crooked half-smiles too.

But it couldn't be denied. He was also slightly crazy.

Maybe more than slightly.

Reading the book she'd found at the library convinced her of two things: (1) It was a pretty serious disorder, and (2) Matthew definitely had it.

The case studies in that book had people whose whole lives got destroyed by compulsive obsessions. Lawyers who

55

lost their jobs because they couldn't stop taking showers. Teachers who left classrooms unattended to run home and check their stoves. On one level, Amy was grateful for this side of Matthew. Without it, she knew he never would have been her peer helper. He'd been normal once, with friends in the smart crowd who went to dances and after-school activities planned by committees. She'd never done any of that, but she remembered seeing Matthew at tables in middle school, selling raffle tickets and carnations. Now she'd learned he wasn't kidding that first day he worked with her. He said hello to no one. He spent passing periods in the hallway too busy tapping lockers and whispering to himself to notice the people who tried to say hi or catch his eye.

Except the days he was with her.

It was electrifying the way he watched her so carefully that he forgot himself. He didn't mumble or tap. Mostly he didn't do anything strange; instead, he focused on details. He fixed a loose screw on the handle of her walker. He found better straws in the cafeteria for drinking her Boost shake. He thought about her and a million tiny ways he might make her life easier. How could she *not* love him?

Because she did, she saw that he didn't want to talk about OCD.

It made his fingers twitch and his eyes flick nervously around the room. It made sweat break out on his upper lip. Instead of talking about it, she asked him if he would mind joining an after-school club with her that met twice a week. The others couldn't stay after school, but Matthew, with no sports, no other jobs, and no place he had to be, could.

The day of the first meeting, they walked together to the yearbook room.

'You're really interested in *yearbook*?' he asked.

'YES. I LOVE DESIGN AND LAYOUT. THAT'S MY THING.'

'Wow,' he said. 'I thought Simon and Garfunkel was your thing.' Ever since he'd told her about the list, he brought it up every chance he could.

She pressed the Pathway button with her fake laugh. 'HA-HA.'

Yearbook was filled with mostly younger kids who already knew one another. No one looked up or acknowledged them when they walked in.

'I have to be honest with you,' Matthew whispered as they moved to a table at the back. 'It's been years since I even bought a yearbook.'

'WELL, THAT'S WHERE YOUR PROBLEM IS.' Amy turned her computer down to a whisper. 'YEARBOOKS ARE CRUCIAL TO POPULARITY.'

'Right,' he said. 'I once had two girls write on the same page that I had a really sweat personality.'

She laughed. She liked the way he said *sweat*. 'GREAT MINDS THINK ALIKE, I GUESS.'

'Sweat ones too.'

They weren't put on layout because apparently everyone wanted layout and only people who'd been working for a year on yearbook got to do layout. They were welcome to do ad sales, the faculty advisor said, handing them a packet.

'You call the businesses listed there and see if they're

willing to sponsor again.' Too late, the teacher realized 'calling businesses' might be a mistake for them. 'Maybe one of you could do the talking,' he said, and awkwardly began to shuffle through some papers.

They returned to the back table, where they sat — again — by themselves. Around them everyone else worked busily. Finally Amy whispered, 'WELL, I'M PRETTY SURE HE MEANT I SHOULD DO THE TALKING, DON'T YOU?'

Two days later, they went back again. They sat at the same table and, again, no one acknowledged them.

'I think you're definitely right about the popularity thing,' Matthew whispered. 'I already feel it working wonders.'

'ME TOO.'

If Matthew hadn't been there, making his jokes and their calls to businesses, she wouldn't have lasted. But with him it didn't matter that no one talked to them, including the advisor. They had each other. Matthew made up voices to use on their calls. She typed up scripts for him to say. Instead of focusing on ad sales, they tried to get people to stay on the phone as long as possible. He talked to hair salons at great length about their whimsical names. ('Hair Today, Gone Tomorrow is so bold,' he said. 'The implication that everyone walks out bald isn't a problem, I guess?')

Soon they made fewer calls and spent the rest of the time talking. No one seemed to notice or, if they did, care. It gave them what Amy really wanted, more time to talk. To tell each other stories, even if it took a while because Matthew was shy and Amy had only one hand with which to type.

They talked a little about the other peer helpers. Matthew

told her he'd been friends once with Sanjay, a long time ago. 'It was in preschool, actually. He was the person who told me there was no such thing as a nap fairy who came in and put stickers on children who were asleep. He said it was the teachers wanting the kids to sleep so they could get a break.'

He also told her he didn't know Sanjay any more. Even during the training week in August, neither one of them mentioned preschool.

'SANJAY'S A LITTLE FOCUSED ON OTHER THINGS NOW.'

'Like what?'

'HE CARES ABOUT GIRLS AND POPULARITY. A LOT.' Out of all her peer helpers, Sanjay was the hardest for her to spend all day with. No matter who he was with, he looked over their shoulder to see if someone better was in the vicinity. He talked a lot about the popular crowd – ostensibly making jokes, but they were the kind of jokes that made it clear he was desperate to be one of them. Sometimes it sounded like maybe he was. 'That's *so* Lisa,' he'd say after talking to one of the cheerleaders for two minutes. 'She can't do Spanish at all. I mean, *nada*.' Occasionally pretty girls sat next to him in the cafeteria and said, 'Hey, Sanj.' Sometimes they ate his French fries for a few minutes while they talked to him.

'And Sarah?' Matthew said. 'What about her? What's she like?' As he said this, he peeked up at her, a little nervous.

'WHY?'

'No reason. Just curious.'

'DO YOU LIKE HER?' Amy tried not to ask questions

like this, but she couldn't help it. Her hand moved faster than her brain could stop it.

'No. I mean I *used* to have a crush on her, okay. Sort of. A little.' His face was bright red. He couldn't stop smiling.

'WHEN?'

'A long time ago. Like ninth grade. It was dumb.'

Amy liked Sarah, but knew her the least of all her peer helpers. She knew her dad was Mr Heffernan, their seventh-grade science teacher, and she knew her mother had died of cancer because it happened when they were all in seventh grade and Mr Heffernan left school for almost two weeks. Beyond that, she couldn't say much. Sarah seemed serious about getting into a good college. She was pretty in a way that Amy didn't think got noticed much in high school, but maybe she was wrong. Maybe Matthew had noticed.

He finally stopped blushing long enough to explain, 'Her mother died around the same time my dad moved out of the house, saying he had fallen in love with someone else. I guess I got it in my mind that we had a lot in common.'

'DYING ISN'T THE SAME AS GETTING DIVORCED.'

'No, I know. I just used to watch her. To see if she was holding up. If she looked like she'd been crying. Stuff like that. It was stupid.'

'DO YOU STILL DO THAT?'

'No. I mean, a little. I don't even know her, really. You know her better than I do at this point.'

Amy knew this shouldn't bother her as much as it did. *We're friends*, she told herself. *This is what friends do. They have crushes on other people and they tell their friends about it.* That didn't mean he was going to start dating Sarah. It didn't mean he'd signed up to be a peer helper so he could meet Sarah. The minute she thought of this, though, she couldn't stop her hand from typing: 'DID YOU SIGN UP FOR THIS SO YOU COULD MEET HER?'

'*No.* God, Amy. I didn't even know she was doing it.'

'BUT YOU SAW HER AT THE TRAINING SESSION AND THOUGHT, *I CAN'T BELIEVE HOW LUCKY I GOT*?'

He laughed and blushed again. '*No.*' But it was obvious. He did think that. She could tell.

She dropped the subject completely and went home that night to think it over. Yes, she was jealous. It was infuriating that someone as sweet as Matthew, with such a good heart and with so many problems to wrestle, would waste his time having a crush on Sarah. Not that anything was *wrong* with Sarah – she just wasn't worthy of him. She wasn't as sweet as Matthew or as considerate. Once, Sarah told Amy she didn't expect to keep in touch with anyone from high school after they graduated. 'I feel like I'm kind of biding my time, waiting for better things,' she told Amy. Amy knew what she meant: better classes, better friends, better boys. She didn't want Matthew to have a crush on Sarah, because Sarah would probably brush him away without thinking twice. 'I'm kind of busy these days,' she'd probably say, or even worse: 'I'm not really into high-school guys.'

There was also, growing within Amy, a feeling so foreign she almost didn't recognize it. *Why doesn't he notice* me *that way?*

She wasn't sure exactly what she wanted or could reasonably expect. Kissing was probably too much, of course. But sometimes Matthew would look at her, or put his hand somewhere surprising — the small of her back, or the inside of her wrist — and she'd feel an electric thrill. Once there was even a spark and they looked at each other. She wanted to say, *There. Didn't you feel that?*

But those moments always passed. He'd shake his head and change the subject.

At their next yearbook meeting, they talked about therapists she'd had in the past: 'MY ALL-TIME FAVOURITE WAS AN OCCUPATIONAL THERAPIST NAMED CONNIE. SHE WAS THE FIRST PERSON WHO TOLD ME ABOUT SEX.'

This time Matthew didn't blush so much as break out in a cold sweat. 'What did she *say*?'

'NOT THE GRAPHIC DETAILS. SHE SAID GIRLS ARE TOLD THEY'RE SUPPOSED TO SAY NO, BUT IT GETS CONFUSING BECAUSE THEY WANT IT TOO. SHE MADE IT PRETTY CLEAR: IT'S OKAY FOR GIRLS TO BE INTERESTED IN SEX.'

'How old were you?'

'FIFTEEN, I GUESS. OLD ENOUGH. SHE SAID I SHOULD WAIT UNITL I LOVED THE PERSON OR ELSE UNTIL I WAS REALLY, REALLY SURE I WANTED TO HAVE SEX.'

'She *said* that?' He laughed nervously as if maybe she was joking.

'YES. WHY SHOULDN'T SHE? DO I LOOK LIKE

SOMEONE WHO SHOULD NEVER TALK ABOUT SEX?'

'*No*. God, Amy. You don't have to keep saying that word.'

'WHY NOT?'

'*Because.*' He looked around. 'We're supposed to be selling ads, right?'

'RIGHT,' she typed. 'SORRY.'

Matthew didn't understand what Amy was saying or why some therapist was telling her to have sex when she was fifteen. It made no *sense*. He was grateful that Thanksgiving came the following week and meant all after-school clubs were cancelled.

He spent Thanksgiving with his grandmother, who'd grown up on a cattle ranch and understood cows better than she understood people. They might be stupid, she said, but at least cows behaved in predictable ways. People, not so much. His grandmother once told him that she was lucky that her husband drank himself to death. Now she was free to do as she pleased and say what she thought. Which she did. Before dinner, Matthew overheard his grandmother ask his mother: 'Are things better? Has he got *any* friends this year?'

He was supposed to be watching a parade on TV, but he turned the volume down to hear his mother's answer. 'Yes, Mother, he does. He was chosen to work with a disabled girl, and he's been doing that mostly. I think it was an honour, actually. She asked for him specifically.'

Amy did ask for him specifically – it was true – but he had no idea how his mother knew this. It made him nervous. Like

63

maybe people knew more things than he realized. He couldn't hear what his grandmother said.

'We haven't talked about that,' his mother said. 'I'm trying not to put pressure on him.'

Mumble mumble mumble.

'That's *your* opinion, Mother. Not everyone is ready for college the minute they graduate from high school.'

This was a surprise. His mother had been worrying about what he'd do next year?

'We've talked about him taking a year off, maybe.' (No, they hadn't.)

'Maybe he'll get a job and save some money.' (He would? What job?)

He strained to hear what his grandmother was saying, but he couldn't.

'All I know is that working with this girl has been *good* for him. It's made him think about someone else's problems. He's *good* at it, Mother. I wish you could hear him talk about her.'

Suddenly he felt even more embarrassed. What had he said?

'He really likes her. I can tell. And she likes him. It's very sweet. They're *friends*. I don't know what she's doing next year, but I assume if she's going to college it would be some correspondence situation. Maybe he could try something like that.'

As disorientating as it was to overhear this discussion, he had to admit he didn't mind the idea of living at home and taking college courses online next year. That solved the problem of telling people what his plans were. He had never asked Amy hers because he didn't want to pretend he had answers himself. Now maybe he could.

In the car driving home, Matthew checked his phone and, to his surprise, found a text from Amy.

Feel like barfing but thinking of you. Don't know why the two together. Happy Turkey day. Heart A.

He laughed out loud, surprised at how relieved he was to hear from her. They'd moved past the awkwardness of their last conversation. They could keep going, apparently, the way they had been. A few weeks earlier they'd started a joke about the girls who wore I Heart NY shirts. He wrote back:

Grandmother's turkey dry as the suede fringe on my cowboy vest that still hangs in my guest bedroom here. Real studs. Fake suede. Maybe I'll show you some time. Hey, thanks for writing. M.

With Amy, jokes were easy, he realized. The other stuff, not so much.

He thought about what his mother had said. He wished he could tell Amy somehow. A few minutes later, he texted again:

Got to overhear my mother's opinion of my job with you. Apparently she approves. We both give thanks that your battery pack needs to be changed.

He got this back:

My battery pack is thankful for you too.

As they got closer to Christmas, Amy told Matthew that she'd thought about buying him a Christmas present but decided against it.

'That's fine,' Matthew said. 'I'm not a big present person.' He wasn't a big Christmas person, either (since it always involved a fake, jolly dinner with his father's new family), but obviously Amy, with her walker decorated in silver-and-gold tinsel, was.

'INSTEAD I'M GOING TO GIVE YOU A POEM.'

'Oh. Okay.'

'A GREAT, GREAT POEM. IT'LL KILL YOU WHEN YOU READ IT.'

'All right. I mean, I hope it doesn't *kill* me, but okay.'

The poem was by Yeats. She emailed it to him, then printed out a copy that she presented to him the next day at school:

> *Had I the heavens' embroidered cloths,*
> *Enwrought with golden and silver light,*
> *The blue and the dim and the dark cloths*
> *Of night and light and the half-light,*
> *I would spread the cloths under your feet:*
> *But I, being poor, have only my dreams;*
> *I have spread my dreams under your feet;*
> *Tread softly because you tread on my dreams.*

'DID YOU LIKE IT?' she said, first thing in the morning.

'Oh yeah. It was great. Except you're not poor.' He didn't

know this for sure. He'd never been to Amy's house, but the clues were all there: the car her mother drove, the cost of her Pathway and the rest of her equipment. Plus the fact that her parents paid him sixty dollars every other week.

'IT'S SYMBOLIC. I'M POOR IN MANY WAYS EXCEPT MONETARILY.'

'Oh.' He nodded and smiled. 'Okay.'

He *had* liked the poem a lot – enough to memorize it, which wasn't necessarily significant. Sometimes his brain inadvertently memorized songs and poems he hated, but he did like this one. The problem was, he couldn't think of anything to *say* about it. 'I like that it was *you* telling *me* to walk carefully.' Right away, he knew this wasn't the right thing to say.

She cocked her head, and stared at him. 'THAT'S ALL?'

'I'm not good at poetry, Amy. I'm not sure what else to say.'

'DON'T YOU HAVE ANYTHING FOR ME?'

Now he understood his real mistake. She'd set this whole thing up so they could *exchange* presents without worrying about his having less money than she did. Why didn't he understand these things sooner?

'I don't have anything. I'm sorry.' He felt tongue-tied and awkward. It was a week before school let out for Christmas vacation. Should he run out and get her a present now? Wouldn't that look stupid since he hadn't thought of it himself?

He put it out of his mind because he felt like he had other, bigger things to worry about. He hadn't asked her yet about her college plans, but he would soon. He'd already decided to sign up for whatever online college programme Amy picked for herself. If they did it together, he'd point out, they could share books and laugh about the crazy people in their discussion groups.

For Matthew, it was both a relief to imagine and a little embarrassing to bring up. He didn't want her to know that he hadn't applied to any schools. That he downloaded some applications that made him too nervous to look at. That, without this vague idea of doing something with her, he had no plans for next year. None.

Now he sat beside her at lunch. She'd been wearing a Santa hat all day that everyone commented on, the way everyone commented on everything Amy wore. He could feel her expectation, like she was waiting for him to say something. It made him mad. 'I told you I'm not that great a reader. Poetry especially. I always feel like I'm missing the point.'

She waited a long time, though he couldn't think of anything else to say.

'MAYBE YOU ARE,' she finally said.

CHAPTER NINE

Amy didn't feel jealous of Sarah any more. That brief, two-day stab of crazy envy hadn't been rational, she realized afterwards. Matthew didn't speak to Sarah, and Sarah could hardly remember his name. (She'd thought it was Martin when Amy asked, casually, how well Sarah knew her other peer helpers.) The jealousy fit was pointless except for the way it sharpened Amy's impulse to tell Matthew how she felt. To say, *Do you feel this too? Do you go to sleep at night thinking about me?*

Between Thanksgiving and Christmas, it hovered in her mind every time she walked beside him and every afternoon that they spent in the Not-Really-Working-On-The-Yearbook Club. Embarrassingly, she understood, the Connie story was a misfire. She'd told it so that he would realize: *Yes, Amy is a regular girl too. One who knows about and has discussed sex with other people.* Then she saw how anxious it made him, as did all her other efforts – her jokey texts, her flashy Christmas accessories, even her poem – which she assumed no one could miss the meaning of. *I have spread my dreams under your feet;/ Tread softly because you tread on my dreams.* How could *anyone* miss what she was trying to say?

The problem, she realized, wasn't her uncooperative tongue. After the rocky start in September, she'd figured out that asking questions made conversations with her other peer helpers easier: at first she asked about trivial matters (*Why do boys wear their pants so low? Why do some of them care more about their hair than girls?*), but as she thought about Matthew more she began asking more personal ones. Starting after Thanksgiving, she asked each of her other peer helpers if they'd ever been in love.

Poor Chloe was still riding three buses every Saturday to visit Gary, her incarcerated boyfriend: 'He tells me to stop, but if I don't go he won't have anyone on family day.'

'DOES THAT MEAN YOU LOVE HIM?' Amy asked.

Chloe wasn't sure. 'I *thought* I did. Now I don't know. I wanted to be a person who stayed loyal no matter what. He needs *someone*. Even his mother won't visit him there.'

From there, Amy got the idea to ask the others the same question. Sanjay grinned, a smile so wide his white teeth stood out against his dark skin. 'I love all the ladies. I tell all of them to come to me when they're in the mood for a little brown sugar.' This was the way Sanjay liked to talk.

'AND DO THEY ALL RUN AWAY?'

'Some do.' His smile didn't dim. 'Some are scared of their animal attraction for me.'

'OR THEY'RE JUST SCARED, SANJAY. BECAUSE YOU'RE CREEPY WHEN YOU TALK LIKE THAT.'

'Maybe I am, maybe I'm not. You might be surprised at some of my conquests on the love front.'

'EVEN THAT WORD IS A PROBLEM. *CONQUESTS*. YOU KNOW THAT, RIGHT?'

'Fine, but I'll tell you this. I'm pretty sure Cindy Weintraub has no problem with it.'

Cindy Weintraub was a varsity cheerleader who had brown hair, and thighs that were infinitesimally bigger than those of her blonde, short-skirted cheerleader sisters. For this reason, Sanjay had zeroed in on her as 'possible'.

'I love all of them,' he said when Amy asked which one he liked best. 'But Cindy has a special place in my heart. She and I know what it's like to be overlooked.'

'BUT IS THAT LOVE, SANJAY?' Amy had never seen Cindy do anything except sit down next to him, say hello and eat some of his fries.

Sanjay closed his eyes. 'If the world were a different place, we'd be lovers by now. As it is, we have to settle for an unspoken but mutual understanding.'

Sarah's response was a surprise. In Amy's mind, Sarah always seemed older than her other peer helpers. More like an adult – which Amy assumed, early on, meant that Sarah would be easier for her to talk with, the way adults had always been. Instead it was the opposite. Sarah seemed overly interested sometimes, and distracted other times. She checked her phone constantly for messages that weren't there. Amy asked Sarah if she'd ever been in love, because she'd asked the other two and she wanted to get as many opinions as she could. She had no idea what Sarah would say.

'Are you asking if I've ever had sex, or if I've ever been in love?'

Amy was surprised. No one else besides Connie had ever brought up the subject of sex with her. 'I'M ASKING IF YOU'VE BEEN IN LOVE.'

Sarah opened her phone and checked it. 'I thought I was,' she said. 'But it was last year and I was an idiot.'

'WHO WAS IT?'

71

'Just this guy. He's twenty-three. He manages a cell-phone kiosk.'

Amy couldn't contain her curiosity. 'DID YOU HAVE SEX?'

Sarah stared at her. 'He's twenty-three. What do you think?'

'YES?'

Sarah smiled. 'Yes, Amy. We had sex.' She shrugged. 'I knew I didn't love him by then. I just wanted to get it over with. That's the thing about sex, I've decided. There's this mystique around it, and the truth is everyone should probably just do it once and get it over with.'

Amy considered this for a minute. 'IT WAS THAT BAD?'

'Not bad, exactly,' Sarah said, turning her yogurt spoon over in her mouth. 'I just don't think it's worth waiting forever, like it's going to be so special.'

'WHAT'S IT LIKE?'

'Painful, mostly. I mean, I'm sorry, but it's true. I'm glad I got it over with, though.'

'WHY?'

Sarah considered the question. 'This way when I'm in college and really fall in love I'll know what I'm doing.'

Afterwards Amy had decided that if she never succeeded in telling Matthew how she felt, maybe it was okay. They *were* friends. Very good friends. They joked around a lot and made each other laugh, but they also talked honestly about hard topics too. All of Sarah's talk about sex made her wonder if maybe it wasn't as great as everyone said and she should be grateful – really grateful – for what she had with Matthew.

72

Over Christmas vacation, Amy IM'd with Matthew as they'd
taken to doing a few nights a week. He told her about
Christmas Eve with his father's family, awkwardness made
excruciating when two people accidentally bought him the
same present.

aimhigh: What present?
mstheword: Don't ask.
aimhigh: Tell me.
mstheword: A tenth-anniversary Calvin and Hobbes. Yes,
I am a fan. I know this tells you too much about both my
maturity and my reading level.
aimhigh: It's fine, Matthew.
mstheword: I love Garfield too.
aimhigh: Are you serious?
mstheword: My whole bookshelf at home is pretty much
Garfield collections.
aimhigh: See, that worries me a little.
mstheword: I had a feeling it would. That's why I've never
mentioned it.
aimhigh: You need someone to make some book suggestions.

After she wrote this, she remembered him saying that reading
made him anxious – that he always worried about making a
mistake.

mstheword: Maybe I do need that. Like who?
aimhigh: I happen to have got the Librarian's Summer

Reading Award every year for ten years. I know that seems remarkable, but there's a secret to winning.

mstheword: What's the secret?

aimhigh: Short books count too.

mstheword: So maybe you know some short books you'd recommend?

aimhigh: I know some very short books.

On New Year's Eve, she asked if he'd like to wait up online until midnight with her.

'Sure,' he wrote back. 'That's probably better than sitting with my mother, who likes to spend New Year's Eve drinking too much wine and crying.'

They talked about music and the movies they disagreed about. He made fun of her for liking *The Sound of Music*. She told him to ask himself why only boys like *The Matrix*.

At 11:59 they counted down together to this: 'Happy New Year, Amy. If I were there, I would kiss the back of your hand and thank you for being my friend this year.'

To which she wrote back: 'I love being friends with you, Matthew, which you can interpret any way you like.'

Had she succeeded in telling him what she wanted to say? Had they – in their own awkward way – told each other? She hoped so.

CHAPTER TEN

Matthew was the one who talked her into signing up for public speaking. It was a required class that most people took in ninth and tenth grade, but Amy never had. She could have been excused, the way she was excused from the swim-test requirement in middle school. No guidance counsellor would insist that Amy take a class that depended on something she couldn't physically do.

Except for this: once Matthew suggested it, she wanted to sign up. It had started as a joke about Amy taking three APs and a fourth year of French. 'Why don't you sign up for something *really* hard?' Matthew said. 'I mean, look at this — only three APs? It's like you never challenge yourself.'

'THOSE CLASSES AREN'T HARD FOR ME,' she'd said.

Matthew shook his head. 'What *is* hard for you, Aim? Seriously. I'm curious.' As she typed a response, he thought of something: 'Public speaking!' He laughed and clapped his hands like it was the funniest joke he'd made all morning.

She deleted the answer she'd been typing and thought to herself: *He's right. That would be a challenge.*

'Why *now*?' Nicole asked when Amy told her the class she was adding to her schedule. 'When you've got so many other things to worry about. It's your second semester of senior year. You'll be hearing from colleges soon.'

Colleges had been such an obsession for Nicole she almost

made a scrapbook of the brochures that were sent to the house following Amy's PSAT scores, which qualified her for a National Merit Scholarship.

'WON'T I HAVE TO DO PRESENTATIONS IN COLLEGE?'

Nicole hadn't thought about this. 'You might.'

'SHOULDN'T I PRACTISE NOW? SO I DON'T EMBARRASS MYSELF LATER, IN FRONT OF STRANGERS?'

Her mother nodded. It made some sense.

Amy asked her peer helpers, all of whom had already taken the class, what they thought of the idea.

'Best class I've ever taken,' Sanjay said.

'*Hard*,' Chloe told her with a mouthful of celery. '*Really* hard. Like, posture is part of your grade. No offence.'

'I think you should do it,' Sarah said. 'I'd love to watch you deliver a speech.'

Matthew shook his head. She could tell he felt bad about suggesting it at all. 'The whole thing was a nightmare. For my final speech, my feet were so sweaty I walked out of my shoes.'

Amy still wanted to do it. She planned to use her Pathway, of course, so the hard part would be standing relatively still, which was strangely a bigger challenge for her than walking. Walking, you're supposed to move and make adjustments. Standing still, you're not. Standing meant willing one side of her body not to move and screaming at the other side to move just an inch. It could be agony. Especially with people watching. But that was the whole point.

You could read a speech someone else had written (people circulated famously brief ones), or you could write your own speech. Amy wanted to write her own. She wanted to explain what it was like not just to be her, but to be her *right now*. To feel as if new doors were opening up. To have real friends for the first time, people she said more than hello to. She wanted to say, *I know this is old news to many of you, but it's great, isn't it? To really be able to talk to someone? To joke around?* If she struck the right balance, she hoped to achieve a message that was subtle, but not cloying. *Appreciate it, people. Having friends is great.* She wrote a few drafts and tried the first one on her mother, who laughed politely throughout and afterwards asked if the assignment was meant to be comedy.

'NO. I WANT TO MAKE IT LIGHT, BUT I ALSO WANT TO MAKE A POINT.'

'Oh!' her mother said. 'It's just that comedy is so hard anyway, and your Pathway can't really do the timing it takes. That's all, sweetheart.'

'YOU'RE NOT HELPING,' Amy typed, turning up the volume so it became a scream.

'Why don't you read one of your old *essays*. Those were so good. This one, I'm less sure what you're trying to say.'

Amy cut most of the jokes and added a different point – something she wanted to say to all of her peer helpers about how grateful she was, how thrilling it felt to hear about their lives and tell them about hers. It was what she'd wanted to say to Matthew for months but hadn't found the right opportunity. Maybe this was it. Then she went a step further and added another point, something she also wanted to say to Matthew.

77

She didn't read this draft ahead of time to her mother. She didn't want anyone to stop her. She wanted to just say it.

The day of her speech, Amy's public-speaking class of thirty swelled to include six extras: her parents and all four of her peer helpers. Two people spoke before her: one pretty good, one not so good. When it was her turn, Matthew stood up and walked over to where she was sitting. She could have walked up alone, but she was nervous enough to be grateful for his hand as she climbed the three stairs to get to the stage.

At the last minute, he squeezed her elbow. 'You'll do great,' he whispered, seeming more nervous than she was.

To simulate the heightened pressure of a speech-making situation, a single light shone on an otherwise darkened stage, where she stood behind a lectern – both hands holding the sides for balance, her Pathway placed on the lectern, a microphone pointed directly down towards it. She looked out at the audience and pressed Play. She listened as the automated voice spoke:

'*We who are disabled know what it's like to have our bodies behave in unpredictable ways. Some mornings I wake up surprised by some new change. A knee that won't bend. A fist clenched tighter than it was the day before. What's this? I think. Yesterday I was fine. Now I'm really disabled.*'

It was meant to be a joke, but only two people laughed – her parents.

'*Making peace with a disabled body is a daily struggle. When I am out in the world, I must not only get from point A to point B, but I must also wear a face that says, "Don't worry! I'm okay!" Failing* to do this means I'd move through a world of concerned strangers offering unwanted help. Making peace means forgiving both my body and the world. For the disruption I will make to any room I walk into, for the conversations I must have about it over and over.

'Oh, to meet someone and not have our first conversation be about my talking board! It would be my greatest wish, but I've started to think recently that maybe it's the wrong one. Talking with my computer, about my computer, I've had a thousand versions of the same exchange, but I've also made surprising discoveries, like this one: We never move from that conversation on to the weather. My obvious struggle opens a door and makes other people more honest about their own struggles. After three years of high school, I understand this is rare.'

She let her head drop so her hair hung in front of her face. She couldn't look at her peer helpers for the next part.

'For the first time in my life, I've got over the barrier of my body and I have made what I consider the first real friends of my life. Doing this has taught me a lot about the world of able-bodied people. I have learned that some people who look fine are more crippled than I am, by fears they can't explain. Other people are held back by shyness, or anger. In making friends, I see the way some people handicap themselves. I believe there are choices each of us make every single day. We can dwell on our limitations or we can push ourselves past them. I may be a non-verbal girl delivering a speech, but I am no braver than a shy person walking up to their crush and asking them out. Or a socially phobic person going to a party. I have learned not to judge people by their limitations, but by the way they push past them.

'I have learned that many people have disabilities they must make their peace with.'

Amy wasn't sure what to make of the silence that followed. Her Pathway had no sense of theatre. No way to raise its voice to indicate a conclusion. No one clapped. Maybe they didn't realize it was over. Finally a light applause started from the general direction of her parents' seats. Others joined politely.

Suddenly it was obvious.

The problem wasn't her computer voice; it was her speech. She felt her face go warm as her legs froze. She had to take two steps from the podium to her walker, but she was afraid she wouldn't make it. Then she knew she wouldn't. She couldn't even turn in the right direction.

How long would it take someone to come help her? Who would it be?

Anyone but my mother, she thought.

Matthew, she thought. *Come save me from this.*

Then the lights came up and she saw: his seat was empty. He was already gone.

'I think Matthew was kind of upset,' Chloe said afterwards. 'Not that it wasn't a great speech, Aim. Seriously. But he might have thought you were talking about him or something.'

Sanjay, standing next to her, rolled his eyes. 'Gee, Chloe, why would he think that?'

Chloe didn't realize he was being sarcastic. '*You know*. He's the locker tapper. He's got his issues, and Amy just talked about them in front of everybody.' She was trying to whisper, but too many nights in loud clubs had left Chloe unable to moderate her voice.

Amy felt her breath go short. Why hadn't this occurred to

her? Other people had watched Matthew too. She had written the speech hoping to make a private point between the two of them. *We both have problems and we have to be brave. Look at me up here. If I can do this, you can too.* She imagined it leading to all sorts of breakthroughs. Matthew getting help, starting medication, showing up at her front door one day to kiss her in gratitude for the inspiration she provided with her speech.

'I think he's pretty pissed,' Chloe said.

Sanjay whistled. 'I'd call him rip-shit mad myself.'

For the rest of the day, Amy didn't see Matthew. That night she texted him from home:

I'm sorry, Matthew, if you took my speech the wrong way. It wasn't about you.

She pressed send and kept going.

It was about all my peer helpers. They all have secrets they don't show the world. I was trying to make a point about friendship. That if we're all honest, we can help each other.

That's all I wanted to say.

Matthew?

Are you seriously not talking to me?

Matthew?

For three days she didn't hear from him.

On Monday, she looked for him all day at school. Unfortunately he knew her schedule well enough so that he could easily avoid her, and her helper that day was Sarah.

'DID YOU THINK MY SPEECH WAS BAD?' she asked at lunch.

'No,' Sarah said. 'I actually thought you were talking about me for most of it. Then I looked over at Matthew and thought, *Oh right – it's got to be him.*'

Just as she was wondering if Matthew would ever speak to her again, she got another surprise: there he was after school, waiting for her outside the classroom door for yearbook. 'Were you saying Sarah and the others have secret problems no one knows about?'

She was so happy to see him that she couldn't help it: she squealed a little. She collected herself and turned on her Pathway. 'EVERYONE DOES, MATTHEW.'

'But it was me you were talking about.'

'NOT ONLY YOU.'

He stared at her. 'The others have fears they need to face?'

She could tell by his tone that he didn't believe her. 'SORT OF.'

He shook his head. 'You shouldn't have done that. What we talked about was private, and you announced it to the world.'

Amy thought about Sanjay and Chloe, how quickly they understood the problem. 'DO YOU REALLY THINK IT'S A SECRET?' He didn't say anything. 'PEOPLE NOTICE,

MATTHEW. THEY CALL YOU THE LOCKER TAPPER.'

'That's terrible.' He shook his head and looked away. 'Why would you *tell* me that?'

'WHY NOT? IT'S THE TRUTH. WHY IS THE TRUTH SO TERRIBLE?'

'It makes me never want to come to school again.'

'YOU COULD DO THAT, OR YOU COULD GO TO A DOCTOR AND GET HELP.'

'Why do you keep saying that?'

'BECAUSE YOU NEED IT.'

'I've read three books. I'm doing what they say. I have a mild case that isn't that bad.' Amy didn't say anything. 'It's helping. I'm *getting better.*'

'FINE.'

'You don't believe me.'

'NO.'

'I don't know what you want me to say.'

'IT'S NOT A MILD CASE AND YOU AREN'T GETTING BETTER. I SEE YOU COUNTING ALL THE TIME. WHISPERING. TAPPING LOCKERS. IF ANYTHING, IT'S GOT WORSE.'

CHAPTER ELEVEN

Matthew knew she was right. He thought he was better on his days with Amy, but that was only relative. It *had* got worse. The first time he told Amy about his fears, he felt such a sense of dizzying relief that he began confessing every irrational fear he'd ever had. For a while, he made funny stories out of the old ones. ('I used to be afraid of touching money,' he'd told Amy over lunch after he'd bought himself a milk. 'I had to pay for my milk with little baggies of coins.') At some point, though, a surprising aftermath hit. Something fired in his brain, like a seizure of panic. The voice returned angrier and more insistent. *You think I'm a joke? Something to tell that girl about?*

It made him stop talking about it completely. If Amy asked how he was doing, he told her he was reading the books and learning a lot. He told her he was doing the exercises in the books, even though he wasn't. Now he sat across from her in yearbook and thought about telling Amy the whole truth. What this was *really* like. How hard he tried to battle the worries. How he reminded himself, every morning: *Think good thoughts.* How he had his own speech composed long before she delivered hers. Only his existed solely inside his head: *Life is good. You are fine. No one will die because of you.*

What if he told her about the internal monologue that got delivered inside his head all day long: *It's just a faucet. It's off. Life is good. It's off. Don't check. You're fine. Okay. Check it once. Now. It's off. It's fine. No one will die or be hurt because of you. You*

84

checked the faucet. Amy is good. Amy is fine. Amy will not die or be hurt by that faucet. You checked the faucet. You can check again after Spanish but not before. If you check before you might get sick or Amy might get sick. She probably will get sick. So don't! Stop! If there's a quiz in Spanish you can check before the quiz because you haven't studied for the quiz so you'll need something to help. There is a quiz. Go! Go fast! Run out like you're sick with no time for a hall pass. You are sick because you knew there was a quiz and you wanted a reason to come back and check. There. You're fine. You're good. No one will die because of you.

Because Amy was looking at him funny, he didn't say any of this. Instead he said, 'It doesn't help to have you stand up in front of the whole school and announce my problems!'

'I DIDN'T.'

'Yes, you *did*. I'm trying to deal with this. I *am* dealing with this, but it's *my* thing to deal with, not yours. You think just because you've read a book, you know what will work for me better than I do. But this is my life. You don't know what's going on inside my head.'

She deleted whatever she was typing and replaced it. 'THEN TELL ME.'

His breath went short. 'I – I can't. It's not that easy.'

'TRY.'

'I don't want to.'

She pulled up what she was typing before. 'IN EIGHTY PER CENT OF PEOPLE WITH OCD, SOME COMBINATION OF MEDICATION, TALK THERAPY AND BEHAVIOUR TRAINING HELPS. YOU'RE NOT DOING ANY OF THOSE.'

He had no answer. She was right. He wasn't. He felt his breath go shallow, like he might start to hyperventilate.

'DON'T FREAK OUT. WHY DON'T YOU LET ME HELP YOU INSTEAD?'

'How?'

'I COULD GIVE YOU ASSIGNMENTS WITH JUST ENOUGH DIRT AND GERM EXPOSURE TO MAKE YOU UNCOMFORTABLE. THEN I'LL MAKE SURE YOU DON'T WASH YOUR HANDS, OR CHECK ANY FAUCETS. I'LL KEEP SCORE AND GIVE YOU MORE POINTS FOR THINGS THAT MAKE YOU REALLY UNCOMFORTABLE.'

He couldn't look up at her. He talked while looking down at his knees. 'I don't think I'm meant to include other people. I think this is a private thing.'

She typed quickly. 'YOU'RE WRONG. YOU'VE BEEN TOO PRIVATE. BEING SECRETIVE MAKES IT HARDER.'

'How would you know?'

'BELIEVE ME, I KNOW.'

'How?'

'GIRLS TRY TO BE PRIVATE ABOUT CERTAIN THINGS TOO, AND IT DOESN'T WORK.'

'What are girls private about?'

'LOTS OF THINGS.' She typed quickly while he worked to catch his breath. 'LIKE PERIOD STAINS. YOU TRY TO BE PRIVATE BUT THEN YOU REALIZE YOU HAVE A BIG, RED STAIN BETWEEN YOUR LEGS AND WHAT YOU REALLY NEED IS *HELP*.'

Why was she telling him this? It made the back of his neck prickle. 'Then you wash it away, right?'

'NOT AT SCHOOL. WASHING IT WOULD MAKE YOUR PANTS WET AND WOULD LOOK EVEN WORSE.'

He felt his throat tighten. He couldn't bear the thought. He shook his head to clear the picture of the bathroom and sinks filled with bloody water. *After this, I can go wash my hands,* he thought. *One quick trip to the bathroom. I'll wash once because I've earned it, sitting through this talk. Or twice, in case the faucets are dirty.* He had long sleeves on, thank goodness. That helped with faucet germs. If everyone turned faucets on and off with protection, there would be no problem with contamination at all. If the world could see –

Something in his brain stopped the train of thought.

A new thought materialized: Amy had done this on purpose. She'd brought up period stains knowing it would make him anxious. Knowing he'd hear it and want, first thing, to get to a bathroom and clean up. His hands were already damp and sweaty. He couldn't wipe them on his trousers, which were covered in chair germs and bus-seat contamination. The safest place was putting them in his armpits. Hopefully that would quiet his heart as well.

Why would she do this on purpose?

Then he realized she'd already told him. *I'll give you assignments that will make you uncomfortable.*

He was plenty uncomfortable now. His shirt was damp; sweat stains were blooming from his pits down to his waist. 'You're not going to let me go to the bathroom, are you?'

She thought for a bit before she typed. 'OF COURSE YOU CAN GO, BUT I'LL ENCOURAGE YOU NOT TO.'

He started to rock. *I'm okay*, he thought. *Amy is okay. No one is going to die or be hurt if I don't wash my hands. I can do it later, after we leave, and everything will be fine.*

That's when Amy's computer started talking again. 'YOUR OBSESSIONS AREN'T RATIONAL. YOUR FEAR MAY SEEM REAL BUT THE DANGER IS NOT. YOU'RE SAFE. YOU'RE ALL RIGHT. YOU'RE HAVING A PANIC ATTACK, BUT THAT DOESN'T MEAN YOU NEED TO WASH YOUR HANDS OR DO ANYTHING AT ALL. JUST RIDE IT OUT.'

He couldn't look at her.

He certainly didn't want her to reach over and touch him. He couldn't bear that. He'd fly apart or scream if she pushed this any further. She would let him go to the bathroom, but he couldn't, not really. This was the therapy he'd been reading about and pretending to do on his own. Confront the fear. Ride through it. Don't use a compulsion to make it go away. He'd thought about trying it. He'd imagined trying it, but, no, he hadn't actually tried it.

Because it was *hard*. He felt like throwing up. He felt like a flu was starting in his stomach and tearing through his body. Like any minute he'd have period stains on his trousers – or, worse, poop.

He folded himself further over and put his forehead between his knees. He took a few breaths. His face went hot and red. His heart pounded. His brain snagged on one thought:

Don't cry in front of Amy. She's seen a lot, but that would be too much. Just breathe in and out. Calm down. Find your voice. Say something so she knows you're not going to cry. He opened his mouth, but nothing came out. His tongue was dry as if all his saliva had turned into the sweat pouring from his armpits. He couldn't speak. He coughed, which made the silence worse.

He felt like they'd been there for an hour when her Pathway started up again. 'YOUR FEAR MAY SEEM REAL BUT THE DANGER IS NOT. YOU'RE SAFE. YOU'RE ALL RIGHT. YOU'RE HAVING A PANIC ATTACK. YOU DON'T NEED TO WASH YOUR HANDS OR DO ANYTHING AT ALL. JUST RIDE IT OUT.'

He remembered a suggestion he read in one of his books. *Make a tape of your own voice telling your brain to relax. Replace the compulsive thoughts with reassuring ones.*

Oh sure, he'd thought when he read it. *That won't seem crazy at all.*

Now he understood.

Replace one voice with another.

Teach your brain which one to listen to.

After it was all over, he felt light-headed and dizzy. The first words he said to Amy were, 'I hate you. I really do.'

'I KNOW. I HATE MYSELF SOMETIMES TOO.'

He took a long drink of water from a bottle in his backpack, and kept going. 'I don't want to make a little project out of this. You fixing me.'

'WHY NOT? I'M HARDLY FIXING YOU. I'M

HELPING YOU. YOU'RE DOING THE HARD WORK. I JUST SAT HERE.'

'Exactly. It's hard. And when –' He wasn't sure how to put this exactly. 'When I'm not in the middle of an attack, it's pretty easy to see how stupid I must look.'

'NOT AT ALL.' She thought for a moment. 'IT'S PRETTY EASY FOR ME TO SEE THAT EVERYONE ELSE CAN WALK AND TALK.'

'It's not the same.'

'ISN'T IT? YOU DON'T THINK I FEEL STUPID MOST OF THE TIME?'

The idea of this surprised him enough to think about it for a minute. No one blamed Amy for the way she looked and sounded. But people *did* blame him for the washing and the tapping and the strange things the voice in his head made him do. Maybe *blame* wasn't the right word. But they noticed. They looked at him funny. They slid their lunch trays away. And their chairs. And their eyes.

How long had he not wanted to admit this? He'd tried so hard to keep his private agony a secret that he hadn't realized how much it showed. Now that he thought about the looks people gave him walking down the hall, in class, even on the bus where he hardly knew anyone, it was like he'd become the contagion of which he was forever trying to rid himself.

It wasn't a secret at all. Everyone knew. His mother. Amy. Everyone he'd walked past these last few years. It was a horrible feeling, like a bad taste in the back of his mouth that didn't go away no matter how much he swallowed.

★

After yearbook, they sat outside on the planter beside the roundabout where Amy's mother picked her up. He thought about telling Amy she was right about a few things: he probably couldn't do this on his own. He probably did need help of some kind. He'd probably have to do all sorts of scary and embarrassing things, like go to a doctor and tell that person all his problems. He knew Amy was right, but his throat felt too clogged to say it.

There was a chance that he still might cry, and he didn't want to add that to the list of embarrassing things she'd seen him do today.

To his surprise she started talking: 'I ASKED IF I COULD HELP YOU BECAUSE I'VE NEVER BEEN ABLE TO DO THAT FOR ANYONE. I WANTED TO SEE IF I COULD. IT'S TERRIBLE ALWAYS BEING THE PERSON WHO NEEDS HELP. I'M SORRY IF I MISJUDGED EVERYTHING. I'M SO NEW AT HAVING FRIENDS THAT I MAKE MISTAKES SOMETIMES.'

'It wasn't a mistake.'

'IT WASN'T?'

'No. It's what I'm supposed to be doing. I just haven't yet because it isn't fun.'

'NO. I'M SURE IT ISN'T.'

He peeked up at her. 'It made me mad, I have to admit.'

'I KNOW. THAT'S WHY I'M SORRY.'

'You want to hear something weird, though?' A car pulled up that looked like Nicole's, but wasn't. Relieved, he kept talking. 'When I went to the bathroom just now I didn't wash my hands.'

'AT ALL?'

'No. I wanted to. But I didn't absolutely *have* to. Usually it feels like there's no choice at all. But this time it didn't.'

'THAT'S GREAT, MATTHEW! THAT'S WHAT'S SUPPOSED TO HAPPEN! YOU'RE RETRAINING YOUR BRAIN!'

'I still want to wash my hands. I probably will when I get home.'

'THAT'S OKAY.'

'I'm not cured or anything.'

'OF COURSE NOT.'

'I guess it's good for me to practise.' He looked at her shyly. 'And maybe have help.'

CHAPTER TWELVE

In the beginning, Amy limited her Matthew assignments to the days he walked her between classes. She printed them ahead of time so that no one overheard her in the hallway, instructing him to do strange, arbitrary things:

Touch honey and leave it on your hands for an hour.
Walk down four halls without tapping any lockers.

It broke her heart the way he nodded with each assignment and then looked away, as if he didn't want her to see his fear. She remembered reading that OCD was surprisingly unconnected to overall brain function. Meaning people with OCD can recognize how crazy their thoughts are; they just can't stop them.

Writing the assignments had another plus: they didn't have to discuss why he did these things or what bad luck he was trying to keep at bay. Given the silence she spent so much of her day in, Amy recognized that with certain matters the less said, the better. Irrational thoughts were irrational. No need to make him feel more self-conscious by insisting on a rational discussion of them.

After a few weeks, he admitted that her repetitions helped. Occasionally she played those again if she saw his hands shaking, or his lips moving. 'THIS ISN'T A RATIONAL THOUGHT YOU'RE HAVING. YOU ARE SAFE. YOU ARE FINE. THE FEAR MAY BE

REAL BUT THE DANGER IS NOT.'

His progress was bumpy. Some days he'd have no problem walking down the hall without tapping lockers; other times she watched him go white as his lips moved: 'The fear is real. The danger is not.'

To take his mind off his assignments, Amy told him more stories. She could see that it helped. As they walked and he concentrated, she played stories that she'd typed in the night before. She told him about trips she'd taken with her parents to France, the Grand Canyon and Disney World. The best part, she said, was usually the motorized scooter they rented for her on the trips. 'YOU CAN'T BELIEVE HOW FAST THEY GO. FEELS LIKE FLYING.'

When he asked why she didn't use one all the time, she explained her mother's philosophy: that if Amy wanted to keep up in the real world, she could never take the easy route. 'Yes, this will be hard,' Nicole would tell Amy as they practised walking four or five hours a day through the first six years of Amy's life. 'But we're not afraid of hard.' When Amy told him this story, she mistyped it. 'You're not afraid of *heart*?' Matthew said.

'HARD.'

'I don't get that.'

'WE'RE NOT AFRAID OF HARD. LIKE, "LOOK, HONEY, EVERYTHING'S GOING TO BE HARD FOR YOU. DON'T BE AFRAID OF IT."'

'Oh.'

'IT'S SUPPOSED TO BE INSPIRING. GOD KNOWS I DON'T APPROVE OF EVERYTHING MY MOTHER

DOES, BUT I THINK SHE WAS RIGHT ABOUT THAT. SHE TAUGHT ME NOT TO BE AFRAID OF HARD WORK.'

'Right. Okay.'

Matthew listened to this and remembered another story Amy had told about her mother. After she was born, the doctor told them Amy would probably never walk, talk, or even lift her head. 'SO GUESS WHAT MY MOTHER DID?' He couldn't guess. 'WHEN I WAS FIVE MONTHS OLD, SHE LAID ME FACE DOWN IN THE BATHTUB WITH ABOUT AN INCH OF WATER IN IT.'

Just hearing the story sent a chill down his spine. '*Why?* You could have drowned.'

'BUT I DIDN'T! I LEARNED TO LIFT MY HEAD.'

It was like Amy had never been afraid of anything. Starting school in second grade had been no problem. Not being understood until she got her first communication device, a DynaVox, in fourth grade, was frustrating but not particularly scary. He tried to imagine being so young, navigating his way through endless days around a huge school when no one understood a single word he said. Another chill ran through him.

'IT WAS FINE!' Amy insisted. 'I WAS OUT OF THE HOUSE, IN THE SAME ROOM WITH OTHER KIDS. I WAS HAPPY.'

Some of her stories weren't so happy. She told one about being in Mr Heffernan's seventh-grade science class. It started as a funny story about Sarah's father, except it wasn't all that funny. Amy loved science, and worked hard on a project proposal for the state science fair. When she was one of four students chosen as a finalist, Mr Heffernan told her she couldn't go. It would be too hard on her, he said.

'That's terrible,' Matthew said. 'Weren't you mad?'

'MY MOTHER WAS. I DON'T KNOW IF I WAS SO MAD.'

She finished the story that night on email:

To: mstheword@gmail.com
From: aimhigh@comcast.net
Subject: seventh grade

When my mom went in to complain that I had a proposal that had been accepted and an A in his class and what more did he want, Mr Heffernan said, 'Yes, but she has an aide assisting her in taking all the tests. I have no real proof that she's doing the work.'

I told my mother it didn't bother me. How was he to know that if Sybil, my aide, had taken the test, I'd have probably earned a C in the class? Embarrassingly my mother kept pushing the issue, even after I asked her to stop. She said if she didn't fight him he'd continue to exclude every disabled kid coming up behind me. He still held his ground. It would never work, he said. It would be too hard on me. He said parking in the city was a problem. Sometimes they had to walk two or three blocks, carrying their projects. The less valid his points seemed, the harder my mother fought, until it became an all-out war of letters and emails. I didn't realize it was happening until years later, when I found copies in my mother's desk drawer.

In one letter, Mr Heffernan wrote, 'With all due respect, you might have a skewed view of your daughter's abilities. Perhaps you haven't considered the disservice it does to her very real accomplishments to insist she's capable of being superior in all her academic subjects. I'd ask you to look again at your daughter – where her genuine affinities lie – and not push her into areas where she isn't interested in achieving.'

The first time I read that, I actually thought he had a decent point. Because academics came so easily to me, my mother wanted me to be great at *everything*. But I've always loved reading and writing most of all, so why did I have to be great at science too? I don't know. Maybe I just admired him for standing up to my mother.

No one else had ever done that.

That night, Matthew surprised himself by composing a longer response than usual.

To: aimhigh@comcast.net
From: mstheword@gmail.com
Re: seventh grade

Your story makes me think about Sarah and what it must be like to have only one parent and have that parent be Mr Heffernan. I always remember this one conversation I had with her in eighth grade. We were dialogue partners in French, which meant memorizing these stilted, fake conversations where teenagers ask each other what time it is and then talk endlessly about the pleasant weather. They always end up going to a cafe and ordering a *jambon sandwich* to trick you into saying it wrong. In France you say *sandweeeech*. Sarah and I had the softest voices in the class, which meant the teacher was always clapping her hands and screaming, '*Répétez! Répétez!*'

I felt especially bad because it seemed like the teacher didn't give Sarah a break, even though we all knew her mom had just died the year before. Then one day, I couldn't believe it. We were in the middle of our dialogue and Sarah started crying. She was turned away from the rest of the class so only I saw it.

We talked for the first time after class that day. She said she wasn't sure why reciting dialogues was so hard for her, but she thought maybe it was because she spent most of the time feeling invisible and doing those dialogues made her realize she wasn't, and that made her even more sad.

So that's why I had a crush on Sarah for a little while. Kind of hard not to, but nothing ever came of it. Partners got switched in French, we were both paired with shouters and we never talked again.

The weird thing now is that even through that whole

training week at the beginning of this year we never once mentioned that French class. I assume girls forget things like that, maybe. Boys don't. Or I haven't anyway.

About your story – I think Mr Heffernan was totally wrong and you're being way too nice by forgiving him. I just looked it up and keeping you out of the science fair is against the law. Nobody can be excluded from a school or activity because of their disability. So, yeah. I guess your mother was right to fight that one.

Do you have another task for me? I can't believe I'm asking this.

On Monday, Amy greeted him with a big smile. She'd been puzzling over his story all weekend, wondering if it might be a hopeful sign. He'd had a crush on Sarah and had done nothing about it. It wasn't *Amy's* body he was scared of – it was *all* girls'. At first it made her nervous, then she got an idea. The more she thought about it, the better the idea seemed. 'I HAVE A NEW ASSIGNMENT FOR YOU.'

He looked especially handsome this morning, in a black T-shirt with a fading guitar logo on the front, which made this even better.

'Okay. What is it?'

'TODAY YOU WILL ASK SARAH OUT ON A DATE.'

'Oh, okay. No thanks to that one.'

'LET ME REPHRASE. NOT A *DATE* DATE. YOUR ASSIGNMENT IS TO INVITE SARAH TO TACO BELL

FOR LUNCH, ORDER TWO BURRITOS, AND EAT THEM. NO BATHROOM TRIPS, NO TAPPING. AFTERWARDS I'LL NEED A FULL REPORT.'

He shook his head. He couldn't look at her.

'Are you *serious*?' he said.

'VERY SERIOUS.'

'Because this is different from any of the other assignments. This involves – one – getting over the fear of stepping into a Taco Bell, and – two – getting over what you obviously understand is a large fear of talking to Sarah.'

'EXACTLY. THAT'S WHY I PICKED IT. PLUS IT'S THE ONLY RESTAURANT YOU CAN WALK TO.'

'Why do I have to do both things at once? Why don't I just go to Taco Bell with you?'

She smiled and almost typed something flirty. *Are you asking me on a date?* But she didn't. Since Christmas vacation, when she'd tried to tell him how she felt, Amy's feelings hadn't changed, but her strategy had. If she was really his friend and helped him get better, maybe he would see what was obvious. That he liked her too. Of course it was a risk as well – sending him on a date with another girl to get him to notice her. But it was a risk she'd have to take. 'BECAUSE I DON'T EAT THERE. IT'S A LITTLE TOO GROSS FOR ME.'

'That's not funny.'

'I'M NOT TRYING TO BE FUNNY.'

'I don't want this assignment. Give me something else.'

'YOU AGREED, MATTHEW. YOU HAVE TO DO THIS IF YOU WANT TO GET WELL. BESIDES, I HAVE A THEORY. YOU SAID YOUR OCD GOT WORSE

STARTING THREE YEARS AGO, WHICH MEANS IT WAS NINTH GRADE, THE YEAR RIGHT AFTER YOU HAD YOUR CRUSH ON SARAH. I THINK THAT MEANS SOMETHING.'

'Like what?'

'LIKE MAYBE THE VOICE BLAMES YOU FOR NOT BEING BRAVE ENOUGH TO ASK HER OUT BACK THEN. THIS IS ABOUT CONQUERING FEARS, RIGHT?'

'I guess.'

'DOES THE IDEA OF ASKING HER OUT MAKE YOU AFRAID?'

'Yes.'

'GOOD. THEN YOU SHOULD DO IT. IT WON'T BE A DATE. PRETEND YOU WANT TO TALK ABOUT ME, SINCE THAT'S WHAT YOU HAVE IN COMMON NOW. THAT SHOULD GET YOU THROUGH LUNCH, AT LEAST.'

'You really want me to do that?'

As she typed, she thought about the question. *Did* she really want him to do this? What if it went amazingly well and a few weeks from now he wrote her to say, *Guess what? Sarah and I are going to see a movie tonight.* Given that Sarah dated a twenty-three-year-old last year, it wasn't likely, but it was possible. She might surprise everyone by looking at Matthew and seeing what Amy saw – his beautiful blue eyes, the way his smile made his whole face light up. Sarah might not care about his non-existent social status, and think, *Why not date a nice boy after all these jerks who never call?* It could happen.

The possibility scared Amy, but she also knew this: Matthew needed to prove something to himself.

Up until now, they'd been working on irrational fears. Shyness around a girl wasn't irrational. If he could do this, it would be big. 'YES,' Amy typed. 'I DO. I THINK IT WILL BE AN EXCELLENT EXERCISE.'

CHAPTER THIRTEEN

Oh, the whole episode was excruciating. His heart thudded audibly; a bead of perspiration trickled down one side of his face. 'Hey, Sarah, what're you doing for lunch?' Matthew said, coming up behind her at a water fountain.

'*Today?*' she said, standing, dripping water from her chin. 'Right now?'

'Not *right* now. It's only ten fifteen. But we have the same lunch block, right? At least I think we do. Never mind. Maybe we don't.'

'I've got C.'

'Me too.'

'Well, I guess that's the same, then, right?'

'I guess it is.'

'If you'd like to go out for lunch, we could. I don't have a car or anything so I couldn't drive us. We'd have to go to Taco Bell, which some people think is gross, I know.'

'That's okay. I like Taco Bell.' She looked around the hallway. 'Sure, why not? Does anyone else want to come, or just us?'

He panicked. He wasn't prepared for this question, even though it was probably a normal one. How many times had he heard someone say, 'We're headed to the Bell, anyone want to come?' Never to him, of course. But people said it.

He couldn't think how to respond. They weren't part of any larger group. They shared no friends, unless she meant Amy. But Amy couldn't come if they were going to talk about her. And Amy couldn't swallow anything at Taco Bell, except maybe refried beans and a little rice. Instead of answering Sarah's question, he let an awkward amount of time pass without speaking. Finally he said, 'So . . . what? Should I meet you out front at eleven twenty?'

Seniors were allowed to leave school for lunch on Fridays only. So far, Matthew hadn't left for lunch once, but he knew most kids piled into cars and drove. Taco Bell was the only place in walking distance. It required taking a route past the field house and down an alley filled with trash dumpsters. Matthew wondered if his brain would let him touch food after walking past so much trash. He wondered if Taco Bell sold any food he could eat with a fork. Would it be worse to eat his food holding it with a paper wrapper, or to wash his hands a few times before they sat down? What had Amy said the rules were? He couldn't remember.

One thing he knew for sure: this wouldn't be like her other tasks, which all involved confronting private fears on his own. He knew this the minute they stepped into the restaurant. Crowded with seniors, the line to order food stretched about seven people long.

'Maybe we should leave,' he said, his mouth dry.

'No, I've been here before. The line goes pretty fast.' Even as Sarah spoke, the line moved forward. 'See?'

Sarah was, if anything, even prettier now than she was in ninth grade. Her hair was shorter and cut in a chin-length bob. She looked older than other girls, but not in the same way other girls looked older, with heavy make-up and revealing clothes. She just looked more comfortable with herself and happier.

Ryan Starling, an idiot who rode on Matthew's bus, turned round and looked at them. 'What are you two doing here?' he said. Ryan was also a star wrestler, which meant his legs and arms bowed a little with all his muscles.

Sarah laughed easily, like what he said was funny, not insulting. 'We live here, actually, Ryan. We eat every single meal here. It's strange, I know, but we can't get enough of it.'

'This *crap*?' Ryan said.

'I know. Weird, right? Do this: order every item off the dollar menu and eat it all in one sitting. Afterwards you'll think, *God, I really love Taco Bell.*'

Ryan leaned towards Sarah and lifted his eyebrows. 'How 'bout you help me eat it?'

'Oh no. Not today. I only let myself do that treat once a week.'

Matthew watched them and wondered: What happened to the shy girl who cried doing French dialogue focused on her? When had Sarah Heffernan become joking buddies with the jocks?

'I'll tell you what. If I order all that food, why don't you sit with me anyway —'

'Not today, Ryan. Let's get dysentery together another time, 'kay?'

After Matthew and Sarah got their food, they sat down at the only empty table left, in front of the drink dispenser.

'How do you know that guy?' Matthew whispered.

'Who, Ryan?' Sarah shrugged. 'I think we had life drawing together last year. He's not as bad as he seems, but maybe that's not saying too much.'

Matthew wanted to ask how she'd grown more relaxed over the last three years while the opposite had been true for him. He wondered if she even remembered the conversation they once had where she'd cried and he comforted her. Instead of asking about this, he asked why she signed up to work with Amy. Right away she grew quiet, as if it were an awkward question.

'It's kind of a long story,' Sarah said. 'Not that interesting, probably.'

'Does it have to do with your dad?'

She started eating one of her tacos one-handed. He'd ordered a burrito, but couldn't bring himself to unwrap it. 'Sort of,' she said softly. 'He asked me to do it. And I didn't have much community service for my college apps.'

He wondered if he should tell her what Amy had once pointed out to him – that technically you shouldn't get *paid* for community service. 'Why did your dad want you to do it?'

'He always felt bad about something that happened when Amy was in his class.'

She told him the story about the science fair that he already knew. 'He didn't let her participate because he always assumed that Nicole pushed Amy to be some kind of disabled superachiever. Like her mother had this agenda to prove the doctors were wrong. He thought it was dangerous for Amy's sake, and none of the school administrators would say no when she signed Amy up for an all-honours schedule. He was convinced Nicole wrote the science-fair proposal.' She shrugged. 'I guess he wanted to know if he was right.'

'He wanted you to figure out if Amy was really smart?'

'Something like that.'

'What did you tell him?'

'I told him I thought he was probably right. I know that sounds terrible – I know Amy's smart enough that she *could* have written the proposal; I just don't think she *did*. I don't think she's *that* into science.' She shrugged as if this wasn't a particularly shocking thing to say. 'I don't know. It's just my hunch.'

Matthew felt his face go red. He'd never be able to eat a bite now. 'How can you *say* that? Of course she wrote it herself! You've seen her writing. You know how good it is.'

'Right – it's just the feeling I get. I mean, look at Nicole. She's way too invested in Amy's accomplishments. Has Amy told you how many colleges she's applying to?'

His heart started to race again. No, she hadn't. 'How many?' he said softly.

'Twenty. I'm not kidding. I know we're all being a little ridiculous with our thirteen applications and our parents breathing down our necks, but *twenty*? Five Ivy Leagues? You don't think that's a bit much? I'm surprised Amy hasn't mentioned this to you. It's almost all we talk about. We're applying to two of the same schools, and they have these crazy essays. *Describe what your life would be like if you lived on the moon. Write an essay from the point of view of one of your hands.* You wouldn't believe what we've had to write about.'

'Where is she applying?'

Sarah rattled off a list: Yale, Brown, Stanford, Columbia. He stopped listening. His breath went shallow. How did he not know any of this? The applications were due months ago.

Amy had never mentioned them once. 'Do you think she'll get in?'

'Oh sure. She's got the grades and the board scores. I think that's what worried my dad. He was talking to the high-school guidance counsellor, who said Amy was probably our best shot at Harvard or Yale this year, and it made him feel bad about what happened when she was in seventh grade.'

Harvard or *Yale?* Was she serious?

'Aren't you going to eat, Matthew?'

'No.' He was really sweating now. And having a hard time breathing. 'I have – I'm sorry . . . I have to go to the bathroom.'

In the bathroom, he plunged his hand into the hottest water he could get from the tap. His skin went from pink to red. He washed his hands, then his wrists, then up to his elbows. He sterilized everything front and back. He rinsed and shut off the faucet with his elbow.

Who did Amy think she was, getting inside his head, telling him what to do when she'd never told him the first real thing that was going on in her life? *Harvard or Yale?* He'd never met anyone who applied to either of those places, let alone had a reasonable chance of getting in. A new, terrible thought occurred to him: *Amy felt sorry for him*. She knew he didn't have the grades or the scores to get into a competitive college. Actually, his grades were okay; his test scores were the embarrassment. He'd taken them twice, the second untimed. Even then, his anxiety was so bad he actually sweated on to the paper on which he was bubbling answers. His second score only went up by fifteen points – such an incremental gain, his guidance counsellor suggested that he should rethink where he wanted to apply. Or even *if* he wanted to apply. 'College can be stressful for some kids. Taking a year off might not be a bad idea. I even encourage it in some cases.'

They never talked about it again because, secretly, he was relieved. Everything about college applications had filled him with dread, especially the essays that encouraged you to 'describe your thought process in coming to this conclusion/opinion/decision, etc.' How could he do this? How could he write, *After thirty-two checks of the faucet, I determined that Pitzer is my number-one school choice, mostly because it has an even number of vowels in its name, which for some reason my brain cares about right now*?

He wasn't sure how long he stayed in the bathroom. Long enough to wash his hands four more times without doing it twice in front of the same person. Long enough to calm down from all the information Sarah had told him. Long enough that, by the time he walked out of the bathroom, Sarah had switched tables and was sitting with Ryan.

'TELL ME ABOUT YOUR LUNCH WITH SARAH,' Amy asked him the next day. 'I'LL NEED A FULL REPORT TO GIVE YOU CREDIT.'

'Why didn't you tell me where you're applying to college?'

'IT NEVER CAME UP. WHAT DIFFERENCE DOES IT MAKE?'

'A lot. You should have told me.'

'*WHY?*'

'Because I had to hear about it from Sarah. It was terrible.'

'WHERE DID YOU THINK I WAS APPLYING?'

He hesitated. What *had* he thought? If he was honest, he assumed she wasn't going to college. That the practical logistics would be too complicated even for a smart girl like Amy.

'I assumed you weren't applying.'

'BUT MY MOM TALKS ABOUT ME GOING TO COLLEGE ALL THE TIME.'

It was true; Nicole did talk about it a lot. 'I guess I didn't picture you going right away. Or applying to places so far away. Are you really going to live in a dorm?'

'THAT'S THE IDEA.'

'And you think that's a good idea?'

'WHAT'S WRONG WITH IT?'

Did she need him to spell out the ways it could be a disaster? Should he remind her of everything other people did for her? 'I just think it's naive. College isn't like high school.'

'WHAT'S THAT SUPPOSED TO MEAN?'

'People will be busy doing their own thing. They'll have cars and be joining fraternities and sororities. I think in college, people tend to be more self-absorbed.'

'WHAT ARE YOU SAYING?'

'You've never been away from home. You tried summer camp and you hated it. You spent the whole time in your cabin sleeping.' She'd told him the story over lunch once. It was her only experience getting to know a group of kids as disabled as she was. The big surprise was discovering how little she had in common with any of them.

'THAT WAS DIFFERENT. I CAN'T BELIEVE YOU'RE EVEN BRINGING IT UP.'

'I don't understand why you're applying to all these Ivy League schools. Is it just so you can walk around telling people you got into Yale?'

'NO. I APPLIED SO I CAN GO TO YALE.'

'But why there? Why not someplace closer – where you can live at home?'

'BECAUSE THIS IS MY CHANCE TO LIVE AWAY FROM HOME.'

'But what if you can't do it? What if it's a disaster?'

She typed for a minute. 'IF I CAN GET IN, THAT'S A PRETTY GOOD SIGN THEY THINK I CAN DO IT, RIGHT?'

He felt like a tennis ball was bouncing around in his stomach. *NO!* he wanted to say. *It's a sign that they want to look good for accepting an intelligent, non-verbal girl.* 'Have you made it clear everything you can't do? That you need help in the bathroom and eating and getting dressed?' He knew it was mean to point these things out, but he couldn't stop himself.

'JUST BECAUSE YOU'RE TOO SCARED TO TAKE ANY RISKS DOESN'T MEAN THE REST OF US SHOULD BE.'

'This isn't about me, Amy. It's about you.'

'I THINK THIS IS ABOUT YOU, MATTHEW. I'M SORRY, BUT I DO.'

CHAPTER FOURTEEN

Amy never expected Sarah to tell Matthew about her college applications, and now she wondered if she'd made a terrible mistake. Helping him get over his fear of going out with a girl was only one of the reasons she suggested the lunch with Sarah. The other reason had to do with a secret she'd been keeping for almost two weeks: she'd been accepted at Stanford and offered a scholarship.

'I DON'T WANT TO TELL ANYONE AT SCHOOL YET,' Amy told her mother after she got the news. 'THERE ARE TOO MANY PEOPLE WHO HAVEN'T HEARD YET.'

'They're going to find out sooner or later, Aim. You don't have to protect people.'

'I KNOW THAT, MOM. BUT LET ME DECIDE WHEN THAT IS. *PLEASE*.'

'Okay.'

'I *MEAN* IT.'

Her mother waved her hands. 'Fine, fine. I'll keep my mouth shut.'

To Amy's surprise, she did.

These college acceptances had left everyone feeling unmoored. She heard more bad news than good about the letters other people were getting from college. Sarah had been wait-listed at Berkeley, but rejected everywhere else. Sanjay had one acceptance, but no offers of even a smidgen of scholarship. Amy waited for a rejection so she could share that first. 'I GUESS BROWN'S TAKING NO ONE,' she planned to say. And then she got into Brown.

'Can we tell people now?' her mother asked.

'No,' she said.

The next week University of Pennsylvania and Vassar welcomed her into their freshman classes. Sarah had got two more rejections and one wait list. Sanjay had got no money from MIT. Chloe, with her 1.9 average, seemed as if she was faring better than anyone else. She planned to start at community college, where she would turn around her study habits and eventually apply to law school.

The only person who never – even once – talked about next year was Matthew.

Amy knew why. If a can of Sprite left unattended made him anxious, how could he face the prospect of filling out a college application? She wished she could tell him the truth: *Of course I haven't talked to you about college. You're working on something harder and more important right now.* She wished she could express how it felt to watch him overcome some of his most stubborn fears: *What you're doing right now is harder than me getting into colleges. Be proud of this. Don't worry about the rest.*

Instead of saying this, she typed, 'YOU DIDN'T TELL ME HOW LUNCH WITH SARAH WAS,' to change the subject.

'Fine.'

'REALLY FINE OR FAKE FINE?' They had ten minutes before the first bell would ring. She didn't want to start walking. She wanted to have this conversation.

113

'I don't know. I'm not sure I like her all that much any more.'

'WHY NOT?'

'She's changed a lot.'

'WAS SARAH MEAN TO YOU? I'LL BE REALLY MAD IF SHE WAS.' It was a surprising impulse. Amy definitely didn't want him to fall in love with Sarah again, but she also didn't want Sarah to have given him any reason to distrust girls.

'I don't want to talk about it. She said some things I didn't like; that's all.'

'LIKE WHAT?'

'Like she thinks her dad was right, leaving you out of the science fair.'

For a long time Amy didn't say anything.

'WE SHOULD PROBABLY GO,' she finally typed.

For the rest of the afternoon, they didn't mention Sarah again.

That night after dinner, Matthew sent her an email:

I'm sorry for telling you about what Sarah said. I made it sound much worse than it was. Sarah likes you. I can't really explain, except I don't think I can keep any secrets from you. Even ones I should.

Ten minutes later, he got this back: *There's something I have to tell you.*

He wrote right back: *You're there! Hurray! You're speaking to me!*

In return, he got this:

I got a scholarship to Stanford. I also got into six other schools, but I'm going to Stanford. I was scared to tell you. That's why I pushed you into taking Sarah out to lunch. I wanted to have something else to talk about.

Though she waited for half an hour, she got no response.

CHAPTER FIFTEEN

It took less than a day for the word to spread. Ms Malone, Amy's tenth-grade English teacher, screamed and began to cry at the news. Mr Hayes, their principal, hugged her. Chloe decorated Amy's locker with streamers, and the editor of the school newspaper emailed her a note about doing a story on her.

I'm not sure about that, Amy wrote back. *A lot of people are getting their acceptances. I don't think mine is such a big deal.*

But it was. That night their local newspaper, the *Franklin County Bulletin*, called to schedule an interview and asked if they might send a photographer over.

'Of course,' her mother said.

Later that same night, the local TV station called. 'I talked for a long time to a woman named Ashley,' Nicole told Amy while she got ready for bed. 'She was so nice and so excited for you, Amy. I said it was fine for their camera crew to come after the newspaper. That way you won't have to get dressed up twice.'

A camera crew for a TV show? 'YOU SAID YES WITHOUT ASKING ME?'

'Of course I did, sweetheart. You have to understand. This isn't just about you.'

Amy didn't understand. 'WHO IS IT ABOUT?'

'You're a role model, darling. For every child with a disability who is struggling right now, wondering if they will ever go to college or have a chance at a normal life.'

Amy wondered if that were really true, or if other kids with disabilities felt the way she did when she went to that camp and was surrounded by other kids with disabilities. Amy liked the idea of inspiring a community she didn't know very well. She wanted to feel a bond with them. The problem was, she didn't. She couldn't stop thinking about Matthew and her other friends. How none of them had sorted out what next year would look like yet. How they were hovering on wait lists and updates from financial-aid offices. Except for Matthew, poor Matthew, who had simply gone silent on the subject altogether.

She wasn't an inspiration to any of them; she knew that much.

Instead of getting angry at Amy for keeping secrets, Matthew surprised himself. He got angry at himself. Angry enough to ask his mother to make an appointment with a doctor.

'For what?' his mother asked.

'You know what for. A psychologist. To do whatever. Talk about my problems. Get medication.' He had a terror of taking pills, but he'd been reading more case studies in his library books where medication was necessary when other therapies didn't work.

'Oh, Matthew, that's wonderful!' His mother clapped her hands. 'It's a wonderful idea!'

In the doctor's office, he surprised himself by staying calm and making more sense about this whole business than he ever had before. The woman's name was Beth – she had red, curly hair and looked too young to be a doctor, though she assured him she was. He told Beth he'd had OCD off and on for at least four years, maybe longer. He said he'd been doing exposure/response-prevention therapy for about six weeks, and it hadn't made much of a difference. 'I waste more time now than I ever did before, obsessing about whatever I'm not meant to be thinking of. I'm just *tired* of it. I'm so sick of the whole thing.'

He described some of his fixations: the hand washing, the water faucets, counting even-numbered objects in a room. He told her his main fear, of hurting other people. That he might have done it in the past, or done it unintentionally. He told her about the can of Sprite, and the terrible fear that he might have hurt Amy as a baby in the hospital. Fifty minutes later, he walked out of her office with a prescription. That night he took his first pill before he had time to worry about what the voice might say. The next morning he woke up expecting to feel different.

He didn't.

It was early and his mother hadn't left for work yet. He walked into the kitchen, where she was reading an article about Amy in the newspaper.

'She really is something, isn't she?' his mother said.

Alongside the article, there was a picture of Amy seated at the kitchen table. She looked beautiful – her hair curly, down around her shoulders, her face relaxed, not into a smile, exactly, but a welcoming look.

'I guess so,' he said.

Take the picture up to your room, the voice said. *You know you want to.*

'She got into more schools than just Stanford,' his mother said brightly. 'Six altogether. Three Ivy League. You probably knew that.'

You didn't know that, the voice said. *You never asked.*

'Where?'

His mother rattled off the list of schools.

She's famous, the voice said. *Or, if she's not famous yet, she's going to be famous soon. Like Stephen Hawking, only prettier. And a girl.*

Here was a surprise: if anything, the pill had made the voice *chattier*.

You'll be sorry, it said.

Sorry for what? his brain answered. He took the article from his mother and carried it into the bathroom. *What will I be sorry for?*

Maybe this was a change. He'd never had an argument with his brain before.

It's so obvious and you don't even see.

See what? Just tell me.

You love her.

No, I don't. I can't believe you said that.

Fine. Whatever.

I don't love her. That's a ridiculous thing to say.

Fine. It doesn't matter. She's pretty much through with you anyway.

He read the article to the end, and wondered if his brain knew something he didn't. He thought: *She's through with me?*

CHAPTER SIXTEEN

'SO I HAVE YOUR NEXT ASSIGNMENT,' Amy said as he helped her out of her mother's car. 'I KNOW YOU'VE BEEN WAITING, AND IT'S A GOOD ONE, TRUST ME.'

Two weeks had passed since his lunch date with Sarah. There had been no assignments since then because now that Amy was semi-famous, she was too busy.

'One article in the newspaper doesn't mean she's famous,' his mother said.

'Don't forget TV,' Matthew reminded her. 'She was also on the news.' Thank heavens Amy looked more like her real self and less beautiful on TV. He was trying not to think about what the voice had said. On TV, her mouth fell open and her head wobbled as the interviewer asked her stupid questions like, 'Is it exciting to have got into so many great schools?' and 'Do you think college will be harder for you than high school or easier?' Matthew liked Amy's answer to the first question ('SINCE I CAN ONLY GO TO ONE SCHOOL, IT DOESN'T REALLY MATTER HOW MANY I GOT INTO') and loved her answer to the second one ('HARDER, I HOPE. IT WOULD BE A RIP-OFF IF IT WAS EASIER, RIGHT?'). It was a great moment of television awkwardness as the interviewer took about twenty seconds to decide whether Amy was joking. Finally she decided yes and laughed.

Maybe Amy wasn't famous compared to movie stars, but in *their* school, for the last two weeks, she was. The old stares she always got walking down the hall had changed to whispers and smiles and even finger waves. Towering jocks from the basketball team touched her shoulder and said, 'Congrats, Aim. Nice job!' like they'd been friends for years. One day Matthew kept a count: thirty-two people said hello to Amy before lunch. 'I could give your mom a list of the names. She could enter it into her database.'

'HA-HA,' Amy typed. 'BUT NO THANKS.'

In the last few weeks, he'd noticed one interesting change. Amy had started eating real food in front of him. Soft, unchokable food like hummus and tabbouleh salad. She still made a mess, though once she'd made the decision to eat in front of him, she didn't seem to care much what she looked like. When he asked why she was eating real food for lunch suddenly, she told him he should be flattered. That she only ate in front of people she felt comfortable with. He *was* flattered until it occurred to him – maybe she was comfortable because now she thought of him as more disabled than she was.

'Come on – you've got a Hi–Bye friend list that's probably sixty names long now. Maybe more. Your mom will be so happy.'

'THESE PEOPLE AREN'T MY FRIENDS. THEY DON'T KNOW ME AT ALL.'

'Of course they don't know you. Hi–Bye friends aren't supposed to know you. They exist solely to promote a feeling of popularity, however superficial that might be.'

'I DON'T LIKE THEM SAYING HI SUDDENLY WHEN THEY'VE SPENT THE LAST ELEVEN YEARS IGNORING ME.'

He could tell by the way her chin jutted out that she was serious. This wasn't a joke. It really bothered her. 'Maybe it's good to learn this now. It'll save you the trouble of pledging a sorority later.'

'I'M SERIOUS. I REALLY DON'T LIKE IT. PEOPLE I DON'T KNOW CALL THE HOUSE. MY MOM GETS THEIR EMAIL AND MAKES ME WRITE BACK TO THEM.'

'Who's called you?'

'WEIRD PEOPLE. A BOOK AGENT SAID I COULD BE LIKE THE KID WITH MS IN THE WHEELCHAIR WHO WROTE INSPIRATIONAL POETRY. I SAID, "DIDN'T HE DIE?" AND SHE SAID, "YEAH, THAT'S WHY EVERYONE LOVED HIM SO MUCH. HE WROTE POETRY IN THE FACE OF DEATH."'

'How are you supposed to be like him if you're not dying?'

'I TOLD HER THAT AND SHE WAS SURPRISED. SHE THOUGHT HEMIPLEGIA MEANT DE-GENERATIVE. I SAID NO, HEMIPLEGIA MEANS ONE SIDE OF MY BODY IS MORE AFFECTED THAN THE OTHER. HEMIPLEGIA DOESN'T MEAN DEGENERATIVE. *DEGENERATIVE* MEANS DEGENERATIVE.'

Matthew felt bad that he'd been so angry at Amy for the last few weeks. It sounded terrible. 'What's the assignment you have for me?'

'OKAY – I GOT THE IDEA FROM CHLOE. SHE SAID THERE'S AN OPENING AT THE MOVIE

THEATRE WHERE SHE WORKS. I THINK YOU SHOULD APPLY.'

She took a bite of tabbouleh salad that only made it halfway into her mouth. The rest got sprinkled on her Pathway and the table.

'You want me to apply for a *job*?'

She nodded. It was hard for her to eat and type at the same time.

That's not an assignment, that's a job, his voice said. He repeated it out loud.

'IT'LL BE FINE. YOU POUR A FEW SODAS, SELL A LITTLE CANDY AND THAT'S IT. YOU'RE DONE.'

'You want me to work *concessions*?'

'DON'T SAY NO AUTOMATICALLY. SAY, "I'LL THINK ABOUT IT, AMY."'

'I'll think about it, Amy. And then I'll say no.'

'I WAS PRETTY SURE YOU'D SAY THAT, SO I FILLED OUT AN APPLICATION FOR YOU. I REALIZE THAT MIGHT SEEM LIKE AN OVERSTEP, BUT SOMETIMES FRIENDS HAVE TO PUSH EACH OTHER.'

He couldn't get over it. *She filled out an application for him?*

'YOU DO IT ONLINE. IT'S EASIER THAN YOU THINK.'

It occurred to him: maybe this was really about college and his future. He'd told her the truth – that he hadn't finished any applications in time – but he told other people he was 'taking a year off to work and make money' before going back to school. It was an easy thing to say, especially when he heard

123

others say it. Amy was making sure it was true.

'Why do I have to work at a movie theatre?'

'BECAUSE IT'LL MAKE YOU INTERACT WITH STRANGERS. YOU'LL ALSO GET OVER YOUR FEAR OF HANDLING MONEY AND FOOD TOGETHER. YOU MIGHT ALSO MAKE NEW FRIENDS.'

He wasn't sure what any of this meant. Did she want him to make new friends? Was she sick of being his only one? The possibility made him sad.

'You can call me Mr Ilson,' the man said at Matthew's interview. Mr Ilson had bright red hair and didn't look much older than Matthew. 'The first thing you should know is that I run a tight ship. Some people think a movie theatre is a pretty easy job. You scoop a little popcorn, pour a few sodas, bam, you're done. That couldn't be further from the truth, okay? Yes, we've only got three screens here.' Mysteriously he made air quotation marks around the word *three*. 'We're not a giant multiplex in a mall, but do we get rushes where the concession line stretches to the door? Sure. Is there a stress factor to this job? You bet there is.'

As he spoke, Mr Ilson tapped the edge of his desk. Right corner, left corner, middle. He detailed the pressures of the job, especially getting the theatres cleaned between every show. 'People think our floor is a giant trash can, I guess. That's what you'll learn after a few weeks. *Please deposit trash in the receptacles on the way out* means nothing to these folks. Nothing at all. Might as well be speaking Chinese.'

As he spoke, the tapping continued.

'Mostly I'll be watching what you're doing *between* rushes. You got time to lean, you got time to clean, okay? You consider yourself a pretty clean person?'

Matthew started. It was the first question he'd been asked. 'Yes,' he said. 'I do.'

'Great, then. Chloe said you're good, and we all love Chloe.' He opened a folder and looked over a calendar filled with pencil markings. 'How's Friday nights and Saturday afternoons for you? You'll have to come in early on Friday to get trained.'

'Okay,' Matthew said.

Apparently that was that.

Four days later, he was wearing a poly-blend smock over a button-down white shirt and was learning how to operate the popcorn machine. Though it was four o'clock in the afternoon, he was exhausted. The night before, he had lain awake for hours worrying about how he'd do a job that involved squirting butter and cleaning greasy surfaces. Except for the French-fry machine at McDonald's, did any after-school job involve *more* grease? Why hadn't he said, 'Fine, Amy, I'll get a job, but let it be at JCPenney. I should *not* be working around messy food'? He didn't say it because he knew what she would say. *That's the whole point. If you want to get better, you don't make the easy choice; you make the hard one.*

Amy could be so unrelentingly *right*. He hated it sometimes. He hated it now.

As he stood there, dead on his feet, a girl named Hannah showed him how to fill the black-with-burnt-oil kettle in the popcorn popper. 'So it's pretty easy. One cup of kernels, a quarter cup of oil, and two tablespoons of this yellow powder.'

Matthew stared at the bright yellow powder she was measuring. 'What *is* that?'

'Who knows? Popcorn-flavour powder, I guess. It makes it yellow and smell good.'

Matthew's stomach turned over. 'You add *chemical popcorn flavour* to real popcorn?'

'I know, right? I gotta admit, though, it tastes pretty good.' She ate some of last night's leftovers – stored in a black Hefty trash bag – as a demonstration. 'Yeah,' she'd said, pouring the old stuff in. 'The machine gets cleaned every night, then the old stuff goes back in. Maybe that's a little gross. I don't know.'

A little? Matthew thought, watching. 'People spend money on food that's been sitting in a trash bag?'

'I know, right? *A lot* of money too. Did you see our prices? That's why I put extra butter on the old stuff.'

Halfway through his shift, Matthew got a text from Amy.

Amy: How's it going? Just asking. Not worried.

Him: Weird. Definitely a weird place.

Amy: Are you busy?

Him: Not really. Have you heard of popcorn-flavour powder? Can you Google it for me?

Amy: No. I mean, I could, but I won't.

Him: If you get it on ur hands, it doesn't come off. Perma-yellow.

Amy: Pretty!

Him: Gotta go. Customers.

In the course of one shift, he learned there was no need to look busy unless Mr Ilson walked out of his office. In between rushes, the other employees did pretty much nothing except talk and text. Usually there were four people working a shift – one to sell tickets, one to tear, two to sell concessions. Because he was being trained, there were five people the first day. Hannah was shift leader, though it was hard to tell how she got that honour given her lackadaisical attitude towards every aspect of the job. 'Bathroom checks mean you're supposed to check supplies, then initial the paper on the back of the door. Usually I don't check; I just initial. If there's no toilet paper, someone will tell us, believe me.'

'Is it bad to check?' Matthew asked, sounding a little strained. He'd made it through three hours just fine. He only had an hour and a half to go.

'It's not bad. You just don't have to,' she said. 'Mr Ilson would have us cleaning the bottom of his shoes if he could.'

'I'll probably check,' Matthew said. 'If that's okay.'

Hannah shrugged. 'Whatever.'

When his turn came for the bathroom check, Matthew went into the men's room. On the back of the door was a grid for initials and, behind it, a laminated list of items to check: toilet paper, soap, paper towels, trash can. On the bottom were three items:

1) *Wipe down sinks and urinals.*
2) *Check the floor for spills.*
3) *Empty trash.*

Wipe down sinks and urinals?

Matthew felt his heart begin to race. Now that he'd read the instruction, he had to do it. But how could he without touching a stranger's pee through paper towels?

He walked back out and found Hannah. 'Are there gloves for cleaning the bathroom?' He was almost sure that wasn't a crazy question. The cleaning ladies at hotels always wore gloves. He'd wanted to steal a box once when he saw one on a housekeeper's cart.

Hannah sat on the floor below the popcorn machine, texting on her phone. 'I don't think so,' she said, not looking up. 'Just skip it. Seriously. Write your initials and take a break.'

He felt his pulse behind his temples. He couldn't skip it. Bad things would happen if he skipped it. He'd lose this job or worse. Someone in his family would get cancer. Amy would die. She'd either die or get very, very angry at him. So angry she'd stop speaking to him completely. He'd have to quit both jobs, the movie theatre and Amy, because otherwise he'd get fired and everyone knew it was better to quit than get fired. *Fired* went on your record, which followed you for life. *Fired* meant no one would hire you later, when you tried to get a real job in an office as an adult.

He could feel his panic mounting, making him sweat through the T-shirt he was wearing under his smock. 'I feel like I should clean the bathroom. I'm just going to clean it for a little while, all right?'

'Fine,' Hannah said. 'Do whatever you want.'

CHAPTER SEVENTEEN

'So I learned a lot of interesting behind-the-scenes secrets about movie theatres,' Matthew said on Monday morning as he and Amy walked between first period and second.

'SUCH AS?'

'Such as the combos aren't any cheaper than buying popcorn and soda separately. I never realized that before. I also learned that as far as popcorn goes, *warm* is not the same thing as *fresh*. And I thought this was interesting: apparently there are no laws expressly stating that the cheese topping on nachos has to contain any real cheese. I would have thought yes, it should have a *little*, but no, apparently not.'

Amy stopped walking and typed: 'WHAT REALLY HAPPENED?'

'It was fine until the end. They have something called bathroom checks, which freaked me out a little. Trigger words, I guess. I was all right.'

'NO, YOU WEREN'T.'

'No, I wasn't. It's true. But I wasn't fired!'

'TELL ME WHAT HAPPENED.'

'I couldn't stop cleaning the bathroom. There were these stains in the urinals. They must have been rust stains, but they looked like they should come off. I kept scrubbing and scrubbing. Finally it was time to close. The manager came in and told me to stop.'

'HOW LONG WERE YOU IN THERE?'

'Maybe an hour . . . I'm not sure.'

The bell rang and the hallways emptied around them.

'AND HE DIDN'T FIRE YOU?'

'No. I'm still on the schedule. I work Monday night.'

'DID HE SAY ANYTHING?'

'He just said, "Better let someone else do the bathroom checks."'

They started walking again. Outside the door to French, Amy started typing again. 'DID HE KNOW YOU'D BEEN IN THERE FOR AN HOUR?'

'I think so.'

'IT SEEMS WEIRD THAT NO ONE SAID ANY-THING AND NO ONE STOPPED YOU.'

It had seemed a little weird to Matthew, but that was because he always lost track of time in the middle of an episode. In fact, they felt too quick. He always needed more time to get these jobs done. Last night he could hardly believe it – when he finally finished up and came out of the bathroom, everyone had gone home except Hannah and Mr Ilson, who were in his office, counting the cash drawer.

'All set, Matthew?' Mr Ilson said, watching Hannah count a pile of fives.

The lobby was dark; the lights around the concession stand were off. Matthew was glad they couldn't see how sweaty he'd got scrubbing around the urinal drains. He nodded.

'We'll see you Monday, then. Good job tonight.'

'The manager said I did a good job.'

Amy cocked her head. 'THAT SEEMS STRANGE. OBVIOUSLY YOU DIDN'T IF YOU SPENT AN HOUR IN THE BATHROOM. THAT WASN'T YOUR JOB.'

Why was she *saying* this? Why couldn't she give him a break? Mr Ilson obviously had. And Hannah hadn't said anything, either. He'd done *fine*. He spent a night with new people, working a job that involved food, grease and money handed to him by strangers who probably hadn't washed their hands before opening their wallets. All things considered, it went as well anyone might have expected.

The next morning, Amy wasted no time telling him what she'd found out. 'CHLOE GOT A TEXT FROM HANNAH. YOU WANT TO KNOW WHAT SHE SAID?'

'No.'

'SHE SAID, AND I QUOTE: "YOUR FRIEND HAS THE SAME THING MR ILSON DOES." TURNS OUT HE DOES ALL THESE THINGS, LIKE HE MAKES THEM COUNT THE MONEY BECAUSE HE WON'T TOUCH IT. HE THINKS NO ONE NOTICES, BUT THEY TOTALLY DO. DON'T WORRY, I DIDN'T TELL CHLOE ABOUT YOU. WHEN SHE SHOWED ME THE TEXT I SAID, "NO, THAT'S NOT MATTHEW'S PROBLEM." BUT IT'S GREAT, RIGHT?'

'Why is it great?'

'BECAUSE HE WON'T FIRE YOU! MAYBE YOU CAN EVEN TALK TO HIM!'

'But everyone hates him. He's an awful manager. He's got a million rules and they do nothing but make fun of him behind his back.'

'OH.'

'This makes me feel about a hundred times worse. Like

131

now I know how people talk about me behind my back.'

'NO ONE TALKS ABOUT YOU BEHIND YOUR BACK.'

'You and Chloe just did. So did Hannah and Chloe.' He looked down at the food for which he'd lost all appetite. 'I feel like I can't go back there now.'

'OF COURSE YOU CAN!' She'd turned the volume up so it sounded as if her Pathway were yelling. 'DON'T DO THAT!'

'I feel like I've got to quit.'

'I WON'T LET YOU QUIT.'

'You're not in charge of me, Amy.'

'NO, BUT I'M A BETTER JUDGE THAN YOU ARE.'

'I could quit this job with you, you know.' Just saying this made his heart begin to race. What would he do if he didn't have his Amy days to look forward to? He didn't even know. Why had he made a threat that would only hurt himself?

She turned her Pathway way down. 'I HOPE YOU DON'T QUIT THIS JOB,' she whispered. 'I'M SORRY, MATTHEW. I WON'T ORDER YOU AROUND.'

For the rest of that day, she gave Matthew no assignments and said no more about the movie theatre. At the end of the day, just before her mother's car pulled up, she said, 'PLEASE DON'T QUIT THIS JOB.'

He didn't say anything until after he'd loaded her walker into the car and opened the car door for her. 'I probably won't quit,' he said, and smiled.

CHAPTER EIGHTEEN

As wet, grey February warmed into March, Amy noticed more changes with Matthew. Little ones at first, but gradually they began to seem more significant. He was looser. At night on IM he was funnier to talk to. At school, he was less preoccupied, though, admittedly, he was still nervous sometimes. If their bodies accidentally touched – which happened all the time, opening doors, getting her books out – he flinched and blushed. 'Sorry,' he'd say. 'I don't know why that just happened.'

The more aware of it Amy became, the more it kept happening. Some days, she'd fixate on some part of his body – his hand or his knee – and stare at it until her wild, uncontrollable hand would reach out and touch him. She used to think his body communicated feelings his brain hadn't acknowledged. Now she wondered if hers was doing the same: trying to say, *Look at me. Would you ever consider being more than friends?* Maybe it was okay for her body to do this, since how could she possibly type such a question and say it out loud? Plus it was thrilling to watch him blush and look down in confusion. Once she touched his elbow and he put his hand over the spot as if he'd got an electric shock. To her, it was a small gesture that said: *He feels this too. He notices these collisions.*

There were other things she noticed: he blushed and stammered more often in her presence while she nervously typed and deleted things she wasn't sure she should say. She wanted to say something definitive, but she didn't want to scare him off. She had no experience, but she knew this much: You had to be cautious. You couldn't scream, 'I REALLY LIKE YOU, MATTHEW!' every time the impulse crossed your mind. You also couldn't point out that his hand had stayed on her back for a longer period of time than was strictly necessary as he helped her stand up after lunch.

As part of his gradual loosening up, Matthew started telling more stories, mostly from his days before OCD. She asked if he'd ever been to any of the boy/girl parties where people played kissing games. He blushed and nodded. 'I'm pretty sure the whole thing was a joke,' he said. They were at a yearbook meeting, though these days they no longer pretended to work on anything. They sat side by side, talking. 'Because the bottle kept landing on me.'

She loved the little crooked smile on this face. 'WHAT DID YOU DO?'

He laughed and covered his face with his hands. 'Sat there and waited for the person to kiss me.'

'DID THEY?' She tried to imagine it and couldn't.

'Yes.'

'AND THEN WHAT?'

'And then nothing. It was the next person's turn and they spun.'

'NO ONE LAUGHED?'

'No.'

'THEN IT WASN'T A JOKE. THEY ALL WANTED TO KISS YOU.'

'Hardly. More like there was a dent in the rug.'

He told her he kissed about seven girls one night, but

he wasn't sure, which didn't sound like him at all. Even in his good phases, when he wasn't preoccupied by making deals with his brain, Matthew wouldn't have lost count of something like kisses. When she pointed this out – 'YOU COUNT EVERYTHING, MATTHEW. HOW COULD YOU NOT HAVE COUNTED YOUR KISSES?' – he said, 'I don't remember. That's all.'

She wondered if maybe it was a good sign. Maybe it meant that he could let go of all his compulsions when the situation was right. He was there, letting seven girls kiss him without bathroom trips or hand washing or sterilizing his mouth in between. Later, when Amy prodded, he could name five of the girls he'd kissed that night and even admitted to having a crush on one of them, Katie Morse. All of which meant: he *had* kissed a girl. Quite a few of them, in fact. It was possible.

Amy watched for more signs that were hard to read, because he was never at his worst on his days with her. 'With you, my brain takes a break,' he told her once. 'I'm not sure why.'

She wanted to say, *Maybe your brain is trying to tell you something*, but she didn't because she had to be careful. 'At last,' he once said, meeting her mother's car in front of school. Because of a three-day weekend, she hadn't talked to him in six days. 'I thought this day would never come.'

She knew what he meant, because she felt the same way after she hadn't seen him for a while. Still she said, 'WHY?' and he looked confused. Having said something so sweet – *I couldn't wait to see you again! Life is harder when I don't spend passing periods with you!* – he retracted like a turtle into his shell. 'No reason. I don't know why I said that.'

Recently these moments happened more often. She felt as if something was shifting between them. He'd comment on her hair, how pretty it was, or he'd say he liked her necklace and then be embarrassed enough to explain: 'It makes your neck look nice.' The first warm day in March, they ate lunch at a table where someone had left a *Glamour* magazine open. Amy lay her fist on a photo spread of spring fashions. 'HOW WOULD I LOOK IN TARTAN PLEATS?' she typed.

Matthew looked at the picture. 'Oh please. You're a lot prettier than *her*.'

'NO, I'M NOT.'

He studied the picture again. There seemed to be no question in his mind. 'Yes, you are. Her eyes look like they're on the sides of her head.'

Amy couldn't believe he was saying this. Did he *really* think it? She pointed to another picture. 'HOW ABOUT HER?'

He shrugged. 'She's okay.'

'PRETTIER THAN ME?' Why was she doing this? She lowered the volume on her Pathway so no one else could hear.

'Different. Not my type.'

'WHAT IS YOUR TYPE?'

'I don't like girls who wear a lot of make-up. Or if you can see their bra strap. I never understand that. Why do some girls do that?'

Recently there had been a change in the school dress policy addressing this very issue, because the nice weather meant spaghetti straps and tank tops and bras were visible everywhere. 'YOU DON'T LIKE SEEING A WOMAN'S LINGERIE?'

'Not in calc, no. Not right before lunch, either.' He smiled as if he knew he sounded prissy. 'Most boys aren't interested in models. It's girls who think they're so beautiful. Boys look at that and see a paper-thin nothing. We're not interested in that.'

'WHAT ARE YOU INTERESTED IN?'

He leaned across the table and whispered, 'Their soul, of course.' He flashed a smile and she laughed. The whole conversation made her so happy that she forgot to close her mouth, and drool slipped out and on to her shirt. She flinched when she felt it and her bad arm spazzed out. 'Oops,' he said, wiping her chin.

That night she brought the magazine home with her. She even tore out the picture and stuck it in the frame of her full-length standing mirror so she could study it and compare herself. For a long time she stood with her walker to the side, and hung her head in the same way the model did. Her hair was prettier. Her good arm was good. Everything else, not so great. She couldn't will her bad arm to uncurl, couldn't loosen her fist or relax the tendons that stood out with the effort of holding her head up. Nor could she do the one thing that would have helped the most: soften her face so that it was pliable and capable of showing the expressions other people took for granted. Her face had only a handful of options: raised eyebrows (for surprise and joy); a closed-mouth O (for worry and concentration); and a wide-open mouth that filled in for everything else. She had no smile of approval, no soft frown of disapproval, nothing subtle. In every photograph of her, she wore one of these three expressions. The only exception was a picture taken when she was asleep, and then her face softened, like she didn't have CP at all. Why was that possible in her sleep but impossible awake? She couldn't say. Just as she couldn't say why her parents continued to purchase large sets of her school-picture packages, as an annual reminder of her inability to smile.

She wasn't prettier than this model: anyone could see that. But their conversation opened up a new possibility: *Matthew saw the world differently*. He didn't like girls with make-up because he would have been afraid of touching anything that could rub off on to his hands. He didn't like bras showing in public because it went against the rules. He couldn't be with one of those girls. *But maybe*, she began to think, *he could be with me*.

The Monday after their magazine conversation, he greeted her with a four-leaf clover and laid it carefully on her board. 'YOU'RE GIVING THIS TO ME?' she typed.

'Yes.' When she asked him why, he said, 'Because you believe in optimistic signs. It's better off staying with you.'

Was that a sign? She wasn't sure. But she hoped so.

About a month after starting his movie theatre job, Matthew surprised her again. 'Can I ask you something?'

She squinted at him. 'SURE.'

'Do you ever think about prom?'

'WHAT DO YOU MEAN?'

'You know. Going.'

Her heart began to race. She shouldn't presume this was his way of asking her. He might be looking for her advice on asking someone else.

She told him the truth. 'NO. DO YOU?'

His expression changed. 'No. I mean, not really. It was stupid.'

The conversation ended as quickly as it started, but she couldn't get it out of her mind. For weeks now, she'd been making jokes about prom with all her peer helpers. This year, the theme was 'What a Feeling!'

'HOW DO YOU DECORATE FOR THAT?' Amy asked them all. 'WHAT DO YOU WEAR?' According to Sarah, who had gone two years ago, prom was famous for being an overpriced disappointment where most people had no fun. It was also famous for being incredibly strict about alcohol and drugs.

The next day she talked about prom with Sarah over lunch.

'Because no one's ever got any booze into the actual event, everyone makes a big deal about trying,' Sarah told her. 'Girls stick little bottles in their bras, or guys hide them in the lining of their jacket. Then they always get caught. It's stupid.'

'SO ARE YOU GOING?' Amy asked. Lately Sarah had got harder to read. Suddenly she was wearing make-up to school and dressing in new, tighter clothes. She looked like all the other girls, glancing around the cafeteria, waiting for something to happen. Amy wished she could just ask: *Is there someone here you like?* But she couldn't. After that one conversation about her old boyfriend, the twenty-three-year-old, Sarah had never talked about her love life.

'I doubt it,' Sarah said. 'I don't think anyone's going to ask me this year.'

There *was* someone; Amy could tell. 'WHO DO YOU WANT TO GO WITH?'

Sarah blushed. 'It's stupid. You'd laugh if I told you.'

'NO, I WON'T.' Amy felt her right side tighten up with a new fear. *What if it's Matthew? What if Sarah decided on that lunch date that she liked him?* 'DO I KNOW HIM?'

'Yes.' Sarah leaned across the lunch table. She smiled as if she were going to say it, and then changed her mind and shook her head. 'I can't explain it. It makes no *sense* –'

Amy could already feel her heart break.

Sarah kept going. 'He's not anyone I would have pictured myself with, but we've started talking more. We went out once, and I can't help it: I just keep *thinking* about him.'

It *was* Matthew. It had to be. If Amy really cared about him, she'd have to let Sarah have him. Taking Sarah to prom would show Matthew what Amy had been trying to get him to see all year – that he was wonderful and sweet and handsome and desirable. With Sarah, he would *feel* this. With Amy, not so much. 'YOU SHOULD ASK HIM TO PROM. HE WANTS TO GO. DON'T WAIT FOR HIM TO ASK YOU.'

'I have no idea what he'd say. I mean – no idea at all. He might say great, but he might say he'd rather go with someone else. Look at me – I'm never like this about a boy. I *hate* myself.' It was true. Amy never had seen Sarah like this before. Her cheeks looked flushed as if she might start to either laugh or cry; she wasn't sure which. 'I just wish he wasn't so obsessed with stupid *cheerleaders*.'

Amy looked up. *Did she just say* cheerleaders*?* 'IS IT *SANJAY*? YOU LIKE SANJAY?'

There was a line of tears in Sarah's eyes. 'It's so stupid, right? I can't *help it*. He makes me laugh and he's *so* good-looking. People don't even see it because he's Indian or whatever, but I'm sorry, he *is*.'

'I SEE IT.'

'You do?'

'OF COURSE. HE *IS* GOOD-LOOKING. HE'D GO TO PROM WITH YOU. HE'D BE CRAZY NOT TO.'

'You really think so?' Sarah smiled as a tear fell down her cheeks. 'I swore I wasn't going to say any of this to you.'

'WHY NOT?'

'I didn't want you to think I signed up for this job so I could meet guys.'

Amy could hardly contain her relief. 'I DON'T THINK THAT.' Even as she typed, though, her heart hammered with a new thought. Maybe this wasn't such a far-fetched idea – that these peer helpers signed up for this job looking for something more than friendship. Maybe Matthew *had* been about to ask her to prom. 'I HAVE AN IDEA,' she said to Sarah. 'I DARE YOU TO ASK SANJAY. IF YOU DO, I'LL ASK SOMEONE TOO.'

Sarah looked surprised. 'Who?'

'I'LL TELL YOU WHO IT IS IF I GET HIM TO SAY YES.'

That night, they stayed up late, IMing their plans for over an hour. ('I think I'm going to make it like a joke,' Sarah wrote. 'Or else I'm just going to tell him you suggested it.'

'Do that,' Amy wrote back. 'Tell him I think you'd make a cute couple.')

Amy had never had a girlfriend before. It was electrifying. She liked hearing how Sarah got so worked up and nervous. It made her feel less alone, pining for Matthew.

After three days, Amy got a text from Sarah on the way to school:

I did it! He said yes. Ur turn now.

'I don't know,' Amy wrote back.

U have 2. U promised. Just ask.

Thursday wasn't a Matthew day, but Amy saw him that afternoon for yearbook club. He met her outside her last class, with one hand outstretched to scoop her backpack off her walker and on to his shoulder. 'Ready to continue our seminal work on the *Gryphon*?' he asked.

Instead of walking, she stopped and sat down on one of the benches outside the nurse's office. 'I HAVE TO ASK YOU SOMETHING.'

'Okay.' He sat down next to her.

'DID YOU BRING UP PROM THE OTHER DAY BECAUSE YOU'D LIKE TO GO?'

'Maybe. Why?'

'BECAUSE I'M WONDERING WHO YOU WERE GOING TO ASK. I'M WONDERING IF IT WAS ME.'

He blushed and looked away. 'I was thinking about

142

it, but I've changed my mind now.'

'WHY?'

'Because, as you keep pointing out, prom is a joke. They've picked a terrible theme. There's no way to decorate or dress for a theme like that. I don't know who's in charge –'

'I WANT TO GO.' She peeked over and saw that he was smiling now.

'You *do*?'

'YES. EVEN SMART GIRLS LIKE ME CARE ABOUT STUPID THINGS LIKE PROM. I WANT TO GO.'

'So okay. Let's go.' Now he was really smiling.

'BUT, IF YOU'D RATHER ASK SOMEONE ELSE, THAT'S FINE. I DON'T WANT YOU TO FEEL OBLIGATED TO TAKE ME LIKE IT'S ONE OF YOUR ASSIGNMENTS.'

'Okay.'

'OKAY WHAT? DO YOU WANT TO ASK SOMEONE ELSE?'

'No. I wanted to ask you. Now I have. Sort of. Except you did the asking, but that's okay. We've got to the same place.'

'WHAT PLACE IS THAT?' She felt a little light-headed and sick, as nervous as he looked in the throes of his panic attack last fall. Her throat was dry, her forehead damp.

She couldn't get over how calm he seemed. He even leaned over to whisper in her ear. 'The place where we sit around and bore each other to death talking about what we're going to wear.'

They skipped going to yearbook completely. It was a beautiful, sunny day. If they were going to prom, Matthew said, they should start working on their tans. They found a patch of grass and he helped her sit down, then stretch out flat. She lay on her bad side, so it was less obvious.

'I know this much. A tuxedo washes me right out. We have to start thinking about the pictures. We'll look like ghosts if we're not careful.'

'SO WHAT *ARE* WE GOING TO WEAR?'

'Funny you should ask,' he said, 'because I already know. My father left behind a tuxedo with a cutaway jacket that fits me perfectly. I have to warn you, I look weirdly good in it.'

She was starting to feel better. She laughed, one of her strange, barking laughs. 'WHAT'S A CUTAWAY JACKET?'

He stretched out beside her and closed his eyes. 'You'll have to wait and see.'

'WHAT SHOULD I WEAR IF I WANT TO CONVEY A SENSE OF IRONIC DISAPPROVAL ABOUT THIS EVENT?' These jokes took a little longer to type. *Convey* and *disapproval* weren't on her word-prediction program.

'You could try a trash bag.'

She laughed again. 'WITH HOLES?'

'Or not. Maybe you could wear one of those tuxedo-decal T-shirts. That might make me look silly, but I don't mind.'

'YOU WANT ME TO WEAR A DRESS, DON'T YOU? YOU WANT TO SEE WHAT MY SKINNY LEGS LOOK LIKE.'

'I know what your skinny legs look like, Aim.' He did – it was May and warm enough now that they'd all started wearing shorts to school.

She rolled over on to her stomach to ask him a serious

144

question. 'WHAT IF IT'S TOO MUCH PRESSURE AND YOU GET ALL NERVOUS AND STRANGE?'

He opened one eye and looked at her. 'I'll try not to.'

They had to discuss this ahead of time. It could be a disaster if something happened, and they hadn't. 'WHAT IF I END UP SITTING IN THE CORNER WHILE YOU'RE IN THE BATHROOM FOR AN HOUR TRYING TO TAKE A SHOWER IN THE SINK?'

'I'll take a pill. Take the edge off. Thank you, though, for planting that idea in my mind.'

'WHAT PILL? YOU DON'T TAKE PILLS.'

'I have some very small pills I take. Prescribed by a doctor. For a while they didn't do anything. Now I find they help me relax.'

She couldn't believe what he was saying. 'YOU'VE BEEN SEEING A REAL DOCTOR?'

He smiled and rolled on to his stomach too. For a second she thought he was going to hold her hand. Instead he brushed some grass from her shoulder. 'For almost six weeks now. It turns out you were right. Medication helps.'

After that, a strange thing happened: Amy couldn't stop her expectations from rising. She imagined herself transformed and beautiful, like Molly Ringwald in *Pretty in Pink*, with her homemade dress and mysterious lace boots. She pictured her hair in an upsweep of loose curls. In the fantasy, her prom face looked like the one she only wore asleep, loose and relaxed. She imagined a photographer asking her to smile and, for the first time in her life, being able to do it.

CHAPTER NINETEEN

Matthew had got the idea of asking Amy to prom a few weeks ago, before he felt any change from the medication. He thought of it the first time prom tickets got mentioned in the homeroom PA announcements, and he saw kids around him poke one another and roll their eyes. He watched the shyer girls look down nervously at their hands. For the first time in years, instead of thinking about himself, he thought about them and wondered: *Do all girls secretly want to go to prom?*

That night he asked his mother what she remembered of her own prom, and she smiled as she poured herself more wine. 'Oh my gosh, I *loved* prom. I couldn't believe it when Jacob Lister asked me. I'd had a crush on him for years and never understood why he didn't date anyone. Then at prom he told me he was probably gay, which was sad in a way, but also brought us closer. I had a wonderful time.'

'Do all girls wish someone would ask them?'

'I don't know if it's changed,' she said, 'but in my day, sure. Lots of people pretended they didn't care, but they would have gone if someone had asked them.'

If that's true, he thought, *Amy should be asked*, but even as he thought this his stomach twitched nervously. When he told his mother what he was thinking of a few days later, she told him it was a good idea, but he shouldn't do it out of pity.

'No, it wouldn't be like that. I feel like she's my best friend. And this is something friends do for each other, right?'

His mother looked unsure. 'Maybe. I don't know.'

'Isn't that what Jacob Lister did for you?'

'I suppose. Though if I'd had my way, we would have made out.'

That was two weeks ago. Since the afternoon they'd spent lying on the lawn, he was surprised by how much fun the buildup was. The next day, Amy told him she was on a special diet to gain weight and grow bigger boobs by prom. 'I DON'T KNOW IF IT WILL WORK, BUT IT CAN'T HURT TO TRY, RIGHT?'

'Your boobs are fine,' he whispered, blushing. The medication had helped, but it didn't work miracles. Some conversations were still too embarrassing to have without blushing.

A week before prom Amy told him she'd bought her dress with her father, actually, not her mother. 'MOM DOESN'T LIKE SHOPPING. PLUS SHE'S NOT SO INTO THIS PROM THING, I GUESS.'

Matthew's stomach twitched again. 'Why not?'

Amy didn't seem to think it was important. 'NO REASON. JUST . . . YOU KNOW . . . PROM IS A CLICHÉ. WANT TO HEAR ABOUT MY DRESS?'

'Yes.'

'I'M NOT GOING TO TELL YOU. . . . OKAY, I'LL TELL YOU THIS MUCH: IT'S NOT TIE-DYED. I THOUGHT ABOUT THAT AND DECIDED NO.'

'Heels?'

'NO HEELS. SENSIBLE ORTHOPAEDIC DRESS FLATS. FLESH COLOURED.'

'Really?'

'NO. BUT I'M NOT GOING TO TELL YOU. I DON'T WANT TO RUIN THE SURPRISE.'

They talked about corsages ('I DON'T KNOW IF I WANT A FLOWER SO MUCH AS A BUTTON THAT SAYS, *VISUALIZE WHIRLED PEAS.* IS THAT TOO MUCH TO ASK?') They talked about boutonnières. ('I'm thinking a yellow rose,' he said. 'Or else a squirting flag pin. Either one is fine.') By then, they'd joked around so much that Matthew began worry that the actual evening might ruin the happy times they'd had leading up to it. With so many unknowns – driving, parking, dancing – who knew what could happen?

At Amy's insistence, they ruled out going to dinner beforehand. 'IT'LL BE COMPLICATED ENOUGH,' Amy said. 'LET'S NOT BRING FOOD INTO IT TOO.'

Indeed it was complicated. Beyond being the first time in ten years Matthew had left the house wearing uncomfortably dressy clothes, it would also be the first time he'd driven with someone other than his mother as a passenger. He passed his test (by the thinnest margin of two points), which meant he wasn't a *terrible* driver, just a horribly overcautious one. He travelled most comfortably ten miles below the speed limit, and overreacted to any movement in his peripheral vision. On the test, he lost points for swerving to avoid pedestrians he was nowhere near. He'd warned Amy a week ago: 'My driving can be a little lurchy.'

She said, 'WHAT'S OUR CHOICE? A LIMO FOR THREE HUNDRED DOLLARS OR YOUR MOM

DRIVNG US? I'LL TAKE THE BUMPY RIDE. I WON'T
MIND, I PROMISE.'

At the time, he'd felt grateful, but driving to her house
he wondered if he should have spent his savings on the limo.
He'd forgotten the biggest problem with driving at night:
headlights coming *at you.*

He got to Amy's house at seven o'clock, where he was
greeted by her father at the door. Matthew had only met Amy's
father once, at the first training session for Amy's helpers. He
was a surprisingly small man – shorter than Matthew – with
a stern expression that Amy said was mostly for show. 'HE
PRETTY MUCH DOES WHATEVER MY MOM TELLS
HIM,' she once told Matthew. 'SOMETIMES IT MAKES
ME FEEL SORRY FOR HIM.'

'Max Van Dorn,' he said, holding out his hand. 'You must
be Matthew.' In the dim porch light, his hand looked greasy,
as if he'd just had it in a bag of potato chips.

I can't touch that hand, Matthew thought. *If I do, I'll be
washing that grease off all night.* 'Better not,' Matthew said,
touching his tuxedo.

'Right, of course. Come on in.' He stepped aside and let
Matthew into the foyer, where they stood way too close to
each other. 'Look, I might as well tell you, Nicole is feeling
a little anxious about this evening. I'm sure it'll go fine, but
anything that isn't her idea to start with, well – she gets
nervous.'

That makes two of us, Matthew thought. 'Okay,' he said.

'Her mother keeps saying Amy shouldn't stay out late, that
she sometimes loses muscle control when she's tired, but I say,

hey! It's prom, right? You're going to give the girl a curfew on prom night?'

In situations like this, the medication didn't make Matthew less nervous. It only made him nervous, with side effects like dry mouth and an eye twitch. Now he tried to swallow, but couldn't. He tried to imagine what her father was saying. *Amy loses muscle control?*

'I say stay out as late as you like. I'm not worried about any curfews. I told Nicole, "This kid knows Amy. He knows her little quirks." Still, she thinks you should have a list of instructions and emergency phone numbers. I told her, "This is a school dance, honey. Not some medical procedure."'

Why did he say *medical procedure*? An image flashed in Matthew's mind of operating on Amy, standing over her open chest cavity, unsure what to do. Finally he managed to end his own silence: 'It's fine. Instructions are fine.'

Mr Van Dorn laughed, then he leaned in and whispered, 'Well, that's good, because you're going to get them.' His breath smelled like mint, as if he were trying to cover up some other smell. Alcohol, maybe. Or the disease he'd just transmitted to Matthew by leaning close enough to breathe all over him.

'Is Amy ready? Because we should probably go.'

'Yes, yes, of course! Just a few last-minute adjustments and then we'll only need an hour to take some pictures. Then you're free.'

Apparently this was a joke too, because they took no pictures. When Amy finally emerged from her bedroom with Nicole behind her, it was clear they had been arguing. Amy's face was bright red, as were Nicole's eyes. They both had damp cheeks. In the terrible awkwardness that followed, Matthew could think of nothing but leaving as quickly as possible.

In the car, Amy sat for a full minute without speaking. Finally she typed, 'YOU LOOK NICE.'

'Thanks,' he said. He started the car and put on his blinker, though he hadn't pulled out of her driveway yet. He checked his mirrors and looked up the street.

'DO YOU WANT TO SAY SOMETHING ABOUT HOW I LOOK?'

'I did, didn't I?'

'NO.'

A car drove past, which threw off his checking. He started all over again. 'I'm sorry, Aim. You look nice too. I wish I wasn't driving. I have to concentrate.'

'WAS THIS A TERRIBLE IDEA, MATTHEW?'

'No. What do you mean?'

'I HAVE A FEELING THE WHOLE NIGHT MIGHT BE A DISASTER.'

For a moment he felt relieved just to hear her say it. This was why he loved Amy, if the word *love* could be applied to someone he was afraid to touch and sometimes didn't even like looking at. He turned the car off. 'Maybe you're right. Do you want to go back in?'

He had Nicole's instruction sheet folded inside his pocket. He'd probably have to spend the first hour of the evening reading through it. With the prospect of that, plus driving this car that now felt like a giant tank, walking Amy back inside and calling it a night didn't sound like such a bad idea.

'NO WAY. I SPENT AN HOUR BUYING A STRAPLESS BRA FOR THIS. I'M GOING.'

He looked over at the folds of her dark-blue dress, tight like a cummerbund around her waist, with a flared skirt that started around her hips. It was a lovely dress, not at all what he'd expected. It looked like a dress Grace Kelly might have worn, with miles of skirt that stopped below her knee and billowed a little when she stepped outside. She looked beautiful. Too beautiful for him to think about for too long or look at too closely. It would only make him more nervous. 'What's a strapless bra?' he finally asked.

'LIKE A TOURNIQUET FOR YOUR CHEST.'

'Can you breathe if you're wearing it?'

'BARELY.'

He worried. There were so many ways this night could go wrong. How many teenagers died every year in car crashes going to and from their prom? Or something else could happen: Amy could have a seizure or choke on a cube of ice. She could die from wearing a dress that required such a torturous bra. 'Do you want to take the bra off?' he asked.

She smiled, one of her wide-mouthed smiles. 'DO YOU REALLY MEAN THAT?'

No, he couldn't say. *Of course I don't mean it.* Taking it off would require his help, and his hands were shaking too much.

'NEVER MIND. LET'S JUST GO. YOU DON'T NEED TO BE NERVOUS. IT'LL BE OKAY. I PROMISE.'

He smiled. 'Look, I'm sorry. I *am* nervous, but mostly about driving this stupid car. Not about you. You're the least of my worries.'

'GOOD.'

They sat for a moment, quiet. 'Are you nervous?' he finally asked.

She didn't answer. She was looking out the car window, back at her house. He wondered if he'd already wrecked the whole night. 'You do look beautiful, Amy. So beautiful it made me nervous seeing you just now. I never do well in unexpected situations.'

She pulled her board in front of her face without turning round. 'YOU DIDN'T EXPECT ME TO LOOK GOOD?'

'Well. Not like this. Not this good.'

'DOES IT SEEM PATHETIC? ME TRYING LIKE THIS?'

'*No.*'

'MY MOTHER THINKS THIS WAS ALL A BIG MISTAKE. FINE TO BE FRIENDS. BUT NOT . . . THIS.'

'What? We *are* friends.' He had a speech he'd wanted to tell her tonight, about how much their friendship meant to him. He'd planned to save it for the end of the night, but he changed his mind and decided to say it now. He'd finally got the car out of her driveway, but now he pulled it over to the side of the road and turned it off. 'I had this dream about a week ago; do you want to hear about it?'

'OKAY.'

'In the dream, you and I were swimming in a pool that had lights and fountains and was beautiful, except the tiles were pieces of broken pottery. They hurt to walk on, so we had to keep swimming. When I got closer to you, I realized you were swimming without a bathing suit on. I asked why and you said, "I never wear a bathing suit. My body rejects them." Don't worry, I couldn't see anything in the dream except that you looked beautiful and you swam perfectly, better than me. I just wanted to keep following you around the pool and get stronger myself. That's what I kept thinking in my dream: *Just stay close to her, keep swimming, and you'll get stronger.*'

'DO YOU KNOW WHAT WATER SYMBOLIZES IN DREAMS?'

'What?'

'SEX.'

'No, it doesn't.'

'I DIDN'T THINK THAT UP. FREUD DID.'

He pressed his sweaty chin to his bow tie. 'Well, I don't think it was about that. I think it was about seeing what a strong person you are. You aren't afraid of things and you're always true to yourself and I've learned a lot from you. You're the first person I've ever talked to about my problems, and it's made a big difference. Telling you about my fears made them more real, but more manageable.' Talking like this made him feel as if a weight was lifting off his shoulders. 'I want us to be friends for the rest of our lives. I feel like you're the best friend I've ever had.' He felt light-headed hearing himself. He knew it might sound silly to her. She might roll her eyes and call him sentimental. Knowing her, she'd probably make a joke to break the tension of the moment, but he didn't care. He'd said what he wanted to. His shirt was wet through, and it was over.

He turned and looked at her, surprised to see tears in her eyes. For a long time, she didn't type anything. She started to, and then stopped and wiped her eyes. Was she crying from happiness? Impossible to say. 'Amy? Are you okay?'

Finally she typed: 'WHY DO YOU THINK I WAS NAKED IN THAT DREAM?'

He sat back as a chill passed through his wet clothes. That was the problem with the speech he'd just delivered. He couldn't explain that part at all.

CHAPTER TWENTY

Amy knew the truth. Her mother didn't have a problem with prom. She had a problem with Matthew. Amy had never told her mother about Matthew's problems, but she'd figured it out.

After her speech, Nicole asked which of Amy's peer helpers she was talking about in the speech. At that point, Amy was so worried that Matthew might never speak to her again that she told her mother the truth, a mistake she regretted every time her mother raised a sceptical eyebrow at the mention of Matthew's name.

'I'm not saying he's a bad person,' Nicole said after Amy told her about prom. 'I *like* Matthew. I'm saying this is too much responsibility for someone who can be unreliable.'

'HE'S NOT UNRELIABLE. HE'S THE BEST PEER HELPER I HAVE.'

'This is different, Aim. You know that. This involves a lot of responsibility. He'd have to drive at night. He'd have to get you there and back safely.'

For two weeks, Nicole suggested alternatives. What if her father drove? What if they went as a part of a group, with Sanjay and Sarah? For the first time in her life, Amy held her ground. 'THIS IS MY CHOICE. I WANT MATTHEW TO DRIVE. I WANT HIM TO KNOW I TRUST HIM.' Typing this, Amy thought of the uncompromising stances her mother had taken with teachers in the past. She almost said: *I learned this from you, Mom. You should be proud of me.* In the end, what choice did her parents have? She'd be leaving home soon, going away to college, making her own decisions every day. How could they not honour this one?

The night before prom, Nicole came into Amy's room. 'I'm sorry we've made this so hard for each other.'

In the light from the moon, Amy could see that her mother had been crying. She felt bad. 'YOU WANTED ME TO MAKE NEW FRIENDS. REMEMBER THE LISTS?'

'I do.' Nicole laughed. 'I suppose I wanted you to make a lot of superficial friends. I didn't want anyone to matter more than your dad or me.' She started crying again, which made Amy feel bad.

'MATTHEW DOESN'T MATTER MORE. HE MATTERS IN A DIFFERENT WAY.'

'I know. It's just hard when you've spent seventeen years protecting your child, who is smart and beautiful and a little more fragile than everyone else's child. No risk seems worth taking.' She looked out of the window, quiet for a while. 'I've never understood parents of kids who play football. How do you sit in the stands and *watch* your child get hurt?'

'THIS ISN'T FOOTBALL, MOM.'

'No, I know.'

'THIS ISN'T EVEN RISKY. IT'S JUST LIFE. I'M HAVING A LIFE.'

'I know.' She blew her nose. 'And that feels risky to me. I can't help it. It just does. I see all the ways Matthew might hurt you, even if he doesn't mean to. Even if he's a nice boy with the best intentions.'

'HE'S NOT GOING TO HURT ME. HE'S THE

BEST FRIEND I'VE EVER HAD.'

'But that's just it, Aim. You want more than that, don't you? You don't want to be just his friend.'

How did her mother know this when she'd been so careful not to show her feelings? She couldn't lie now. 'MAYBE.'

'That's what I'm most scared of, I suppose. I see you changing in all these ways – looking through magazines and trying on dresses. I'm scared that he'll never love you the way you want to be loved. I want to spare you that, sweetheart. It's a terrible feeling. That's all.'

Except that wasn't all. The next afternoon, an hour before Matthew was due to pick her up, her mother appeared in her doorway again. She wasn't crying this time. Her lips were a thin line of determination.

'There's one more thing,' she said. 'Your dad and I have talked about this. We're letting you go tonight, but we don't want you seeing Matthew over the summer. You've got your summer classes to concentrate on and college to get ready for. This may not even come up, but in case it does.'

Amy was beginning to understand her mother's obsession: 'CAN I SEE MY OTHER PEER HELPERS?'

'Of course, dear. But with Matthew . . . we think he has some issues he needs to sort out.'

Nicole must have been talking to Ms Hynes, the guidance counsellor who still oversaw the peer-helpers programme. This wasn't only about Matthew's OCD. Of all her mother's 'concerns', this was the real one: she knew that Matthew wasn't going to college.

'HOW ABOUT IF HE SORTS HIS ISSUES OUT? COULD I SEE HIM THEN?'

'If he's better a year from now, of course you can see him. We'd love to have him come over and say hi.'

'A YEAR FROM NOW? ARE YOU SERIOUS?'

'He isn't well, Amy. You've had so little experience with boys that you don't see this yet, but your father and I do – we don't want you to think the only person who will ever love you is someone who has such serious problems himself. You're smart about so many things, but not about this. You don't see what's obvious to everyone else.'

'WHAT'S OBVIOUS?'

She hesitated for a moment, and then said it: 'He's not *good enough* for you. Of course you think he's wonderful and should be your best friend, but he's not and he shouldn't. He's not *worthy* of you, Amy.' Her face was flush with emotion. 'He's not as *smart* as you are. Wait a year and you'll see. Meet some boys at Stanford and you'll understand.'

Outside the door, she could hear her father talking to Matthew. She lowered her Pathway to a whisper. 'WOULD IT BE BETTER IF I WAS GOING TO PROM WITH SANJAY?'

Two weeks ago Sanjay had got off the wait list at Caltech and been accepted into their engineering programme. This week he'd told Amy he'd come up with his first potential patent as an engineer. He was grinning from ear to ear when he told her what it was: a way to stash a quart of booze in her walker so they could sneak it into prom. 'Hiding it is one level of brilliance,' he said. 'Dispensing it will be a whole other

159

level of genius.' Sarah sat beside him as he laid out his plan, smiling as if this would all be very funny.

Though their relationship wasn't clear, Amy feared there was an imbalance of feelings on Sarah's side. 'I can't explain why I like him, I just *do*,' she'd told Amy. 'I keep thinking he's got all this potential if only he'd relax and be himself.' For his part, Sanjay seemed happy to have a date that would get him to prom, and thrilled at his plan to win popularity with the booze once they get there.

'It's gonna be *great*,' he kept saying. 'People will bring their punch cup over to Amy, stick a straw in the screwhole. It'll take two seconds. Shazam! Mixed drink! We'll be the first people to get booze into prom!'

It was the first time Amy had sat in the cafeteria with two peer helpers at the same time. Technically it was a Sarah day, not Sanjay, so he was there voluntarily making them laugh with his idea. He kept going with his argument: they wouldn't get in trouble, because what chaperone would take the time to inspect Amy's walker? If someone did suspect something, Amy would excuse herself to the bathroom and empty it out. 'We'll go down in the history books,' he kept saying until Amy couldn't say no. It felt too good to be sitting there, scheming with friends. This was what she'd wanted this year to be: after seventeen years of academic achievement, she wanted the chaos and jumble of real people in her life, with their stupid ideas and senior pranks.

'Of course we'd feel better if you were going to prom with Sanjay,' Nicole said now. 'Unfortunately you're not.'

'JUST BECAUSE HE GOT INTO COLLEGE?'

'No, sweetheart. Because he's got a good head on his shoulders. Because he doesn't need your help or your pity.'

Amy wished she could tell her mother what the good head on Sanjay's shoulders had talked her into doing. *You want to know how trustworthy Sanjay is? Pick up my walker and ask yourself why it feels two quarts heavier.* She didn't, because she wanted her night with Matthew more than she wanted to prove her mother was wrong.

Now she looked over at Matthew, driving in a hunch with his face inches from the wheel. Maybe she shouldn't have forced him to drive just to make a statement to her parents. At the speed Matthew was going, they'd make it to prom just as it was ending.

'YOU'RE DOING GREAT. YOU'RE A GOOD DRIVER.'

'It might be better if we don't talk. I've got a turn coming up.'

He wasn't doing great. He was a terrible driver. His foot arbitrarily went up and down on the gas in response to whatever was going through his mind. Being thrown against the seat belt was leaving a mark on Amy's shoulder. The dream speech had been sweet, but after he'd delivered it he'd looked ashy pale and ill about the implications of what he might have just said.

After they got to the Sheraton and made their way inside, Amy studied the other girls milling around in the lobby. There was no one she recognized from any of her classes. 'I guess we're meant to get in line and take pictures first,' Matthew said.

'They're sixty dollars for the cheapest package. I didn't know what you'd say, so I didn't pay yet.'

Behind them a group of about ten kids appeared, laughing and calling out to one another. All the girls hugged and touched one another's hair. No one looked over at them. She leaned towards Matthew. 'DO WE KNOW THEM? ARE THERE TWO PROMS HAPPENING HERE?'

He looked over at the group she was pointing at. 'Yeah. They're with us. I took Spanish with one of those girls.' They watched the group for a while. More joined. To Amy's eye, it was sad; everyone looked like an overdressed movie extra paid to stand around, pretending to have fun.

After they got their picture taken, Matthew told her he should go to the bathroom and read her mother's list of instructions. 'I'll be right back. Do you need anything?'

No, she shook her head – and wondered how long it would be before she saw him again. Then she looked up and saw Sanjay coming down the hallway with Sarah behind him, trying to keep up. He looked surprisingly good in his tux.

'You look *fantastic*, Amy,' he said. 'I've already heard people talking about you.'

'WHAT WERE THEY SAYING?'

'Just that you're *here*! They can't believe it! Did you have any problems at the door?'

'NO. I TRIED TO TELL THEM MY WALKER WAS FILLED WITH BOOZE BUT THEY DIDN'T BELIEVE ME.'

Sanjay's expression froze. 'You're joking. That's a joke, right?'

162

'YES. THAT'S A JOKE.'

'Okay, look. I want you sitting someplace where the chaperones won't notice a lot of people coming over to talk to you.' They walked inside the ballroom, which was loud and dark with a spinning, mirrored ball over the dance floor. Sanjay sat her down next to a table with its pink, floral centrepiece and glass–mug mementos that said: *WHAT A FEELING! Coral Hills High School Senior Prom, Class of 2014.* 'I want you hidden for a little bit. Like behind this potted plant.'

'MATTHEW'S IN THE BATHROOM. YOU HAVE TO TELL HIM WHERE I AM.'

'I will, don't worry,' Sanjay said, and explained how this would work: he'd send people over in groups of three or four to sit with her for a few minutes and fill their cups from her walker. 'Don't worry about talking to them. I'll remind them of everything.'

Remind them of what? Amy wondered. *That I can't talk?*

She watched as he fastened the contraption he'd engineered – with clear tubing and a spigot he'd taken from a five-gallon thermos dispenser. 'This way, there's an on/off switch. I'm telling people half a cup at a time, tops.'

He seemed to think the demand would be overwhelming, that no one would think twice about drinking something that had been sitting in a metal walker. (Sanjay had spent an hour after school cleaning it out. Still Amy wondered, 'WON'T IT MAKE EVERY DRINK TASTE LIKE METAL?' 'Just wait,' Sanjay said. 'I guarantee no one will care.')

By the time he finally got the spigot and hose attached,

Amy noticed that Sarah had walked away, as if she didn't want any part of this.

'Okay,' Sanjay said, pouring his first cup. 'Alpha test completed. Plan operational.' He could hardly mask his delight.

'WHERE'D SARAH GO?'

'Never mind Sarah. She's having a little issue about nothing.'

'WHAT'S HER ISSUE?'

'I told you. Nothing. She thinks I'm overinvested in this idea. I told her I'm doing this for *you* so you can have fun and talk to all these people.'

'COME ON, SANJ. I DON'T REALLY WANT TO TALK TO THESE PEOPLE.'

He flashed her a look. 'Well, don't tell Sarah that. I'm going to start telling them they can come over.'

'DON'T FORGET TO TELL MATTHEW WHERE I AM.'

'I will, I will. Don't worry.'

Brian Campbell walked over first, the quarterback of the football team. Amy had taken two classes with him in tenth grade, but had never talked to him. She laughed when he caught her eye and bent down on one knee in front of her walker. She laughed again – stupidly – as he worked to get the spigot open. It took almost a minute for him to get the device to work. A minute that Amy filled with two awkward laughs, a hiccup, and silence. 'Thanks, Amy,' he said when he was done.

Roger Altiers stepped up next. They'd had eighth-grade

math and three years of French together. 'You're Amy, right?' he said. She nodded. 'So, hey, Amy, what's up?' After that, everyone who came up greeted her by name as if Sanjay had told them to. For a few minutes, it was so disorientating that she started to get scared. She wanted Matthew to come back so he could explain why everyone who'd never spoken to her before suddenly knew her name, but she didn't see him anywhere. That's when she realized how trapped she was. She couldn't move because her walker wasn't hers any more. It was everyone else's joke of the night: get your picture taken, your coat checked and stop by Amy's walker! She watched Sanjay and saw how carefully he picked the people to point in her direction, dragging it out forever, like they were starting meaningful friendships. She overheard him a few times, reminding people of the classes they'd had, of how they'd known each other since third grade.

It made her even sadder than she'd felt when she'd first walked in.

CHAPTER TWENTY-ONE

None of this was going the way Matthew wanted it to. Picking Amy up and talking to her parents had made him more nervous than he'd expected it to. So nervous it wasn't until they were inside the hotel lobby that he *really* saw how lovely she looked tonight. But why did seeing Amy in her dress awaken such a panic? Was it the neckline shaped like a *U* so he could see her collarbone and the sprinkling of freckles across her chest? Was it how he felt standing beside her, waiting to get their picture taken? Was it letting himself really look at her body for the first time? He almost couldn't believe it. She was *beautiful*.

Amy's body had always been a mystery to him. He recognized parts of it, of course. He'd seen her barefoot before and knew the way her toes stuck up and her ankles went rigid. Her feet were her most despised body part, she once told him, because they were the main thing that kept her from walking better. The one time he saw her feet up close, she'd scraped her ankle and he examined it to see if she was all right. Doing that, he surprised himself by discovering that he didn't mind holding her strange foot in his hand. In fact, he started rubbing it, wondering if he could soften the stiffness with a massage. When had he ever done anything like that? Now he thought about tonight and a new fear skated down his spine. How did he expect this evening to end?

Too late, he realized: they'd thought too much about the logistics of getting here and not enough about what they would *do* here. She'd already told him she didn't want to dance. She also told him about Sanjay's stupid plan to spike other people's drinks.

'Do we have to drink?' he asked her nervously.

'OF COURSE NOT,' she said. 'I'M ONLY A CONDUIT. IT'LL BE OVER IN TWENTY MINUTES, HE PROMISES. TOPS.'

Matthew didn't care about that. He didn't care about seeing Sanjay or Sarah or any of these people they were supposedly friends with, but weren't really. The only thing he really wanted to do was find a quiet spot to sit down with Amy and talk.

With all the joking around and preparation for prom, they hadn't been able to do this for a while, which meant he hadn't got to tell Amy what had been happening with him. How the world had begun to feel different with his medication. How he'd noticed certain changes, especially at work, where he was getting to be friends with the rest of the staff. *It's like I don't have to spend so much time in my head. I can actually have conversations*. If they found a spot to talk, maybe he could ask what was going on earlier tonight with her parents. Why her father had seemed so nervous and her mother so angry. They obviously weren't as happy about Amy going to prom as he'd thought they'd be. Nicole had barely spoken to him and no one had taken any pictures. Thinking of this reminded him of the note from Nicole that was still in his pocket. 'You don't have to read this now,' Nicole had said when she handed it to him. 'You can wait until afterwards.'

He'd slipped it into his pocket before Amy could see what it said on the outside: *Instructions for Matthew.* Surely even Nicole could see how this might be hurtful. The implication that he was taking Amy to prom as part of his job. Getting paid to be her friend and answering to her mother, who signed the cheques and could give him 'instructions'. He remembered Nicole saying he could read this afterwards, but now he couldn't wait. He wanted to know what she had to say to him:

Dear Matthew,

Please understand this is not about you personally. This is about our responsibility to protect our daughter, who is more inexperienced and fragile than you probably realize. We understand that you have your own issues that you've struggled with this year. We were disappointed that you didn't disclose these problems before you began to work with our daughter. If we'd known about them, we would have made a different choice, and not taken the risk of letting Amy become attached to someone who has difficulty controlling his actions. Please understand that we do not dislike you personally. As her parents we have to protect Amy. It is our duty. In our view, it is dangerous for her to become too attached to you. I'm sure you understand this. After this evening, we'll ask that you not see Amy again.

    Many thanks,
    Nicole and Max Van Horn

I'll wash my hands once, he said to himself. *Maybe twice. Because this letter is cruel and unfair, I'll let myself wash them twice. I won't check the faucet. I won't need to, because Amy doesn't agree with her parents. If she's here with me now, it means she doesn't agree with them. It means she doesn't think I'm a dangerous person.*

Maybe you are dangerous. Maybe they're right.

For the first time in weeks, the voice was back.

No. I don't believe that. The only danger for Amy tonight is from Sanjay and his stupid plan.

Sanjay is fine. Sarah likes Sanjay. Everyone likes Sanjay. You're the problem.

He couldn't leave the bathroom. Even if Amy needed him, he couldn't leave yet. He was starting to sweat. His shirt was soaked through. He'd have to wash his arms if he ever wanted to get clean. Maybe his armpits too.

The bathroom door opened. A boy he didn't recognize walked in. 'Are you okay, man?'

No, he tried to say, but nothing came out.

'You look a little sick.'

I am, he didn't say.

'I could get you some water. You want some water?'

The boy was nice enough to leave, but then he didn't come back. Matthew sat down on the bathroom floor because standing had started to make him dizzy. He'd never get clean now. There were floor germs and sink germs and shoe-bottom germs. He was probably sitting right now on dog shit from the bottom of someone's shoe. Nicole was right: he couldn't control this. He couldn't control his pounding heart or his shaking hands. He couldn't walk out of this bathroom. He couldn't find Amy and tell her not to worry, that he'd be fine in a few hours.

What would Amy say anyway?

Hearing this surprised him. He knew what Amy would say. She'd said it many times. *This feeling will pass. The fear is real but the danger is not. You don't need to panic. Ride it out.* He could almost hear her saying it. Like she was in the room with him. Like he'd brought her Pathway with him, though of course he hadn't.

He took a deep breath and let his own brain conjure her words for himself. *The fear is real*, he made his brain tell itself. *The danger is not.*

After a while he looked around. He had no idea how long he'd been in there. When he finally came out, it felt like there were twice as many people in the hallway than before. Most of the boys had their jackets off and a few had loosened their ties as well. A couple was fighting near the doorway.

Matthew was better now. Calm enough to find Amy and apologize for leaving her. She wasn't where he left her, which made him nervous. How long had he been gone? He opened the door to the ballroom, which was pitch-black inside except for a mirror ball flashing. He shut the door and went back up the hallway, where he saw a surprise, sitting on the carpeted floor: Sarah, wearing a magenta dress with a corsage pinned to her shoulder, crying like he'd seen her do once before, in eighth grade.

He went over and bent down beside her. 'Are you okay?' he said softly.

She shook her head but didn't answer.

'Technically I don't think you're supposed to start crying until *after* prom is over. You never know. You might still have fun.' He always surprised himself after a panic attack – how

170

calm he felt. How reasonable. It was like all the adrenaline in his system had been used up and now he could sit here in peace.

'I hate Sanjay.'

'Oh right. I have to admit I don't love the guy, either.'

'Why is he so obsessed with getting these cheerleaders and football players to pay attention to him? We're never going to see them again, right?'

'Right. I mean, we can only hope.'

'He thinks this whole idea gives him power over them. I told him that's not how it works. If you care what they think, *they* have all the power.'

'You're probably right,' he said. The more he thought about it, the more right she was. Maybe it even applied to the note in his pocket. *If you care what they think, they have all the power.* Maybe he could just throw it away. Maybe he could just not care what Amy's parents thought.

'Are they done with the booze?'

'No. It turns out two quarts goes a lot further than you'd think. He's going around offering it to people he's never talked to before. They're saying no thanks and he's trying to talk them into it. Meanwhile, there's other idiots who've gone back five times.'

He wondered if this was the explanation for the couple fighting in the hallway, for the girls with mascara running down their faces. Maybe those people were all drunk. He asked her if Amy was okay, which produced a fresh wave of tears. 'I don't even want him to drive me home. I don't want to talk to him. I don't want to look at him.'

She was crying so hard, he put his arms round her. 'We can drive you home,' he said, surprising himself. Like driving wasn't a problem for him. Like now that he'd done it with one girl in the car, he could do it with two, no problem.

CHAPTER TWENTY-TWO

'Do you want to try some?' Sanjay asked Amy after about thirty people had visited her walker. Though it was still half full, the demand had died down. People were either starting to feel the effects, or not interested in kneeling next to Amy's walker for a third or fourth time.

'WHY NOT?' Amy said.

As awkward as all the logistics had been, she liked the way a little vodka had made everyone more relaxed in her presence. She wasn't the disabled girl any more, or the superachiever from the newspaper article. She was someone they could joke with. Two people told her how pretty she looked. One boy said he'd be back to ask her to dance later. If booze could lower the walls that had existed between her and all these people for the last twelve years, why not try some of it herself?

Mixed with punch, it tasted terrible at first and then it didn't taste like anything at all. Just a little sting in the back of her throat. And a warm feeling as it travelled down. She smiled, one of her crazy, open-mouth smiles. 'SANKS,' she typed, though Sanjay didn't seem to get the joke. 'I SHOULD GO FIND MATTHEW.'

'Yeah, maybe you should. Last time I saw him, he was hitting on my date.'

Amy's head lurched at this, though Sanjay didn't seem to care. He was still scanning the crowd for popular faces he hadn't approached yet. 'Oh my God, she's here!' he said, breaking into a huge smile. 'Cindy Weintraub is here! I didn't think she was coming!'

It didn't occur to Sanjay that Amy might need help standing up. Or securing the spigot hose so she didn't fall over. At least one person was kind enough to see her coming and hold open one of the double doors for her. As she plodded towards it, she intentionally tried to empty her walker of the last of the booze.

Then she saw, through the open door: Matthew sitting on the floor with his arms round Sarah, who was bent over with her face in his chest. He looked like he was kissing the top of her head. Kissing, and talking, and laying his cheek on her hair. Amy stopped walking. She felt as if something was squeezing her chest. As if she couldn't breathe. Or move.

'Are you going out?' the boy holding the door said.

'NO!' she pressed, just as a song ended, so her computer shouted.

Everyone turned to look at her. Everyone except Matthew and Sarah.

She staggered back, afraid she might fall or something worse. She looked for Sanjay to help her back to her chair. Anyone. The room started to spin. She heard a voice near her. 'Are you okay?'

She tried to press 'NO', but accidentally pressed 'THANK YOU'. She got caught in the spinning strobe lights on the dance floor, which made her feel even dizzier. She stood for a while, on what must have been a corner of the dance floor, and waited for the crowd growing around her to move away.

Just as she feared she was going to fall over, she felt hands on her waist and arms round her. 'You're okay,' a voice whispered. 'I've got you.'

It's Matthew, she thought, closing her eyes and falling back, grateful.

When did she realize that it wasn't? That the panic, the crowd, the flashing lights had made her confuse one rented tuxedo jacket for another? She'd *thought* it was Matthew. She clung on tight, her cheek pressed to his shoulder. She cried, wetting his shoulder, as if it were him. She punched his back and growled and screamed into his chest and then, when it was all over, she realized: it wasn't him.

It was Sanjay's voice in her ear: 'It's okay, Aim. It's okay.'

He walked her back over to the side of the room and a table full of her new, drunk fake-best-friends. They all clapped when she sat down like she was putting on a show and now it was over. 'Just stay here,' Sanjay whispered in her ear. 'I'm going to figure out what's going on with those guys.' He left a drink in front of her with a straw she could reach without any help.

'Are you okay?' a boy named Andrew, sitting across the table, said. Amy had spent tenth grade watching him and, based on that year of observation, assumed he was gay. Now he had his arm round a girl who looked like she was falling asleep on his shoulder.

Amy nodded and tried to smile. Her Pathway had come loose and was dangling by one Velcro strap from her walker. Without it, she couldn't answer him.

'Kind of a shitty night, right?' Andrew said. 'A bunch of people are saying that.'

Amy looked around, confused. She'd assumed everyone else was having fun. She wished she could ask him what he meant, and then another boy appeared out of nowhere and leaned over Amy's lap to grab a cup on the table. 'This music is lame,' he said. 'I asked the DJ where he was from and swear he said Suck City.' The whole table laughed and he noticed, for the first time, who he was leaning over. 'You got anything more in your little contraption?' he said to Amy.

He didn't wait for a response.

'Can I have some? Like, all of it?' The table laughed again as he opened the spigot and tilted her walker to drain the last of it into his plastic cup. 'It won't be enough to save this night, but thanks anyway.' When he put the walker back, her Pathway banged against the leg and spun helplessly from its Velcro tether. There was more laughter as the boy drank the whole cup in one swallow and walked away.

'That guy is a freakin' animal,' Andrew said.

Amy tried to point with her good hand to her dangling computer. She was terrified it might have got vodka on it. Andrew didn't understand. 'Mostly he's a nice guy. He doesn't mean to seem like a dick. He just does sometimes.'

She pointed again. 'Ma – ooo,' she said.

Andrew shook his head. 'I have no idea what you're saying.'

She saw the yellow battery light blinking. 'Ooo-hhwah?'

'Are you okay?' He looked across the table at another couple Amy didn't know. 'Somebody should get that guy who brought her over here. I think she's starting to freak out.'

176

She wasn't freaking out. She was trying to get someone to rescue her Pathway so she could use it, but he would never understand. None of them would.

'What's his name?' the girl sitting across from him said.

'I don't know. The Indian guy. Or Spanish. Whatever he is.' Andrew came around the table to sit next to Amy. 'Tell him we don't know what to do – she's spazzing out.'

Amy tried to keep her head still, and look less spazzy, but there wasn't much she could do. Her bad arm shot out and hit him in the chest.

'Go!' he screamed at his date.

'Fine,' she said, and leaned over to whisper. 'But what's her name again?'

'It doesn't matter. He'll know who you're talking about. Just go.'

Eventually Sanjay came back and the table emptied quickly. 'Here's what I found out,' he said. 'Sarah wants to go home and Matthew wants to take her. I said fine, if he's going to do that, why don't I just take you home. He said that should be up to you.'

Amy felt sick to her stomach. She feared the vodka she'd drunk was about to come back up. Driving here she'd had the premonition that they should turn round and go back home, and obviously she was right. Matthew wasn't having a panic attack this whole time. More like the opposite. He was having a burst of confidence and a breakthrough with Sarah. Now he was looking for an excuse not to have to bring her home. 'TELL HIM IT'S FINE,' she typed after Sanjay returned her Pathfinder to its proper spot. 'I'LL GO HOME WITH YOU.'

Surely Matthew would find her and say goodbye, she assumed. He'd feel bad about leaving with Sarah and want to apologize and Amy would say, *No, don't. It's fine. I'm happy for you. Go have your night with the girl you've loved since ninth grade.* She'd hate him and hate the fact that her mother had been right, but she'd get over it at some point.

But that never happened. She sat alone again for a long time. When Sanjay came back, he told her they were already gone. 'Maybe we should just go too,' he said.

They walked quietly out to the parking lot. In Sanjay's car, she asked if Matthew had said anything else before they left.

'Look – as far as I'm concerned they can go fuck themselves. Who knows what they did? Sorry, Amy. I'm not supposed to swear around you. Did you know that was one of your mother's rules? *Please refrain from cursing around Amy.* It's funny. The minute someone says that, it actually makes you want to swear more.'

As they drove, she calmed down enough to type. 'SORRY ABOUT MY MOTHER.'

'Fuck it. Don't be. You're mother's all right. What do any of us know about having a kid like you? For years she doesn't know whether you'll live or die. Then it turns out you're smart and she has to spend sixteen years proving that to a world full of people who don't want to believe it. It must have been fucking hard. I don't blame her.'

She'd never seen this side of Sanjay. She wished the kids at that table had been nicer about him. Or at least remembered his name. He wasn't a bad guy; he just tried too hard with people who were never going to be impressed by someone like him.

He turned on the radio, and drummed on the steering wheel as he drove. 'The stupid thing is, I like Sarah. I do. Maybe I'm even scared of how much I like her.'

Amy had so wanted to say this tonight that she went ahead and told Sanjay: 'I LOVE MATTHEW.'

He turned and looked at her. 'No shit, really?'

'I THINK MAYBE I'VE LOVED HIM ALL YEAR.'

'Wow. I had no idea.'

It was only eleven twenty when they got home, which meant her parents were still up and sitting in the living room. They looked confused at first and then – Amy could tell with one glance – relieved that it was Sanjay bringing her home. It meant her mother was right: Matthew had lived up to her expectations of failure. Amy was grateful for this much: her mother didn't ask where Matthew was or what had happened. Instead they greeted Sanjay as a hero and offered him a glass of champagne from a bottle they had opened to celebrate the night. 'Here's to prom!' her mother said. 'May we let the whole business rest in peace, now.'

'Hear, hear,' Sanjay said, lifting his glass, a slow smile spreading across his face. For the first time, Amy wondered how much he'd had to drink tonight. He seemed fine at prom as she watched him fill cups for other people; now she tried to guess how many of those he'd had himself. Not that he seemed drunk, only that he seemed bolder. 'Amy was beautiful tonight,' he told her parents. 'I wish you could have seen her. The belle of the ball.'

Nicole took a sip and put her glass down. 'Really? Is that true, Aim?'

'NOT REALLY.'

'It *is* true. Everyone came up and talked to her tonight. I'm not kidding. I have pictures.'

Nicole's eyebrows went up in surprise. Amy tilted her head in Sanjay's direction. He was already holding up his phone to show them pictures. 'Right here,' he said, smiling and shaking his head. 'Here's Amy and Brian Campbell, quarterback of the football team, having a nice chat.'

He held out the phone. Amy squinted and saw the blurry proof – yes, it was Brian half kneeling beside her. Her mother clapped a flat hand on her chest. 'Oh, Amy, look! You *did* talk to him.'

Sanjay thumbed to the next picture. 'Amy and Andy Robbins. Vice president of the class. Headed to Northwestern.'

'I remember Andy! You were in elementary school with him.'

Sanjay kept going. Amy with Willa Samuels, Amy with Dorie Rogers, Amy with Tyrone Michaels, the basketball star who was so tall his head didn't fit in the picture frame.

'They were all so happy that Amy was *there*. They wanted to come over and congratulate her on Stanford and tell her how much it meant getting to know her this year.'

Nicole blinked back tears. 'Oh, Amy, this is so wonderful!'

Why is it wonderful, Mom? she wanted to ask. *Why is it wonderful that I've come home with a different boy than I left with? Why is it better to have had meaningless conversations with people I'll never see again than to have had a decent goodbye with the boy I love?* She couldn't say any of that, of course. Or let herself think about it too much.

They kept talking for a while. No one mentioned Matthew or wondered why none of Sanjay's pictures included him.

'This makes me so happy, Sanjay. I can't tell you how nervous we've been all night.'

'I'll bet.' He smiled one of his big, million-teeth smiles. 'But we were all there together. Matthew, Sarah. All of us. We were looking after each other.' As he said this, he surprised Amy. He reached over and squeezed her bad hand. No one ever touched that hand – not even Matthew, who'd got over his fear of touching other parts of her body, like her feet and her back. Sanjay slid two fingers into her curled fist, loosening it a little so he could rub the back of her hand with his thumb.

Nicole looked down and smiled. 'We should leave you two alone,' she said, clapping her hands together once. 'Max, what are we thinking, staying up this late when it's still their big night?'

Her father looked around, a little confused. 'Everything all right with Matthew, then?'

He looked at Amy as he spoke, though Sanjay answered. 'He's fine now. I just got a text from him. He got a little sick at the start of the night. He asked me to bring Amy home, which of course I was happy to do. Like I said, we were there as a group.'

Amy was pretty sure this wasn't true, but she didn't say anything.

'Wonderful, then,' Nicole said, standing up. 'We *thank you*, Sanjay, for all your help. I don't mind admitting I was a little bit nervous about letting Amy go off with Matthew. Not that we don't trust him. But we trust you more!' Her mother looked a little giddy with relief to have the night over. Sanjay stood up so she could hug him before they left the room.

After they were gone, Amy was surprised. She didn't feel as sad as she expected to. She *had* got through this. Matthew had left her alone for two hours, and when she finally saw him again he had his arms round Sarah, but look – here she was!

Her mother was right – thanks to Sanjay.

Even if she'd hated the reason everyone came up and talked to her tonight, she also had to admit that it made all her old classmates seem less mysterious. And now here was Sanjay, alone beside her, holding her hand. 'Are you tired?' he said.

He still looked gorgeous, the white of his shirt against his dark skin, the black of his bow tie, the same colour of his eyes. Thankfully her hand was steady enough to type. 'NO. NOT TIRED.'

'Do you want to show me around your house?'

It was a strange request, especially given that it was close to midnight. She stood up. 'SURE,' she said, and started to move around. 'KITCHEN,' she typed, and gestured. 'DINING ROOM. OFFICE/STUDY.' She moved slowly down the hall, surprised to discover her parents had already gone to their room and closed the door. 'AND MY ROOM,' she said when they got to it.

It was a little embarrassing to have Sanjay see her room, with its little-girl mementos. Pink walls, a pile of stuffed animals in one corner, a pile of books in the other. She was about to explain why she held on to one and didn't shelve the others, when Sanjay produced a surprise from behind his back.

'Ta-da!' he said, pulling out the bottle of champagne and two glasses.

He stepped inside her room and closed the door behind him. She smiled when she understood what he was thinking.

'Don't worry about your parents,' he said. 'They practically dimmed the lights for us.'

CHAPTER TWENTY-THREE

Starting at eleven fifteen, when he found out that Amy had left with Sanjay, Matthew spent the most of the night furiously texting messages. After he'd driven Sarah home and got back to his room, he sat down at his computer and wrote Amy an email:

To: aimhigh@comcast.net
From: mstheword@gmail.com

All right, this is it. I draw the line at twelve texts. I will assume you're fine because everyone says you looked fine when you left with that jerk, Sanjay. I hope you had a nice time. I drove Sarah home and let her tell me every icky detail she could think of about him and, believe me, there were a lot. Maybe you two have fallen in love so I shouldn't be saying this. If you have, I'm sorry. I'll keep them all to myself. Just write when you get this so I know you're alive; then I'll drift out of your life forever. Matthew

PS Did anyone ever tell you that technically you're not supposed to go home with a different date than you went to prom with? Not that we care what other people think, but if we did, other people might call that strange, or even slutty.

PPS That's all, I guess. Never mind this last PPS.

In the morning, he wrote again:

To: aimhigh@comcast.net
From: mstheword@gmail.com

I've decided maybe you got drunk and must have been momentarily so disoriented that you accidentally got in the wrong car. Thanks for an almost great night that I will now try to forget for the rest of my life. Do I sound mad? I'm not mad. I just think Sanjay should get in a lot of trouble for what he did. Supposedly one girl spent all night throwing up whatever it was that she drank from your walker. So that's one story you might not have heard.

Who knows how many people acted irresponsibly and drove home drunk?

I know I sound like I'm mad and I'm trying not to. But that's because I hated everything that happened last night, Amy, and I'm trying to think of reasons why I should blame other people and not you. I wanted to have a *nice time* with *you.* Not to spend a whole evening talking to other people and wondering where you were. I know some of it was my fault. I had a regrettable episode that freaked me out a little bit in the bathroom. It had to do with the 'instructions' I got from your mom, but it was over in thirty minutes. I made sure of that. I said Sanjay can have you for thirty minutes, so I gave myself that much time to do what I had to do in the bathroom. And then I stopped.

I'm not proud of staying in the bathroom for half an hour, but I *am* proud of the fact that I walked out. I pulled myself together and dried my hands and I walked out to find you. I thought to myself, *Amy's mother isn't in charge of her any more and she doesn't get to decide who she'll be with. Amy decides that. And for tonight, she's picked me.* That's what I thought anyway. Until I saw Sarah crying in the hallway, and she said Sanjay had been fascinated by you ever since he saw you on TV and in the newspaper. He thinks you're going to be some big celebrity soon and he wants to work as your manager and promote you. That's what she said.

I don't understand any of it, Amy, but I especially don't understand how you could leave with him and not see what a terrible thing that was to do to Sarah and me.

Maybe he was laying it on a little too thick, especially since Sarah had helped him put Nicole's note in perspective. By the time they got out to the car and were driving home, she wasn't crying any more. Mostly she wanted to say mean things about Sanjay. 'He never really wanted this job with Amy. He just needed to make money for college next year and this was the best way to do it. He thinks Amy's a spoiled rich girl, that underneath this show of being so close to her parents, she's furious and getting ready to explode.'

'Explode how?'

'Like really rebel. Look at the way her mom controls every aspect of her life. She even picked the friends Amy was allowed to make this year. We all had to send in a résumé and she decided who was 'qualified'. I mean, is that screwed up or what?'

He had to admit: hearing Sarah say this made him feel better about the note in his pocket.

To: mstheword@gmail.com
From: aimhigh@comcast.net

Oh, Matthew, I'm still so confused about what happened last night. Didn't you tell Sanjay that you wanted to take Sarah home? Isn't that what you said to him? I thought that I was being a *good* friend. I saw you and Sarah together in the hallway. You had your arms around her and I assumed this was your golden opportunity. That you'd loved her for years, and I didn't want to be in the way of you getting together with her. I thought if I looked for you to say goodbye, you'd have to say, 'No, Amy, don't go,' even if you didn't really mean it. I thought you'd feel guilty about wanting to be with Sarah.

To: aimhigh@comcast.net
From: mstheword@gmail.com

I meant *you and I* could give her a ride. She was mad at Sanjay and didn't want to go home with him. Why would I have wanted to leave without you????

She felt a little dizzy at all this. How badly she'd misread the situation. She wasn't sure if she should be honest and tell him what she'd wanted to last night. Then she decided, *What the hell*.

To: mstheword@gmail.com
From: aimhigh@comcast.net

I had to assume that all your kindness towards me and your gestures that seem almost romantic sometimes (or could be if you're a seventeen-year-old girl with a crush on your best friend) aren't meant romantically. How could they be, when neither one of us knows what my body would do in such a situation? So if I really am your friend and I want what's best for you, don't you see? I have to assume it isn't me. At least that's what I thought last night.

I made a mistake, Matthew. First letting Sanjay involve me in his scheme with the booze and then letting him take me home. I wish I had more experience with all this so I could understand it better. Does this make any sense?

I'm sorry I left. I'm sorry I hurt you. Most of all, I'm sorry we didn't get to have our night together. Can we try again? Maybe without the dress and the tux? Just a night out?

Two minutes later, he sent this back:

To: aimhigh@comcast.net
From: mstheword@gmail.com

Oh, okay. Yes, we can try again.

Two weeks later, Amy told her parents she was going out to dinner with all her peer helpers as a thank-you for all their help this year. She got one hundred fifty dollars cash to pay for dinner, and was allowed to have Matthew pick her up, though her mother raised a sceptical eyebrow at this.

'Why can't Sanjay give you a ride?' Nicole asked, a nervous edge in her voice.

'HE DOESN'T HAVE A CAR, MOM! HE BORROWED ONE ON PROM NIGHT.'

'Sarah can't take you? Or Chloe?'

'NO. THEY'RE MEETING US THERE.'

'I don't like the idea of Matthew giving you a ride. You remember what happened last time.'

Yes, I do, Amy thought. *Last time I left early and abandoned him because I was scared.* 'IT'S JUST A RIDE, MOM. I'LL BE FINE, I PROMISE.'

She *was* fine. They weren't meeting up with anyone else. They went to a park near Matthew's house and sat near a playground where he'd played as a boy. Matthew packed a picnic, filled with all the soft foods Amy liked most and two cans of Boost, which he claimed to have developed a taste for. 'It's. a little like Muscle Milk, which I also try to drink regularly. I'm sure you can tell just by looking.'

They ate their hummus and tabbouleh salad, strawberries and shortcake, and afterwards they went through a list of things they wanted to do over the summer. Amy had about six books she wanted to read. Matthew had to work five shifts a week. 'They're all in the evening, though, which leaves my days a little free,' he said. 'I'm not sure what I'll be doing before four.'

'YOU COULD COME OVER TO MY HOUSE WHILE MY MOM IS AT WORK,' Amy said. 'WE COULD HANG OUT AND SWIM.'

At first he thought she was kidding; then he looked at her face. 'Are you serious?'

She stared back at him, unembarrassed. 'YES.'

'But your mother wrote me this note. They don't want me to see you –'

'I DON'T CARE WHAT MY PARENTS SAY. THEY AREN'T HOME DURING THE DAY. YOU SHOULD COME OVER.'

Sneaking behind her mother's back? Was this one of her dares? 'I could do that. I mean – sure, I'd like to do that.'

CHAPTER TWENTY-FOUR

Graduation came and went, a hot, sticky non-event. Afterwards Matthew and his mother ate dinner at an Outback. He ordered a filet mignon and she ordered a Dewar's on the rocks, and then, when his meal came, another. 'You seem better these days,' his mom said. 'Do you think all that stuff is helping?' She waved her hand, a little embarrassed, because she meant the medication, and the doctor.

Though he'd been going for three months, they hardly talked about it at all. He told her he didn't want to overanalyse every little thing, or check in with her all the time. Apparently she took that to mean he didn't want to talk about it at all, so he hadn't had a chance to tell her, 'I *am* better. I hope.'

She smiled and ate one of his French fries. 'That's great!'

In the beginning it had felt like a fog rolled into his head and, when it cleared, it had left behind something strange: silence. There was no voice in his head. Since then, he couldn't believe how much more time he had in the day. Hours, it felt like, where he could do what he wanted. Listen to music, surf the internet, text Amy. He'd spent the week before graduation doing all this and still had time left over to start a reading programme too. If he wasn't going to college, Amy told him, then he *had* to start filling in the gaps of his education. 'We haven't even graduated yet,' he told her.

But that didn't matter. Everything was over except for the paperwork and parties. Some seniors had stopped coming to school at all. With extra time and nothing to do, Matthew started reading. He read all of J. D. Salinger, who was surprisingly funny until he got so weird and impenetrable.

'HE NEVER GOT OVER HIS TIME IN THE WAR,' Amy explained.

'Or in prep school,' Matthew guessed.

He liked the books and he liked the feeling of accomplishment that came with finishing another one, especially as the summer began to unfold. He spent most of his mornings reading while he waited to go over to Amy's house, where he would swim until it was time to go to work.

With these loose, unstructured days, he had more time to think about what Amy had written in her email. He never mentioned it when he was with her, but the words always hovered in the back of his mind. *If you're a seventeen-year-old girl with a crush on your best friend*. He lingered over those words: *crush* and *best friend*. He couldn't do anything about them just yet, but they buoyed him with an unexpected self-confidence. They propelled him to do and say things that surprised him.

They flirted now. At least it felt as close to flirting as he'd ever got. In the afternoons when he went over to her house for a swim, he spread suntan lotion on her shoulders and brought her presents like Cheetos, which she loved and her mother refused to buy. Amy always clapped and hugged the bag and he understood something was happening.

The ground beneath their feet was shifting, but he also sensed something else. A hesitation on her part. A little reluctance. Something he couldn't pinpoint but made him pause.

★

Every day, Amy thought of new ways to tell Matthew what she wanted to say. She'd program her Pathway to say, 'I LOVE YOU, MATTHEW MALONE!' or she'd lower it to a whisper. 'I THINK I LOVE YOU.'

It never happened.

Even though it was there, between them, every afternoon.

She could feel it in his attention. The way he read every book that she suggested and loaned him. The way he arrived every day, twenty minutes after her mother had left. The way they dwelled on certain subjects and avoided others – like prom, for instance. And next fall.

All through July and the first half of August, he seemed so much better, so much easier with himself, playing games in the pool, diving showily, shaking his hair over her dry body stretched out on a deck chair. 'You should come swimming with me,' he said one afternoon, in the second week of August, just after they'd eaten a little lunch at the outdoor table and returned to the lawn chairs beside the pool. Neither one of them wanted this time to end, though they both knew it would. 'I understand your commitment to tanning, but maybe you could do both at the same time –'

'YOU'VE MISTAKEN ME FOR SOMEONE WITH FOUR WORKING LIMBS.'

'Come on – you used to swim a lot, didn't you?'

'AS A TODDLER WEDGED IN SWIM RINGS, YES.' She used to love the water, the thrilling buoyancy of it, the way her body floated beneath her. 'THE LIFE JACKET I'D REQUIRE NOW IS SIGNIFICANTLY LESS FLATTERING.'

'Do you have it?'

'I'M NOT PUTTING IT ON, MATTHEW.' This whole summer she hadn't gone in the water once. She told Matthew she didn't like it, that her skin reacted to the chemicals in the pool. Instead she lay on a deck chair, reading and typing and watching him. She never told him the real reason – that she was scared of being in the water with him. Scared of needing his help. Scared of his arms around her. Scared of his dream coming true.

'All right. Why don't I hold you, then? Float you around a little.' He stood beside her, a puddle of water spreading out from his feet.

'I DON'T THINK SO. YOU'D FEEL SO BAD IF I DROWNED.'

'There's where you're underestimating me. You don't realize that I've been working out all summer. Once a week, at least.' He did have more muscles, she'd noticed. Still she had too many memories of humiliating moments when her body betrayed her. Therapeutic horseback riding with her favourite instructor, Glenn, who she once kicked so hard he buckled over and dropped down to his knees. She was 112 pounds of contracted muscles that obeyed no orders she gave them. 'I HAVE THIS LITTLE PROBLEM WHERE I KICK PEOPLE SOMETIMES. MY LEGS THINK IT'S FUNNY.'

Amazingly Matthew held out his hands. 'I'll take my chances.'

Without another word he bent over, scooped her up off her chair, and carried her down the pool steps into the water. It happened so fast, her body had no time to tense up or flinch.

She buried her head in his neck and when he got them into the water up to his waist, he turned her round so his hands were clamped under her arms, round her chest. She floated for a few minutes with her eyes closed, her head back against her shoulder. If her heart hadn't been beating so hard, it would have been relaxing.

'Remember my dream?' he whispered into her ear. 'Where you were a great swimmer?'

Her hand twitched to type a response.

'Where we got in the water and it was like you were *fine*. I still think about that sometimes. I know what you said swimming dreams are about, and maybe you were right, but I still think it was about something else.'

What? She wanted to scream. *What was it about?*

He didn't answer the question that she couldn't ask.

Instead they floated around the pool until they had to get out, because her mother would be home soon.

All summer they'd danced around similar moments, where they almost said something and didn't. Where their bodies spoke for them. Where he brushed an eyelash off her cheek or adjusted a twisted strap on her bathing suit and they'd look at each other for a moment longer than was technically necessary. And then the moment would evaporate. She never pressed those times or mentioned them after they were over. She never wanted to ruin one by shining too bright a light on it and saying, *Look at this. What's happening here? Are you scared too?*

CHAPTER TWENTY-FIVE

For the whole month of August, Matthew tried to think of somewhere special he could take Amy for their last day together. Restaurants were out. She felt too self-conscious ordering food in public and eating it. Though they talked a lot about movies, going to see one seemed pointless. How did sitting in the dark, staring at a screen constitute a memorable time together? He wanted it to be memorable. Something she could look back on after she started making her supersmart Stanford friends.

Finally one afternoon he worked up the nerve to broach the subject. 'So I have this idea of something we could do on August twenty-sixth.'

'WHAT'S AUGUST TWENTY-SIXTH?'

He was surprised she had to ask. The date hovered in his mind like a cliff. 'Your last day in town. You leave the next morning.'

She smiled. Or her version of a smile. 'OH RIGHT.'

'So here's the thing. I have an idea for something, but you'll probably hate it if I tell you ahead of time. Can I surprise you?'

'YOU ALREADY HAVE SURPRISED ME.'

'No, I'm serious. This will be an unusual, festive outing. Not exactly once in a lifetime, but close. It won't involve any fancy dress or other people.'

'BOOZE?'

'None. Unless you request it and even then I'd probably say no.'

'SOUNDS GREAT.'

He picked her up as early as he possibly could without violating the never-to-be-seen-by-Nicole rule they'd enacted at the start of the summer. It had become a game by that point, keeping him a secret.

Is your mom in the room? he'd IM at night. *Does she know you're talking to me?*

Ixnay and ixnay, Amy would write back. Bad pig Latin was their code for *Yes, she's in the vicinity.* Once he asked her what would really happen if her mom found out about him coming over in the afternoon. Amy considered the question. 'IT'S NOT THAT SHE DOESN'T LIKE YOU. SHE WORRIES THAT I LIKE YOU TOO MUCH AND YOU'LL DISAPPOINT ME. I'D PROBABLY HAVE TO SIT THROUGH A LONG SPEECH TO THAT EFFECT.'

'That sounds like she doesn't like me,' he said, but he was smiling. Amy just said she liked him too much.

'SHE'S SPENT EIGHTEEN YEARS OVER-PROTECTING ME. IT'S INGRAINED.'

'Would it be reassuring to her to find out that I've been so ridiculously reliable? That I've broken her rule and come over here every single day?' This was the question he'd been wanting to ask for a few weeks: Was it worse to sneak around, or did sneaking around over time prove something about his sincerity? *See, I really do like your daughter. I come over when I'm not being paid. I even come over when I'm not supposed to! I'm an obsessive-compulsive control freak and I break rules to see her. My blood pressure rises and my heart hammers every single time and I still do it! It makes me crazy and here I am.*

Amy thought for a minute. 'MY MOTHER DOESN'T SEE THINGS WITH THAT KIND OF PERSPECTIVE. I WISH SHE DID.'

Amy was scheduled to leave for Stanford with both parents early on the last Sunday of August, driving up the coast of California, arriving at school in the afternoon, in time to pick up the scooter they'd ordered from a medical-supply company. 'GUESS WHICH PART OF THIS I'M MOST EXCITED ABOUT?' Amy said.

'Six hours in the car with your mother?'

'MY SCOOTER! I'M ALREADY CONSIDERING NAMES FOR IT.'

'How about Wildfire?'

'THE RUNAWAY HORSE?'

'She ran calling Wildfire –'

'PLEASE DON'T SING. I BEG YOU.'

'Fine.' He smiled. 'No singing. No drinking.'

This was how they got through the awkward business of acknowledging what was going on: *Yes, you're leaving for a life I won't be a part of. It will be exciting in ways I can't imagine. Now let's not discuss it any more.*

Earlier that morning, he packed a cooler full of the food Amy had the least trouble with and the most limited access to: pound cake was a favourite, as were Pop-Tarts, neither of which Nicole would buy for her because they had too many trans fats.

'What's wrong with trans fats again?' he asked her in the car, as he tore open a Pop-Tart package for her.

'SEIZURES,' she tried to type, but the food got in the

way. Her computer said, 'SEA SHARES.'

Still, he knew. Nicole had spent their whole training week preparing them for seizures that had never happened. 'Pop-Tarts cause seizures?'

'NO ONE KNOWS WHAT CAUSES THEM. TRANS FATS ARE A THEORY.' She went on, explaining the connection that he didn't understand.

'When was the last time you had a seizure?' he asked.

She thought for a moment. 'FOURTH GRADE?'

'Are you kidding?'

'NO. WHY?'

'You haven't had a seizure in almost ten years and your mom acts like one could happen any minute?'

'THEY'RE PRETTY BAD WHEN THEY COME.'

'But don't you see what it says?'

'NO. WHAT?'

'She's scared about things she doesn't need to be so scared about. Maybe she still sees you as vulnerable in ways that you aren't any more.'

Amy tilted her head to consider this. 'MAYBE.'

He could hardly get over the irony of the argument he'd just made: *Maybe you don't need to worry so much. Go ahead and eat Pop-Tarts.* If he needed any more proof this medicine was working, here it was.

A few minutes later, she looked at him, surprised. 'YOU'RE GETTING ON THE HIGHWAY?'

'Have to,' he said. 'Just for a little bit. We're almost there.' He told her he was taking her to a beach he'd heard kids at work talk about. It was uncrowded and had a breaker of rocks, which meant animals swam in, closer to shore than usual. Sometimes you could see seals in the water, Carlton had said. After he parked, Matthew explained, 'I know you don't like beaches, but I thought if there were seals . . .'

'IT'S WONDERFUL, MATTHEW. IT'S PERFECT,' she said, and it was. They saw seals and later, on the horizon, dolphins jumping out of the water, all of it so magical neither of them knew what to say. Matthew reached over to squeeze her hand. She squeezed it back. To walk down to the water and put her feet in, he had to hold her hand the whole way. Standing in the surf, he held both her hands and none of it felt awkward. They laughed as the waves swallowed their ankles and the sand dug itself out around their feet. The biggest surprise came on the drive home, when she told him she'd never been to the beach before. 'Are you serious?' he said. 'We live in Southern California and you've never gone to a beach?'

'NO. MY MOM ALWAYS SAID IT WASN'T SAFE.'

He thought of what Sanjay had said to Sarah, that Amy had been too sheltered her whole life. 'Things are going to be different starting tomorrow,' he said. He didn't want to sound sad about her leaving, so he kept his voice upbeat. 'You're going to start doing a lot of things you've never done before. Drinking coffee. Wearing ponchos.'

He looked over at her face and decided: maybe he should stop talking about tomorrow.

When they got home, Amy's parents were out at a charity fund-raiser. There was a note on the counter promising they'd be home by ten, which meant they had four hours alone in the house to do whatever they wanted.

All day they had been touching each other. Ever since he'd carried her across the sand to a spot on the beach. Without her walker, he had to hold her hand, which he did for most of the day. Standing calf-deep in the water, he discovered this: holding her hand for so long made touching her in other ways easier. Spreading sunblock on her shoulders. Brushing sand from her face. Small gestures that conveyed such intimacy that anyone watching would have assumed he was her boyfriend.

Inside the house, Amy surprised him. With wall-to-wall carpeting and strategically placed furniture, Amy could get around without her walker or any help from the front door to the kitchen. She paused at each chair and lurched a bit between the sofa and the kitchen island, but other than that, it was a triumphant display of independent navigation.

'Look at you.' Matthew whistled. 'It's like you don't even need peer helpers any more.'

'IF ONLY STANFORD WOULD AGREE TO SCATTER SOFAS AND EASY CHAIRS BETWEEN EVERY BUILDING.'

Matthew laughed. 'You're gonna do great. You'll have your scooter. You won't have anything to worry about.'

'I'M STILL SCARED.'

'Of what?'

She blushed. It was remarkable, actually, how little they'd talked about this. 'EVERYTHING.'

'Oh well. *Everything* is a lot, I guess.'

She sat on a barstool at the kitchen counter. He laid her Pathway in front of her. 'MOSTLY FRIENDS. AND

WHETHER YOU'LL WRITE TO ME.' She didn't look up as she typed. 'I HAVE THIS PICTURE OF MYSELF SITTING IN A DARK DORM ROOM ALONE, WAITING FOR YOU TO COME ONLINE.'

'Oh no, Aims. It won't be like that.' Secretly he loved the image. He had a similar one of himself, sitting in his bedroom at home. 'You'll turn on the lights and read while you wait.'

'HA-HA.'

He came over and slid on to the stool beside her. They'd never spent any time together inside her house. During the day, when he came over to swim, Carlotta, the housekeeper who loved Amy and kept their secret, was always working inside. Now the empty house and the clock ticking above the wall stove felt a little daunting.

'What should we do?' he said. 'Are you all packed? Do you need help with your stuff?'

'NO.'

'So.' He looked around the immaculate kitchen. Not so much as a saltshaker was left out. 'Should we do something symbolic? Pack a time capsule and bury it in the backyard? Draw up a list of your ten best memories from high school?'

'NO.'

'Are you hungry?'

'NO. I'D LIKE TO SHOW YOU MY ROOM.'

Maybe he'd never come inside the house for this simple reason: he was scared of being alone in her bedroom.

'Great!' he said too brightly. 'I'd love to see it.'

Sliding off her chair, she wobbled a little. He caught her bad hand in his and put another hand on the small of her back.

'Lead the way,' he said, close enough that he could smell the ocean and the beach in her hair.

Her room was different from what he'd expected. Frillier and filled with a younger girl's things: stuffed animals, music boxes, needlepoint throw pillows. Only the books stacked up on the floor and bedside table reflected the Amy he knew now.

'Wow,' he said, standing in the middle of the room. 'Do all these guys have names?' He pointed to a pile of stuffed animals.

'ABOUT HALF,' she typed. 'LET'S NOT TALK ABOUT THEM.'

'Okay.' He looked around for something else. Two large suitcases were packed but still open against the far wall. He recognized the neatly folded T-shirts on top and, beneath those, shorts with elastic waistbands. Suddenly he felt everything all too keenly, standing here in her room. He knew her too well – her clothes, her smell, the quirks of her body. If he kissed her now – as he wanted to do, as he'd been thinking about all day – what would happen tomorrow? Wouldn't it make her leaving worse?

'COME, MATTHEW. PLEASE. SIT WITH ME.'

She had a big bed. Four-poster. He sat down beside her, afraid once again that he might ruin everything by crying in front of her. This moment had a thousand possibilities. He didn't want to wreck it with that one.

'I WANT TO TALK ABOUT SOMETHING BEFORE I GO. SOMETHING THAT HAS TO DO WITH YOU AND ME.'

He nodded. She'd pretyped all of this, which he was used to by now, though it was still unsettling. Like she'd known all along what would happen and how this day would end with both of them here, in her room.

'SINCE THE FIRST TIME YOU TALKED TO ME, I HAVE HAD A FANTASY ABOUT YOU AND I BEING BOYFRIEND AND GIRLFRIEND. IN THE BEGINNING OF THIS YEAR, THAT'S ALL I WANTED. THEN I GOT TO KNOW YOU – THE REAL YOU – AND SOMETHING INTERESTING HAPPENED. IT SEEMED LIKE IT WAS MORE OF A POSSIBILITY AND ALSO A SCARIER POSSIBILITY. LIKE IF IT HAPPENED, NOTHING WOULD BE THE SAME AFTERWARDS. OR NOT FOR ME ANYWAY.'

Her Pathway paused. 'Not for me, either,' he said. He feared his heart was beating louder than her computer could talk. He expected her speech to continue but it didn't, so he kept going: 'You're my only friend, Aim. You've got lots of people who love you. I've got you. That's pretty much it.'

'THAT'S NOT TRUE. WHAT ABOUT YOUR PARENTS?'

He'd told her about his sometimes sad mother and his distant dad. He'd told her they were nice people who wanted everything to work out okay, but didn't know how to help make it happen. 'Right – they're there, but when I think about what matters the most in my life, it's you, Aim. You're the only person I think about with any feeling like happiness.'

He feared he was saying too much. Like now that he'd

204

started, he wouldn't be able to stop, no matter how hard he tried.

'I know I'm not supposed to want to kiss you because you might freak out or that's wrong to want, but I can't help it, Amy. I do want to kiss you. I do. I keep thinking about it and trying to get myself to stop and I can't. Is it such a terrible idea? I don't see why it's a terrible idea. We don't have to have sex or anything like that. I mean, obviously. We'd just take it nice and slow and we'll be helped on that front by being a thousand miles apart starting tomorrow. So we could just have this great, long-distance relationship. I think that sounds okay, right?'

'NO,' she typed. 'I'D WANT MORE.'

'Okay. More's okay.' His heart speeded up. 'I don't mind formalizing it, but how? Should I give you a bracelet or something? Or an eight-by-ten picture to put on your desk?'

He could tell she was struggling with what she wanted to say. She kept typing and then erasing what she'd typed. He'd never seen her do this so much before. Finally she pushed Play. 'I'D WANT TO HAVE SEX.'

His face went red. He couldn't believe she just said this. 'Okay,' he stammered.

'SEE, I CAN TELL YOU'RE STARTING TO PANIC.'

'No, I'm not.'

'YES, YOU ARE. YOUR FACE IS ALL SWEATY. I'M SORRY, MATTHEW. I KNOW I'M NOT SUPPOSED TO THINK ABOUT SEX, BUT I DO SOMETIMES. I CAN'T HELP IT. ARE YOU OKAY? YOU LOOK LIKE YOU'RE HYPERVENTILATING.'

'I'm not.'

'THIS IS WHY I DIDN'T WANT TO TELL YOU. I KNEW IT WOULD ONLY MAKE YOU NERVOUS AND START THINKING ABOUT STD'S.'

He hadn't until she said this. How could he have forgotten about STDs? Now she was saying something else, but he was having trouble listening because he couldn't stop thinking about STDs.

'THAT'S WHY I TRIED IT WITH SOMEONE ELSE FIRST. ONE OF US HAD TO KNOW SOMETHING, RIGHT?'

She looked at him, but he didn't understand. 'Tried what?'

'SEX. I CAN TELL YOU THIS MUCH. IT'S PROBABLY BEST TO LOWER YOUR EXPECTATIONS.'

Wait a minute. His brain struggled to catch up. Surely she wasn't saying what he thought she was saying. 'You watched a porno?'

Matthew had done this once, which was more than enough, thank you very much. Body parts bouncing, faces twisted into expressions of pain. He imagined what she was trying to say. *I want to have sex, but I don't want to have sex sex, like they do on pornos.* That was okay. In fact, that was how he felt. *I want to have sex someday, but I don't want to look like that in front of you.*

'I HAD SEX!' Her face didn't match the words her computer was saying. Her mouth hung open, her eyes widened in a look she usually used for something surprising or very funny.

Did she think this was funny?

His heart began to slam against his chest. He struggled

to find his voice. 'You haven't seen anyone except me all summer.' Who could she have had sex with? A gardener?

'NOT THIS SUMMER. AT THE END OF SCHOOL.'

Not Sanjay. He would puke if she said Sanjay. He would have to wash his hands, then go home and get in the shower for a week or maybe even a year.

'IT WAS SANJAY. I ASKED HIM TO DO IT. HE WAS NICE ABOUT IT, BUT IT WASN'T THAT GREAT. IN FACT, IT WAS HORRIBLE. BUT I'VE THOUGHT ABOUT IT AND I KNOW IT WOULDN'T BE THAT WAY WITH YOU. I SHOULD HAVE LISTENED TO WHAT THEY SAY IN BOOKS. HOW YOU SHOULD LOVE THE PERSON FIRST. IT WAS ALL LOGISTICS WITH SANJAY, AND THOSE WERE SORT OF ICKY. I WANT TO FIGURE IT OUT IF IT CAN BE DIFFERENT! WE DON'T NEED TO HAVE SEX NOW, BUT WE'D HAVE TO SOMEDAY, RIGHT?'

He didn't say anything.

He concentrated on breathing. He stood up and went into her bathroom.

In therapy a few weeks earlier, Beth had asked him to describe his most irrational fears. *Stains*, he said. *Blood, wine, grease. Things that won't wash off no matter what you do.* He wasn't sure where this fear came from, except from years of watching his mother try to get oil stains out of his father's work clothes, bent over, rubbing folds of material against itself, working up a little dome of foam. Once, towards the end, he saw his mother in the laundry room, crying as she scrubbed the knees of his father's pants. Matthew wished he'd never seen that.

He wished she hadn't looked up and seen him standing there in the doorway. That they hadn't looked at each other long enough for her to say, 'I've tried everything, Matt. There's nothing I can do.'

Maybe she was talking about the stain or maybe she was talking about the marriage. He was never sure. Stains were a patchwork of mistakes you couldn't get rid of. They showed the world your real self, even the parts you didn't want it to see.

He hesitated and then he told Beth this, as best he could.

'That's great, Matthew. That's a start.'

It wasn't great. He sounded stupid. He wished Beth had different hair so he could concentrate better. Not red. And not so curly. An image flashed in his brain while they were sitting there: Beth naked, wearing only her hair and her Birkenstock sandals. He started to sweat. 'I'm afraid of bodies,' he told her. She wrote it down. 'I'm afraid of what happens when bodies lose control.'

Beth nodded. It looked like she was writing a short story. He'd said two things and she was writing five. 'That's pretty common, actually, especially in adolescence. Your body is changing in ways you have no control over. Your brain starts worrying about everything else it can't control.'

Every time Beth said something like this, it felt like she missed his point. His point was – he was scared of other people's bodies. He was scared of what they might do. Standing in Amy's bathroom, he understood what he couldn't say, even to Beth: he was scared of Amy's body. He could touch her when it felt clinical or necessary. He could even carry her into the pool and float her in the water, because she needed help to swim and he could give her that help.

But touching . . . just for touching?

How could he do that? Sex produced sweat and terrible, embarrassing stains. Once, washing his sheets, his mother said to him, 'You're worse than your father.'

He knew what she meant. There were stains on his sheets. He was worse than his father.

Why did Amy think he could handle this when he obviously couldn't? What did she want from him? She kept saying he was better, but he wasn't. Maybe he could have handled a kiss. He was gearing up for a kiss. He had his mind so focused on the chance of a real kiss that he thought he could do it. He could taste her lips. He wouldn't be scared.

And then – before any of that could happen – she started talking about sex? About wanting it and practising for it and doing it, so she'd be ready for it?

Of course he left her house.

How could he stay? In the car driving home, he went over his choices and decided he had none. If he kissed her it would be almost the same thing as kissing Sanjay. His germs would still be there. His traces. Sex was only one part of everything Amy would soon be more experienced at than he was: making new friends, going to parties.

Why had she pushed this their last night together? What had she said when he was in her bathroom? 'I'VE WANTED THIS ALL SUMMER! I HAD TO SAY SOMETHING!'

She wanted to move ahead of him. She wanted him to see: *Look, I'm an adult now, with experiences you can't even imagine!*

Soon I'll have hundreds of them and I'll completely forget you and this year we've just spent pretending to be friends. He didn't call her that night or answer her texts.

How could he?

She was moving on without him. She'd made that much perfectly clear. The next day, he let her drive away with her parents without so much as a goodbye message on her phone from him.

CHAPTER TWENTY-SIX

EMAILS WRITTEN BUT NEVER SENT:

Dear Matthew,
It wasn't fair of you to walk out of my house without
saying goodbye. In fact, I think it was horribly cruel.
It wasn't easy to tell you what I did. I could have
said nothing, because, as you know, not talking is a
speciality of mine. I told you because it was a hard secret.
I'd been keeping it all summer and I didn't want to do
it any more. I told you because we *know* each other,
Matthew, in ways that are wonderful and also sometimes
hard. I might wish some things about you were different,
just like you might wish there were some things different
about me –

Dear Matthew –
That wasn't fair. Like, not at all. Be mad at me, fine, but
at least have the decency to stick around and *talk* about
it. I feel like you hide behind your OCD sometimes. You
say, 'I have no choice, my brain makes me stand in the
bathroom for an hour,' but you *do* have a choice. You
were making a different choice all summer long. Hanging
out with me, going to work. As long as no one challenges
you or behaves in any unexpected ways, oh, guess what!
OCD cured! But if someone is a *person*, who admits to
having made a mistake – you don't stick around for *thirty*

seconds and talk about it? Suddenly you're all, where's the nearest bathroom? My hands, my hands. I've got to wash my hands.

I'm not trying to be mean – I'm telling you that's what it feels like to be around you sometimes. Sarah said you did the same thing in Taco Bell. That she started talking about her dad and you didn't like it and all of a sudden you had to use the bathroom for twenty minutes. If you'd come back to my room like any decent human being to at least *say goodbye,* I would have told you that I like Sanjay fine but I *never* want to have sex with him again, and that should be enough for you and me to stay friends. If you're going to rule out being friends with anyone who's ever had sex, your world is going to get pretty small. I'll tell you that much right now.

You should consider – long and hard – the self-indulgence of your illness and think about someone else for a change. Seriously.

Dear Matthew – It's been two weeks and I'm just writing to say I'm sorry things ended so badly between us. That's not how I wanted it to go at all.

Dear Matthew,
I saw this kid at school today who reminded me of you. He was walking on his tiptoes tapping and flinching. Maybe he just has Tourette's, and it's not like that's what you really look like. I guess I'm forgetting what you looked like so I'm filling in gaps by staring at crazy people

and wondering if that's what you look like these days.

Don't take this the wrong way, of course.

Matthew –
I've been here for a month and it's not going so well. I'm
more isolated here than I ever imagined I'd be. I live in
the only room that could accommodate my scooter, a
handicapped-accessible apartment beside the infirmary
where an RN is on call all night long. I'm three buildings
away from all the other freshmen, close enough to hear
the noise of their parties but too far away to roll over and
be invited to any of it.

Here is the truth I can't tell my parents, so I'm writing
you a letter that I know I won't send: I'm lonelier than
I've ever been in my life, Matthew. It's worse than before
I got my peer helpers. Back then, at least I had teachers
and therapists who knew me well. Right now I have a
handful of administrators who've met me once and check
in sometimes. I also have a student affairs liaison who
is supposed to help with logistics if I 'want to go to a
sporting event or a concert'. She actually said that. 'A
sporting event or a concert.' How about if I want to hang
out and *meet people*? How about the logistics of adding
one or two people to my friends list, which is, at present,
zero names long?

One thing that I have now learned about college –
there's *way* too much free time. You're hardly ever in
classes, especially if you're only taking three because
your mother was worried about putting too much pressure

on you. Having three classes means on Tuesdays and Thursdays I only have one hour of my day filled. Ten to eleven, I'm all set. The rest of the time I'm rolling around campus wondering, *If I got a service dog, would more people talk to me?*

I spend about half my days completely alone. Of course, I have a PCA to help me get dressed and eat breakfast, but she leaves by eight o'clock and I don't see her again until nine at night. There are plenty of days when she's the only person I've talked to.

Now that I'm telling you this, I know I won't send this letter so I might as well say it all. I've never felt this alone before. I don't know how much of it is my housing situation, how much is the way I left things with you, and how much is the reality I've learned since I got here: people don't like talking to a girl who uses a machine to answer. I don't know why it's never occurred to me before because it's pretty fucking obvious. A voice-generating device is weird. It's awkward and slow. I'm the person people glance at their watches while talking to. I'm the bore on the park bench who might be crazy, but you should still be nice to for a minute or two. That's how I feel. Some days I'm convinced that I *am* that crazy person on the park bench. Like I'd avoid me if I could.

The other day I stayed after class hoping to talk to my American Lit teacher. He's blond and smart and in his lectures it's clear he has some of the same feelings I do about *Huckleberry Finn.* (Spoiler alert: they're mixed!) I planned what I wanted to say. I even typed it in during class, so there'd be no awkward pauses. It was a little joke about something he'd said that day. Before you came along, my best friends were always teachers and I thought maybe I could do that again. Make friends with a professor. This one seemed young and pretty funny. I don't know. Maybe I was too eager. I hadn't had a real conversation with anyone in days. My hand was twitching to type. I rolled up to the front of the class, where a few students were talking to the teacher. I waited. I got my joke ready. Then before I could press Play, the professor looked at me and said, 'Why don't we make an office-hours appointment?'

Before I could answer, he gave me a time two weeks away.

Do you see what I'm getting at? I'd wanted to make a joke. I'd wanted to do it in front of other students so they knew: *Ha! Surprise! The rolling girl is funny!* I'd wanted to be casual like everyone else. But no. Obviously that teacher will need some time to ready himself. He'll need to tell his wife, 'I'm meeting with that girl today.'

Nobody knows me here. Nobody knows I'm not usually as sad as I must look these days. Nobody knows that I was happy all summer. I shouldn't even write these letters I don't send. It doesn't help. I don't know what I'm hoping to accomplish with them.

I suppose I want to keep them, so I have a record of this time. So I remember exactly how hard it was. So I don't sugarcoat it or pretend, *Oh yeah – it wasn't that bad.* It was and it is. That bad.

Note to future self (and pretend Matthew): this is bad.

Dear Matthew – There's one more thing I didn't get to tell you that night in my bedroom. Here it is: I love you. I'm in love with you. I have been for a long time. This might seem like a strange thing for me to say given the fact that we aren't speaking to each other. But I've decided that it's possible to love someone for entirely selfless reasons, for all of their flaws and weaknesses, and still not succeed in having them love you back. It's sad, perhaps, but not tragic, unless you dwell forever in the pursuit of their elusive affections.

So let me not become Miss Havisham dining for twenty years on the wedding cake my true love never showed up to eat. Please, God, no. How many young women have I watched weep their days away over disinterested men? To all of them, I want to say, *Look up. Get a life, because he has.*

I've written you about a dozen different times, trying to get it right, but when I read over the letters I realize this is what I'm always trying to say: I loved you. I always did, even when I joked and teased and pretended not to. You are the fantasy man I've given myself in my wildest dreams of a happy adulthood – smart and funny and challenged in some ways as seriously as I am. But we tried for a year to let our fears rest and trust our instincts and it never really worked. I'm crying as I write this because I'm having to admit that if it was meant to happen it should have by now. And maybe I'm not as generous as I pretend to be, because in this instance I can't seem to say, *Friends is enough* or *Let's be whatever you want us to be*. It's not what I want.

Suddenly I'm afraid of things that never scared me before. I'm scared of going home after this lonely, horrible semester and seeing you again, so much better than you used to be. I'm scared of you telling me you've started dating someone and you've fallen in love. I'm terrified of one day getting an invitation to a wedding where I'll have to go and watch you marry somebody else. Surely you can see the problem in all this, Matthew. I don't have the same choices and it's not really fair. You were angry at me for being with someone else, but surely you understand: you have the chance of getting better. Soon you *will* be better, and then you'll have half the world to choose from.

I had a tiny window of opportunity. For a little while I seemed like a celebrity – that article and being on TV gave me a short time where my accomplishments momentarily erased the body I'm attached to. It's not that I want to deny the reality of my body or the way people see me. This is me; these are my twisted legs; these are my thumbs that will never voluntarily unfold from my palm. I could hate all these quirks, but what would be the point? Where would it get me? Better to look in a mirror and see the truth: I won't have too many propositions in my life. If I get one that's even a little tempting, I'd better consider it. What happened with Sanjay wasn't

too much more than that. I thought, *Here's my chance!*
I know I don't love him. I may not even like him all that
much, but how many chances am I going to get? I wanted
to try it. I'm sorry, but I did. I wanted to see if my body
could manage it. Yes, I wanted to try it with someone
other than you so I'd know what to expect if it happened
with you. I thought one of us should figure this out, so we
don't both panic. That's what I meant when I said I *was*
thinking of you.

Part of me has always admired people who can be
casual with their bodies. The girls who can bump hips with
boys and not even think about it. Or walk with their hand
in their boyfriend's pocket. Or talk about sex like it can be
a big deal, but doesn't have to be.

Sarah is like that. She seems a little older than the
rest of us because she is, in a way. Not having a mom
means she takes care of her dad, but she also takes care
of herself. She's funny about sex. I know you don't
want to hear this, but I have to tell you so you
understand what I was thinking. She says she likes
having sex as long as she's in charge, which means
usually she is. She tells the boy exactly what he can and
can't do. No, she doesn't always love the person, or even
like him all that much, but she says for the time being
that's okay. She'll know what she's doing when she gets
to college, where she plans to meet someone she *will* fall
in love with. That's what she said. That's what was in my
head. (And, yes, I'll admit, maybe I wondered if she was
having sex with you. Maybe I wanted to pre-emptively

hurt her, just in case she was.)

I don't know, Matthew. To me the idea of getting some experience made sense. I didn't want to be so innocent. That's all. Now I worry that you'll never understand this or find a way to forgive me. I know if I don't find my way with you, it's very unlikely I'll meet someone else who will look at me the way you have, or will not be put off by this body of mine. I know the reasons you left my room that night are complicated and not solely about your fear of my body.

I do give you credit for that much, Matthew.

More credit than you probably realize.

Because even as I say this will never work out, part of me still hopes that it will. Part of this whole plan of mine, in fact, has to do with you, with taking a stand. I want to say, *Let's don't wait forever for our lives to start. Let's begin them ourselves. Let's be fearless for once and say, we can do this.* I don't know if I'll have the courage to send this. I hope I do someday.

Dear Matthew –

I have written you quite a few notes and sent none of them. All of them were written in various states of despair. Mostly I'm relieved that I never sent them, but now I've got a new problem and I need to talk about it with someone. I'd rather talk to you, if we can find our way back to our old friendship and good conversations. I don't know. Can we?

Oh, Matthew, I miss you. All the time. Constantly.

Is that saying too much? It probably is.

I can't seem to write to you without conveying some version of the truth, and then I lose my nerve because the truth is too painful for you to know right now. Or something like that.

TEXT SENT, OCTOBER 30:

Hi, Matthew, can we talk sometime? I have a problem I need your help with. Lots to catch up on. xo Amy

CHAPTER TWENTY-SEVEN

Working at the La Tierra Theatre had taught Matthew a lot about joining a group of misfits. After six months on medication and five months on the job, he felt as if he had joined such a group for the first time, or sort of anyway. Sometimes it seemed as if they were all touched by misfortune, biding their time. Chloe with her incarcerated boyfriend, who (thank heavens!) she'd finally broken up with; Hannah helping her single mother support three kids; Carlton starting his fifth year of community college. Matthew stood out among them only because he was the quietest and the most thorough cleaner. Every shift he gave the nacho-cheese dispenser a scrubbing while other people took their breaks and went outside to smoke. He regularly dusted the slow-selling candy boxes and Windexed the candy glass where customers pointed. In between their busy times, his co-workers sat on the floor behind the counter and asked if he folded his underwear too. 'It depends, I suppose,' he said. 'Sometimes.'

Gradually they started talking to him more. The girls first. They told him the gossip among the staff and funny stories about Carlton's band, which was called Caribou and had made the mistake of making Hawaiian shirts and leis their signature wardrobe, so now they were stuck at every gig looking like middle-aged men on beach vacations.

One night Hannah invited him to stay after work with the others. 'How many people think Matthew should get high with us behind the screen tonight?' she announced to the group.

On the night shift, only two people stayed to clean and close after the last show. The others went home or, lately, retreated to a set of beanbag chairs behind the screen on the stage that used to be a real theatre where live shows were performed. There, it was possible to watch the movie backwards through the gritty screen. Though the story was confusing and hard to hear, apparently that didn't matter. Chloe raised her hand, as did Carlton and Sue, who wasn't supposed to leave the ticket booth but always did to lean over Matthew's freshly sprayed counter to grab handfuls of popcorn. 'Oh, I do, I do,' Sue said chewing. 'Matthew high would be fabulous. We'd let you bring your Windex but no paper towels, 'kay? You'd have to just be with us. In the beanbags.'

When he got there, he only pretended to smoke, pinching his lips and sucking air loudly around the end of the joint. He didn't want to get high – he couldn't on his meds – but he wanted to pretend and see what these girls would do.

'See, Matthew,' Hannah said after ten minutes in the flickering lights that felt like Batman's cave. 'Spend a little time back here and you won't care any more which way the candy boxes are facing.'

After a few minutes, she was right. He didn't care.

They'd become a group with inside jokes. Some nights they stood outside after work to finish telling their stories. Once Hannah asked if he'd mind waiting across the street with her for a bus because she hated waiting alone; it freaked her out. He'd never had another person admit to being scared and ask for his help.

'Of course,' he said, and stood with her for almost twenty-five minutes. When the bus finally came, she said, 'Oh my God, sorry this took so long. THANK YOU!' as she hopped on.

'My pleasure,' he called after her. And it was.

After years in isolation, belonging to a group felt a little intoxicating.

He also understood, with the fuzzy-edged clarity medication had brought, that these friendships were different from the one he had with Amy. He understood on some level that he'd made a terrible mistake, walking out of Amy's room their last night together. Even if he was angry he should have stayed and talked to her. After all, they'd been friends for a year by that point. Friends let their friends have sex with other people. Friends even let their friends talk about having sex, which he'd learned from listening in on Sue, who regularly told Hannah about the 'hilarious sex' she'd had with someone who'd just bought jujubes from Matthew. He might have failed to get into (or even apply to) any colleges, but he'd learned a lot the last five months – more than he was ready to admit to Amy. *I know you're right*, he'd have to tell her someday. *It wasn't terrible, what you did. I just don't like thinking about it.*

He even had a revelation with his therapist, Beth. The real problem with his type of OCD – chronic fear of hurting other people – was that you thought so much about not running over children, not sideswiping pedestrians, not poisoning strangers with germs on your hands – essentially not killing a world full of strangers – that you ended up hurting the people you loved most. He saw that now.

He tried to talk about it with Hannah the night he stayed late and pretended to get stoned with them. They sat side by side in two beanbags wedged close together. She asked him what was happening with his love life, the way girls did sometimes as a joke.

'I don't know about love life,' Matthew said. 'I had a very good friend for a long time. I guess in a way, I thought of her as my girlfriend, except not really. Then we had a fight and she went away to school and it made me realize – I don't know. How much I miss her, I guess.'

Hannah turned, punched the blue Naugahyde of her beanbag to make a pillow. 'Oh God, this is my fantasy! Where those just-friend boys suddenly realize they love me.'

'I don't know if this was like *that*.'

'What happened?'

He thought for a moment. 'Well. I realized I loved her.'

Hannah gasped. 'Oh God, that's so sweet.' She turned to Carlton and Sue, who were sitting behind them. 'You guys – listen to this. Matthew is in love. Tell them –' She waved her hand, but he didn't repeat the story. The others were too stoned to care, and the movie was almost over, which meant they'd need to clean the theatre and lock up in a few minutes.

After that night, Hannah asked him about it a couple of times. Did anything ever happen? Did he ever tell her how he felt? Every time she asked, his heart began to race.

'I tried to tell her when we went to prom, but I don't think she understood what I was saying.'

'What happened?'

'She went home with someone else.'

Hannah's eyes bugged out a little. 'From *prom*? Are you serious?'

He hated the picture this gave Hannah of Amy. 'We were all friends. I had disappeared for a while. She thought I left without her.'

'Oh, wow. Had you?'

'No, of course not.'

All this explained why he was so happy, after three months of silence, to get this text:

Hi, Matthew, can we talk sometime? I have a problem I need your help with. Lots to catch up on. xo Amy

He'd been waiting to hear from her for so long. Short as this note was, it felt significant. He liked the fact that she had a problem with which she needed his help. Recently he'd been thinking along the same lines himself, making up reasons to get in touch with her. He never wrote his notes down, but he composed them in his mind.

— I had a horrible night at work. The ice machine broke down and my register was sixteen dollars short. In case you're wondering, the answer is, yes, it comes out of my paycheque. I know sixteen dollars isn't the end of the world, but at the end of a long, pointless night it feels like it might be.

Or this:

— Just wanted to tell you my father's new wife is pregnant, which is (of course) very gross because it means they almost certainly had sex. For my mother, it means an excuse to become even more depressed.

And the overwhelming thing he wanted to write:

— I don't know what I'm doing with my life. I read a lot because I was tired of hearing your voice in my head saying I haven't read

enough. I write because I hear you say, 'If you really want to get better, you need to keep a journal. You need to write down your feelings.' So I'm doing that too, except the minute I start to write everything down, I feel like a character. I start explaining backstory to my journal so it understands where I'm coming from, even though my journal is me. Does that happen to you?

He didn't write or send that letter. Instead he sent this:

Good to hear from you, Aim. Sure. Write back to me. I have no news and nothing in my life has changed much. Except, of course, I'm sorry about . . . well, you know. Everything.

Then he waited. For an hour without moving from the computer. Then longer. He had to go to the bathroom, but didn't dare move. Finally he ran and came back, zipping his fly in front of his computer. Without washing hands because he didn't have time. Amy was back in his life with a problem she needed his help on and he didn't want to disappoint her again. He waited four hours, reading a little and playing music. Before he left for work, he fired off another text:

Have to work. World might end if people can't buy their movie snacks. I'll have my phone if you text me. Otherwise, home by ten thirty. Don't leave me hanging. Just want to know if you're okay.

She did leave him hanging. The next day at noon, he still hadn't heard from her. He would have called her house if there were any way of ensuring he'd get her father on the phone, not Nicole, whose last communication to him was a direct request not to contact Amy ever again after school was over. He allowed a full day to go by before he tried an email:

To: vandorna@stanford.edu
From: mstheword@gmail.com

Okay, you've got me a little bit worried now. You write out of the blue and then disappear out of the blue. What's the problem? I hope school is okay. I've thought about you a lot, Amy. I'm still working at the movie theatre and, believe it or not, it's got sort of fun. Or it's not terrible anyway. Hey, it turns out you were right way back when. Having a job is good for me.

Another day passed, and he wrote:

To: vandorna@stanford.edu
From: mstheword@gmail.com

I'm writing to every address I have and texting your old number. If I don't hear from you by tonight, I'm calling your mother. And you know how much your mother wants to hear from me.

Twenty minutes later, he wrote this:

To: vandorna@stanford.edu
From: mstheword@gmail.com

Okay, Amy, now I'm freaking out. A few minutes after I
wrote that note, your mother called me to say that you've
LEFT school? After two months? I don't need to tell you
she's going out of her mind. She must be to have stayed
on the phone with me for as long as she did. (Over an
hour! She cried twice, and twice I said, 'Don't worry,
Nicole. We'll find her.' It was like we were old friends,
Aim. You would have been so proud of us.) But that's not
the issue, of course. The issue is *you* and *what the hell is
going on*? I don't think this has anything to do with me.
I'd like to imagine I had that much impact on your life, but
I can't believe that's true. Still – if that's one small piece
of what's going on – please know that I think about that
night, and you, every single day, and every single day, I
write these notes in my head where I try to explain to you
how sorry I am and how much I miss being your friend.
    And then I don't send them.
    This whole fall has felt confusing and hard and I keep
trying to figure out why, and then I remember – oh right.
It's because I can't log on at night and IM with Amy.
I'd give anything to hear from you. Email. Letter. Morse
code. Even if you just want to yell at me, that's okay. I
just want to know what's going on.

To: aimhigh@comcast.net
From: mstheword@gmail.com

Aim? Just trying this account. Copying a message I sent to your school account.

To: mohdis@mit.edu, heffernans@berkeley.edu, chloe.mcglynn@yahoo.com
From: mstheword@gmail.com

Hi, everyone – Hope you're all well and school is going along okay. Hard to believe five months has passed since graduation, right? I'm writing to ask a favour of you. I've recently been in touch with Nicole again and apparently Amy has had a hard time in her first semester. Two days ago she left school and Nicole is trying to figure out where she is. She's heard from Amy by email saying she's not in danger, but Amy won't tell her where she's staying now or what's going on.

I told Nicole I'd write to you guys and see if you've heard from Amy this fall. If you haven't, that's fine, but let me know that. And, if you have heard from her, I'd love to know when and how she sounded. Thanks. Hope you're all well.

To: mstheword@gmail.com
From: heffernans@berkeley.edu

Hi, Matthew – Thanks for getting in touch. I have to get back to you later because I'm headed into a lab right now. But I'll write to you tonight.
Sarah

To: mstheword@gmail.com
From: modhis@mit.edu

No word. Sorry. Hope everything turns out okay.
Sanjay

That night at work, Chloe, who had quit a month earlier to concentrate on her classes at community college, stopped by during a lull between movie start times. 'Can I talk to you for a second?' she said, and looked at Sue, who was staring at them. '*Privately*.'

They walked back to the staff-break room that Matthew tried to keep as tidy as possible, though it was mostly a losing battle. Most people didn't bother with the lockers provided; they piled their things in heaps around the room. Today there was a grocery bag in the middle of the table with an open Tupperware container and the remnants of someone's dinner still clinging to a fork.

'Just let me tell you this before you start cleaning,' Chloe said. Matthew stopped. He was bent over the Tupperware, about to carry it over to the sink. He looked at Chloe. 'I saw Amy about two weeks ago. You remember that guy I was telling you about, Marcus, who I'm starting to date?'

Matthew nodded. Mostly he remembered the collective relief they all felt when she broke up with Gary, her incarcerated boyfriend. Chloe kept going. 'Marcus invited me up to San Francisco to see this band he loves, and I asked if we could stop by Stanford on the way and say hi to Amy – I just had this feeling like I should see her – I don't know why.'

Matthew swallowed. He'd had that feeling every single day and forced himself to ignore it.

'I have to tell you, when I first saw her, I almost didn't recognize her. She looked really sick, with black circles under her eyes. Her face was really thin, but then her hands and legs were kind of swollen. I don't know if that was from being in the scooter. Like maybe not walking is bad for her? Marcus said he once knew someone who had gland problems who looked like that.'

Did Amy have a gland problem? Not that he remembered.

'That wasn't even the worst part, though. When I went to hug her goodbye, she started to cry and couldn't stop. I've never seen a nervous breakdown before, but I swear that's what it looked like. I don't know how else to describe it. She was crying so much she couldn't type anything. It kept going for about ten minutes, but it felt like a lot longer. I never figured out what it was about because she was crying too much to type anything. I told her I'd come back the next day and she finally typed, 'JUST DON'T TELL MY MOM. PROMISE YOU WON'T TELL MY MOM.' The next day, we didn't get there until three in the afternoon. I said we'd take her out to lunch, so I felt bad that we were late, but I texted her a few times. She didn't text me back, and when we got there, she was gone. No note, nothing. Her room was locked and we couldn't find her anywhere. We left and I still haven't heard back from her. I feel so bad about the whole thing. I haven't called her mom yet because I keep thinking there was something important she was trying to tell me but she couldn't get it out. Instead she just begged me not to tell her mom. Which makes me feel like I shouldn't tell her mom, right?'

Matthew couldn't stay. There was a line forming and he could hear Hannah asking Carlton, 'Where's Matthew? Please don't say the bathroom.'

He thanked Chloe for stopping by and spent the rest of his shift trying to decide what to do next. That night, he emailed Sarah:

To: heffernans@berkeley.edu
From: mstheword@gmail.com

Sorry to be writing again so soon, but it turns out Chloe saw Amy before she left school and she didn't look good at all. Supposedly she couldn't say much and she couldn't stop crying. I guess I'm writing to you because I have to ask someone: did Amy ever seem depressed to you? Or even suicidal? I keep thinking no, it's impossible, but I know she was different with each of us. Maybe she talked to you about this? Sorry if I'm writing too soon but it's been twelve hours. I'm panicking a little and you must be out of that lab by now.

A few minutes later, he got a text:

She's not dead. I can't tell you where she is or what's going on, but I can tell you she's not dead. You can also tell her parents this. Sarah

He answered:

Thank you for writing to me. If I promise not to say anything to her mother, can you just tell me: did she get in touch with you at Berkeley? Is she staying with you now?

A half-hour later, he got this:

She's not with me, but, yes, I helped her move out of the dorm. Bad situation all around. I'm shocked her parents let that go on as long as they did. She promised she'd contact her parents after November first. You should wait until then and she'll get in touch with you too.

Matthew looked at the date today: October 27.

Why is she waiting four days?

She has her reasons. Don't ask.

Is she getting emails?

I don't know. I think so. Don't worry. She's okay now. Or

better anyway. Staying at school was the problem. It was bad this semester, but that was only part of the problem. That's why she's being mysterious about it. I can't say any more than that. I'm sorry.

That night after work, he went home and composed a long email.

To: aimhigh@comcast.net
From: mstheword@gmail.com

So, Amy,

I don't know if you're reading these emails, but I'm going to write to you anyway because there are a few things I need to say. I'm sorry for what happened at the end of the summer: that's the main thing.

I've spent a lot of time trying to understand what happened between us. You always said I never read enough, that all my problems would be solved if I read more novels. So I've been trying this fall, going through some of the books you suggested, and I have to be honest. Usually I'll get halfway into *House of Mirth* or *Anna Karenina* and I'll think, *My God, have I really just read two hundred pages about a garden party?* Then I'll pick up *All Quiet on the Western Front* and I'll think, *Jesus, is this war ever going to end?* It's not that I don't like the books; I do. You're right – they're great books, but I keep feeling like they're all about people who are horribly trapped by their circumstances. They're hard to read, aren't they? Don't you feel that too? Maybe it brings me to my real point. Do you remember the conversation we had about *The Awakening*, the book you were reading at the beach this summer? It turns out you left the book under the passenger seat in my car. I found it a few weeks ago and started to read it. When you first told me about it, I thought it sounded like another one of those set-ups you love so much, where characters are trapped by a society that forces them to do nothing for most of the book. (I'm sorry, Aim, but those are some of your favourite stories. Where the plot creaks along for hundreds of pages and finally the earth cracks open when a glove gets removed or a teacup dropped.) I expected this story to be like that, but it isn't. Or yes, it is, and, even so, I've got caught up in this world and have even fallen a little in love with Edna, and the ocean and those magical beach nights where she finally claims herself. I didn't read it until now because I always assumed it was all about sex. Now I have to say, I don't think it really is about sex. It's about her claiming a life for herself, and unfortunately the only thing she can do to make that happen is have sex with someone who isn't her husband.

So, yes, Amy, I see why you love this book and why you wanted me to read it, but I also want to say: Please don't forget how Edna is being a little childish too – stamping on her wedding ring and smashing the crystal vase. She married her husband to get away from her parents, and then she spends the rest of the book getting away from him. Okay, I think, but maybe she should have seen what was coming? I got to the end when she only sees the ways everyone has tried 'to possess her, body and soul'. But would that really be the end of the world, Amy? To be possessed that way? What I'm trying to say is: I don't think you have to tear up all your relationships to get away from people's expectations of you. You can just *not do* what they expect, right?

I don't know if you've left school because your parents put too much pressure on you to go to the most high-pressure, competitive school possible, or if it's something else completely.

My guess is that this book doesn't explain everything. I keep going over what you said that night after we got home from the beach. I understand what you were trying to say, but I also have to say I don't believe there's such a thing as casual sex for people like you and me. How could there be? We don't have casual relationships with our bodies. They're unpredictable, humiliating things that have failed us so much it's hard not to hate them, and impossible to imagine being naked with another person and relaxed at the same time. I don't know. Maybe that's not it at all. Maybe this whole thing is my fault for things I haven't even imagined yet. So I'm reading your books, and (yes, it's true) emailing Sanjay, who, I'm sorry, is a jerk. Maybe I shouldn't say that, so if it offends you, consider it a typo. Pretend I meant to say *jock*.

But not worthy of you, Aim. Not worthy at all.

Don't disappear forever, Amy. Don't die making a point

that no one understands yet. Let us find you, and, when we do, tell us what you're trying to say.

I read that final scene with Edna walking into the inky ocean to make her last statement to the world and I thought about the dream I once had of you and me swimming together, strong and whole. Please write back to me. I don't know where you are and I need to hear from you. (I also read that ending and wondered if all of this is all some elaborate suicide note on your part. Please, Amy, don't let it be that. Please. I beg of you.)

Love, Matthew, who is sorry for being about three months late saying all this.

Instead of hearing back from Amy, he got this:

To: mstheword@gmail.com
From: hannah302@hotmail.com

Hi, Matthew – I just wanted to write you a quick note to apologize for what happened after work last week. I didn't mean to startle you with that big beanbag move. I promise I'm not a crazy stalker. I'm just sick of having stupid things with jerky guys who aren't worth all the effort I put into thinking about them. I guess I was thinking, *Yes, Matthew can be a very strange person, but in a sweet, good-hearted way, and maybe after all the jerks I've gone out with he is the one I should get to know better.* I don't know what you're thinking, or if I scared you, but I wanted you to know that I like you. That's all. It's fine if you don't feel the same way. Or not fine, but it's okay. That's all. Maybe you're still thinking about your old friend, I don't know.

Hannah

Three days ago – the night before he got that first text from Amy – he stayed late at work and ended up side by side again with Hannah, in their beanbags. There was a new girl named Reenie with them, who asked, after everyone had been there for a few minutes, 'So is this where everyone plays truth or dare?'

Matthew panicked for a second and wanted to say, *No. Not* at all*!*

Then he thought about Amy and how her old assignments were a little like truth or dare. He felt like Amy was watching him and would be mad if he said no. He felt like that a lot. Even though he was hanging out with new people, it was like she was there, watching everything he did.

Of course, they played. This crowd was born for playing truth or dare. On Hannah's turn, Sue said, 'Okay, Han, you've got to tell someone something you've always wanted to say but haven't had the guts.'

Right away, Hannah looked at Matthew and he got nervous. *She's going to tell me I'm weird and I clean too much*, he thought. But no. She didn't say anything. Instead she leaned forward on her hands, and she kissed him.

At first he thought she'd made a mistake. Like she'd fallen down with her lips accidentally on his. Then he understood: this was a kiss. It had been five years since he'd had one, and he wished there'd been more time to ready himself. Loosen his jaw and warm his lips, maybe. He kept his eyes open too long and did nothing with his hands. It wasn't a great kiss, but it wasn't terrible, either. And afterwards he felt no need to rush to the bathroom and wash anything. So that was good. In truth, he didn't think too much about it afterwards. In fact, his only thought driving home was: *If Amy had been here, she would have been proud.*

But she wasn't there, of course; that was the problem. He wrote back to Hannah:

To: hannah302@hotmail.com
From: mstheword@gmail.com

Can't write much now. Have a friend in crisis. The one I told you about. Thank you for your note, though. You didn't scare me. I'll talk to you on Friday.

CHAPTER TWENTY-EIGHT

If Amy's mother wanted numbers, here was one she could have.

One.

In the three months since Amy started college, she'd made exactly one friend. Hard to know exactly who to blame for this: the school, for deciding that Amy should live in an apartment next to the health-services office? Or her parents, who agreed so easily without ever consulting her? Amy wasn't told about her housing assignment until they had arrived on campus for the first day of orientation and were standing in the office of the student housing administrator, who spoke quickly to her parents, highlighting all the pluses of the apartment without giving Amy any time to even ask a question.

Outside the office, alone with her parents, Amy fired off all the questions she wasn't allowed to ask in the administrator's office. 'WHAT ABOUT LIVING IN THE DORM? WHAT ABOUT THE ROOMMATE I'M SUPPOSED TO HAVE? HOW AM I GOING TO MAKE ANY FRIENDS?'

Nicole steered them over to a bench and sat down. 'The school went over your health records and they didn't think a regular dorm room was a good idea, Aim.'

'SO I HAVE TO LIVE IN THE INFIRMARY?'

'Of course not. You won't be *in* the infirmary. You'll be *next door*.'

'I DON'T WANT TO LIVE THERE. EVERYONE WILL ASSUME I'M SICK.'

'No, sweetheart, it's not like that,' Nicole said. 'You'll be in a more comfortable apartment, with your own refrigerator for your own foods. You'll have an alarm system and a registered nurse next door, twenty-four hours a day, for any emergencies that crop up. It's safer this way, that's all.'

'I DON'T NEED A NURSE! I DON'T NEED ANY OF THAT.'

She saw her mother exchange a look with her father. Something to the effect of, *You need to speak up here.*

'Here's the thing, Aim,' her father said, placing a hand on her shoulder. 'We know that you'd rather be in a dorm, but the college has some reasonable concerns about the safety of that. We talked to the people in the housing office for a while. We told them your personal-care needs and some of our safety issues, and they were pretty clear that a dorm wouldn't work. They couldn't provide the monitoring you would need.'

'I DON'T NEED MONITORING! I NEED HELP IN THE MORNING AND AT NIGHT DRESSING! THAT'S ALL! I DON'T NEED A NURSE!'

Her dad stepped away. He never lasted long if Amy really protested something. Nicole kept going. 'The nurse won't do any of that. You don't have to see the nurse at all. They assured us that the apartment is very separate.'

It was gradually becoming clear to Amy – all of this had been decided a while ago. Though she'd been given a dorm room in the packet that arrived weeks ago, she didn't have one any more. 'YOU DECIDED ALL THIS WITHOUT *TELLING ME*?'

'We thought it would be better if you were here and you

241

could see the place. They sent us pictures and it's lovely.'

In her original welcome packet, Amy's dorm assignment was on the freshman quad. After she opened it, she spent hours on Google Maps studying the exterior of her dorm building and the grounds around it. She memorized the paths that looked wide enough for her scooter to navigate. She imagined herself rolling along with a classmate beside her. But now it was clear: she could protest all she wanted, but she wouldn't be living in a dorm this year.

Was this a punishment for the summer she spent seeing Matthew behind her mother's back? They were never caught, but Amy always wondered if Nicole suspected something. Early in the summer, her mother heard about the vodka-at-prom story from the mother of another classmate who told her she was so sorry about the way Amy had been used by the other kids at prom. When Nicole confronted her, Amy tried to argue. 'NO ONE WAS USING ME! I AGREED TO THE WHOLE THING! IT MIGHT HAVE BEEN A STUPID MISTAKE, BUT IT WAS *MY* STUPID MISTAKE.'

Nicole refused to see it that way. 'It never would have happened if we hadn't hired those peer helpers. They assumed you were desperate for friends and would do anything they asked you to. Turns out they were right, unfortunately.'

The surprise after that was the absence of any punishment. Amy kept expecting something. That her mother would insist on signing Amy up for another online college-credit course over the summer. Something rigorous and ridiculous like statistics or medieval French literature. But no. Apparently she'd waited until now to exact her revenge.

Nicole sat down on the bench across from Amy's scooter and laid out all the other decisions they'd made without consulting her, including this: they would only hire professional PCAs to help with her needs.

'HOW ABOUT SOME DISCRETION MONEY?' Amy suggested. 'IF SOMEONE HAS A SIMILAR SCHEDULE AS ME, MAYBE I CAN HIRE THEM FOR A LITTLE HELP TAKING NOTES AND GETTING ME LUNCH?' Surely that wasn't a crazy idea. Some flexibility in those first few months when she might be the loneliest?

'Absolutely not,' Nicole said. 'We've tried that once and we've learned our lesson.'

What could Amy say to this? *No, you're wrong? Matthew and the rest of them have been wonderful friends?* She had made mistakes too. Worst of all with Matthew, who she misjudged so terribly their last night together. He'd walked out of her house without saying goodbye. Since then, he hadn't texted or got in touch with her once.

'OKAY, MOM,' she said, and started her scooter towards the apartment where she would live alone, in the back of a building that was mostly administrative offices. The following morning and every morning after that, Amy rolled out of her room to greet secretaries in business suits arriving for work. Because she had no dorm or resident advisor, Amy spent orientation week sitting by herself, on the side of all the activities, watching as her peers completed scavenger hunts and tossed water balloons back and forth to one another. The few people who spoke to her had evidently not heard that they needed to wait for a response, because three separate

243

times Amy typed answers to questions only to look up and realize the person had walked away.

For those four days of orientation – the longest four days of her life – only the personal-care assistants who came in the morning and evening to help her dress and undress heard her speak. Otherwise her glorious Pathway with its humanoid voice and amazing capacities went unnoticed by a single classmate. Amy tried to change that when classes started. She preprogrammed a funny introduction of herself. She studied her class syllabus so she could ask questions about supplemental reading. She was prepared for every possibility except the one that happened: three lecture courses with professors who never took attendance and only left five minutes at the end for questions and comments. Amy raised her hand, but was never called on. Her second weekend of college, she didn't bother leaving her room at all. She stayed inside, ate yogurt and rice cakes, and listened to the thrumming bassline of party music across the quad.

By late September, she felt as if she'd become a professional recluse. She went to classes and forced herself, for one meal a day, to eat in a cafeteria. Beyond that, she stayed inside, spending time on various chat rooms and discussion boards. Just as she was beginning to wonder if she might be truly losing her mind, one afternoon a 'personal message' showed up in her Shakespeare discussion mailbox. It was from a boy named Brooks whom she'd noticed in class, mostly because he talked a lot and had pale hands and the long, thin fingers of a pianist.

Brooks: Hello, Amy. I wondered if you might like to talk privately sometime. I believe we share similar readings on some of these plays.

She pictured his hands in class, carving pictures in the air as he spoke. Sometimes he kept his fingertips pinched together like the conductor of an invisible orchestra. Once she'd even had the thought: *He looks weirder than me.*

Amy: Sure.
Brooks: You seem to know your Shakespeare pretty well.
Amy: The plays, yes. The sonnets, not so much. As a poet, I'd say Shakespeare was a wonderful playwright.
Brooks: Yes, I agree.

Amy couldn't help it. The relief of talking to another human being again was so huge she laughed out loud, alone in her apartment.

Amy: Who are some other writers you like?
Brooks: Hard to say. I tend to like writers less the more I read of their work. I start finding their shortcuts, the similar points they make over and over. Like Shakespeare, for instance. How many times is he going to write about the way words fail to describe our deepest emotions? We get it already.
Amy: Maybe words failed him.
Brooks: Exactly.

It wasn't always clear if he understood her jokes. Probably not, judging by how serious he was about his literary passions. Shakespeare was okay, but his real love was reserved for early horror writers like H. P. Lovecraft, whom he talked about a lot.

For a few weeks, their exchanges went back and forth. She enjoyed them enough to imagine that she'd found her first friend on campus, and one day she asked him if he'd like to have lunch after class. 'I don't know about that,' he wrote back. She waited for him to explain. 'It's not you. Or your scooter. That's not the problem.'

Though she was alone in her room, her face burned red with shame. Obviously it was the problem. 'Why not, then?' she typed.

'It's me. I'm socially awkward face to face. I hardly ever eat with anyone. I get repulsed easily by other people chewing. You should see some of these guys on my floor. They eat like animals.'

She wrote another letter to Matthew – one of the many that she'd written but not sent over the last two months. Then she got into bed and cried as she had so many nights since she arrived.

Though Brooks never spoke to her, even once, in class, she kept up their online conversations because he was interesting enough in his own strange way. He had Asperger's, she decided, or something that made him unaware of the hurtful things he sometimes said. If he didn't understand, how could she blame him, she decided. Their book discussions and nightly chats kept her going through the end of September and into October, when a strange feeling took over her body. It felt like a flu that came in waves, then drifted away. *I'm sick*, she'd think, grateful for an excuse to stay inside even more. And then, after she settled herself into bed, it would pass. *Wait. No, I'm not sick.*

One rainy Saturday night, they found each other online and Brooks spent twenty minutes telling her the plot of his favourite Lovecraft story, 'The Outsider'. It was about a narrator who'd lived alone in the catacombs of a castle basement, surrounded by books his whole life. One day he decides the time has come to venture into the world. It takes him a full day of crawling to find his way out of the dungeon, and when he finally emerges he discovers the world he's only known from books is in the grip of terror over a monster that's been unleashed in their midst. He wants to help, because even though he's only been in it for a few minutes he loves the world. Even with everyone screaming in fear and running around him, he loves the colours, the buildings, everything. When he finally sees the monster, he realizes they're right. It's terrifying, a hideous thing covered in scales and warts with teeth that stick out in every direction, but he's determined to stay brave and save this world that he's only ever known and loved through books, so he goes to kill it, and when he does his hand hits a mirror.

As Brooks told this whole story one sentence at a time, posted as another IM message so it read like a monologue interrupted every few seconds by his user name, Amy prayed this wouldn't be the ending. He was the monster everyone feared! Locked in a mirrorless dungeon for years to save his book-loving heart from the truth about himself!

Please, no, she thought. *Let him recognize the similarity to my story.* Surely it occurred to him: she was as isolated as this 'outsider'. Since arriving at Stanford, she'd felt just as monstrously alone.

For a long time, she couldn't think of anything to say.

Brooks: Amy? Are you still there?
Amy: Yes, I'm here. I have to ask you – am I like that monster?
Brooks: No. My God. I can't believe you'd say that.
Amy: You tell a whole story about someone who has lived in isolation and enters the world only to discover the extent of their freakishness. You have to admit, there are parallels.
Brooks: Oh. I guess so.
Amy: I lived a very isolated life for a long time. All my friends were teachers and books. I don't think I even realized it until last year, when I made real friends for the first time. I loved it so much I felt like I would do anything for those people. I *did* do anything. It was wonderful.
Brooks: And what happened?
Amy: I don't know. It didn't last. I discovered the extent of my own freakishness, I guess.
Brooks: You should really read this story.

She hadn't ever asked him this question, but she had to now:

Amy: Why did you want to be friends with me?
Brooks: I told you: I liked your comments on the discussion

board. Plus, I'm from Orange County, so I read that newspaper article about you. I thought you'd be someone I should get to know.

She shouldn't have asked. It only made her feel worse – he was a boy obsessed with the idea of freakishness that she represented. Even if he couldn't put it into words, she understood. Instead of typing any more, she pushed herself away from the computer and felt a wave of nausea roll up through her body. She was truly alone. Worse than alone, because she'd shared too much time with a boy who was casually, unthinkingly cruel.

The nausea stayed with her for the rest of the night.

For three solid days afterwards she was sick. On the fourth morning, she woke up and, still wearing her nightgown, walked down the hall to the infirmary. 'I FEEL LIKE I'M DYING,' she told the nurse. The room seemed distorted, the walls wavery. She wondered if the nurse would scream and run away from her.

She spent all day in the infirmary, hooked up to an IV bag to replace her fluids. She heard the nurse say the word *dehydrated* so many times it lost meaning. She imagined the nurse was saying *de-hydra-headed*. She wanted to ask about this, but the nurse never stayed by her cot long enough for her to finish typing the strange word. At the end of the day, just as Amy was finally beginning to feel better, the nurse reappeared with a doctor beside her, an older man with white hair and glasses perched at the end of his nose. 'Maybe you realize this already, Ms Van Dorn,' he said, 'but it seems there's something more than a stomach flu going on.'

249

Strange how Amy looked at his face and knew right away. Strange that it hadn't occurred to her before.

A stupider girl would have known a long time ago. Would have realized that she'd taken a risk a long time ago, on a night she was trying to prove something to herself.

After Amy had recovered enough to return to her room, she only spent one day agonizing over what she should do. The next morning, she called a cab and asked it to take her to the closest Planned Parenthood clinic in East Palo Alto. There she sat in a waiting room with a dozen other women, many seemingly younger than she was.

When Amy's name was called, she followed the nurse to the exam room and told her right off the bat, 'I CAN TALK. I USE THIS. IT TAKES A LITTLE TIME.' She was tired of people walking away too quickly.

'Fine,' the nurse said, snapping on rubber gloves. 'You need help getting undressed?'

She appreciated the tired woman's straightforward question. 'YES,' she typed. 'I DO.'

As the nurse quietly helped her out of her clothes, Amy got the reassuring sense that she'd seen a lot worse than a disabled girl who'd accidentally got herself pregnant.

After the doctor confirmed the news, Amy nodded and typed, 'IT'S TOO LATE FOR AN ABORTION. I DON'T WANT ONE ANYWAY. I WANT INFORMATION ON HAVING THIS BABY AND PUTTING IT UP FOR ADOPTION.'

The doctor was a woman with messy blonde hair piled

on top of her head. 'Fine.' She nodded. 'In my experience, there's no reason a young woman with CP can't carry a baby full-term. You might have some balance issues and need to use this scooter all the time. You'd be considered a higher-risk pregnancy, which involves more prenatal testing and more regular check-ups.' She went on for a bit about monitoring her blood and protein in her urine.

Amy wanted to laugh right there in the office. This doctor wasn't saying no! She wasn't pointing out all the reasons Amy shouldn't do this – her disability, her schooling, her future. She took Amy at her word. She found pamphlets on adoption and gave them to her.

Over the next few weeks, as Amy wrestled with every minor medical problem a pregnant woman can go through – anaemia, swollen joints, brain fog, haemorrhoids – she wondered why her first impulse wasn't to have an abortion. She could have, the nurse told her. In the second trimester it was harder, a more invasive procedure, but it was possible.

'NO,' she'd told the nurse. 'I DON'T WANT THAT.'

But now it had to be said: she also didn't want a baby or to feel sick all the time.

So what *did* she want?

She lay in bed as tears leaked from her eyes down to her pillow, and thought about the notes she'd been writing to Matthew but not sending. If this 'friendship' with Brooks had taught her anything, it was this: she wanted to see Matthew. She wanted to talk to him. Though he had no part in this, she wanted to share it with him because he would understand this first instinct of hers – to honour this unlikely baby's existence.

251

To think this whole semester might have been a waste, except for this.

Two weeks later, Amy almost made it through an entire weekend visit from her mother without a fight. Almost. There was talk of her looking 'tired' and 'run-down'; there was even a mention of her thickening waist, but Amy ignored it all. She was determined to keep her pregnancy a secret, but she wanted her mother to see another truth: that Amy regularly talked to no one beyond her PCAs. That she spent ninety per cent of her time alone. That she was isolated in a way that no one should be.

Sunday night over dinner, Amy laid it out as plainly as she could: 'I DON'T TALK TO ANYONE IN MY CLASSES. OTHER FRESHMEN EAT WITH DORM FRIENDS. THEY GO INTO TOWN TOGETHER. I DON'T DO ANY OF THAT. I DON'T EVEN TALK TO THE NURSES NEXT DOOR. I DON'T TALK TO ANYONE. IF YOU ASK AROUND, YOU WON'T FIND VERY MANY PEOPLE WHO KNOW HOW I SPEAK, BECAUSE I ALMOST NEVER DO HERE.' It was hard to say all this, but important. She typed it in ahead of time so she wouldn't lose her nerve or skip any parts.

'NO ONE KNOWS ME HERE. AT ALL.'

Nicole sighed and put her fork down. 'Amy, it breaks my heart to hear you say this, but I also don't think that it's true.'

'YES, IT *IS*. YOU NEED TO KNOW WHAT THIS IS LIKE. I'M NOT HAPPY. I HAVEN'T BEEN IN MONTHS.'

'I *know* you have friends.'

Why did her mother insist on believing this? 'I *DON'T*.'

'What about this boy, Brooks? Hasn't he been writing to you?'

Amy's insides went cold. How did she know this? 'YOU KNOW BROOKS?'

'Dad knows his father. They sat on a board together. He's nice, right? I know he's very smart. He was valedictorian of his class. Dad wrote to his father and asked his son to get in touch with you.'

Amy felt sure that if she didn't keep swallowing, she would throw up her dinner all over the restaurant table. Even Brooks, her cruel frenemy, wasn't really hers. This whole life was her mother's arrangement.

'This is what you always do, Aim. You *overdramatize*. I know you're lonely, but you *do* have friends. It's hard for everyone in the beginning.'

Amy said very little for the rest of her mother's visit. After Nicole left, she felt too sick to get out of bed. For five days, she didn't go to classes or leave her room. Chloe came to visit, and she couldn't say the one thing she wanted to say to her old friend: *Take me with you. Don't leave me here. I'm scared I might die.*

The night after Chloe left, after she'd humiliated herself by sobbing uncontrollably for almost twenty minutes, she texted Matthew for the first time in almost two months. When she didn't hear back from him right away, she panicked and wrote to Sarah at Berkeley. 'I need help,' she wrote. 'From a friend. Please come.'

A few hours later, Sarah was there. 'This isn't good,' Sarah said, looking around the room, littered with dirty laundry and empty Boost cans. 'You want me to drive you home?' It was a six-hour drive, but it was also a Sunday. 'I'm happy to do it,' Sarah said.

'NOT HOME. SOMEWHERE ELSE.'

As Sarah cleaned up, she made other suggestions. 'How about another relative? Or my father's house?'

Amy jumped on that. 'YOUR FATHER'S HOUSE? ARE YOU SERIOUS? COULD I GO THERE?'

'I'll call him and ask. I think he'll say yes. But what should I say when he asks why you're not going to your parents' house?'

Amy thought about the old fight between her mother and Mr Heffernan over the seventh-grade science fair. About her mother's determination and Mr Heffernan's quiet insistence: *You do Amy's real strengths a disservice by insisting she excel at everything.*

'TELL HIM I HAD A FIGHT WITH MY MOTHER.'

Sarah smiled and shrugged. 'Okay,' she said.

Watching Sarah throw clothes in a duffel bag and books in a box, Amy felt better than she had in weeks. The air began to clear. It was like she could breathe again. She would be around an adult who had stood up to her mother. She would be closer to Matthew. She would call him up and see him again.

In the car driving down, they talked about music and Sarah's life, mostly. Anything to avoid the subject of Amy's escape from school. She hadn't explained it, because she couldn't yet.

When they pulled up to Sarah's house – a small ranch at

the end of a cul-de-sac – her father was standing at the end of the driveway, both arms raised like some invisible team had just scored a touchdown. 'You made it!' he said. He looked much older but much happier than the last time Amy saw him, which was probably five years ago.

'Thanks for this, Dad,' Sarah said when she got out of the car. 'She only needs to stay a week or so. After that, she can go home.'

'That's fine, that's fine, I'm happy to have her!' he said.

Amy hadn't told Sarah about the pregnancy. Who knew what Sarah was thinking (or her father, for that matter)? But for now Amy was grateful that so few questions had been asked.

Inside the house, Mr Heffernan had an odd mix of food laid out on the counter: a sleeve of Girl Scout Thin Mints, a loaf of pumpkin bread, some petrified clementines. 'What is this, Dad – dinner?' Sarah said, carrying in Amy's things. They laughed in a surprisingly easy way. Before Sarah left, she apologized to Amy. 'I wish I could stay longer, but I have a class in the morning.' She hugged Amy, then stood in the kitchen, whispering for a few minutes with her father.

Amy said nothing about the baby because she hadn't told anyone yet. She was afraid if she did the arguments against it would begin to pile up. She was too young, her own health too fragile. It was too big a risk. She hadn't told anyone because she hadn't wanted anyone to talk her out of it.

To her shock, no one this whole time – not even her mother – had guessed. Her stomach was growing, her breasts enlarged, and still it wasn't a possibility anyone considered.

But a few minutes after Sarah left, Mr Heffernan pointed at Amy's swollen ankles. 'Judging by that oedema, I'd guess you're either pregnant or have a rare tropical disease.' His eyebrows lifted up. 'Beriberi, perhaps?'

Amy surprised herself by laughing. She'd been crying almost constantly for two months, and now she felt fine. 'NO,' she typed. 'NOT BERIBERI.'

'Ah,' he nodded. 'Pregnant, then, perhaps?'

If she told the truth, he might make her go home to her parents. But what other choice did she have? She had to find a doctor here and get seen soon. 'YES, I AM HAVING THE BABY BUT NOT KEEPING IT. UNCONVENTIONAL, I KNOW.'

'Yes.' He nodded. 'Quite unconventional.' For a long time he didn't say anything. Then he nodded, his eyebrows raised again. 'Some might say brave.'

CHAPTER TWENTY-NINE

Two days after he wrote his last long email to Amy, Matthew finally heard back from her:

aimhigh: Got your note, Matthew. Thank you. I loved it.

He laughed out loud in relief, and clapped his hands.

mstheword: You're alive! Hurray!
aimhigh: Yes. I'm alive.
mstheword: Are you okay? Chloe said she saw you about a week ago and she got a little worried. She said you seemed upset.
aimhigh: You could say that. Did she say anything else?
mstheword: Just that you looked different. Like maybe you were sick.
aimhigh: Did she say I looked pregnant?
mstheword: No.

Pulsing cursor. No response.

mstheword: Are you?
aimhigh: Yes. Maybe I shouldn't have just said it like that. That's the big news. The other big news is I'm home. Or sort of home. Nearby anyway.
mstheword: Where?
aimhigh: I can't tell you. My parents don't know. Don't tell them.

mstheword: Why not?

aimhigh: I want to do this my way. They won't let me. Just trust me.

mstheword: Okay. But what does that mean?

aimhigh: I'm having the baby and putting it up for adoption. My mom will freak out. She'll say there's a seizure risk with pregnancy.

He didn't type anything for a little while. He was trying to figure out how long it would take him to Google seizure risks before he got back to her.

mstheword: Is there a risk?

aimhigh: Slight. But there's a seizure risk with everything. Don't Google it. Just trust me.

He stopped typing *seizure* into the search box, which was taking a while because he couldn't remember how to spell it. After that, they messaged for almost an hour. She told him the highlights of her semester. ('Almost none. One weird friend I didn't like very much.') He told her his. ('You were right, I think. Working is good for me. Gets me out of my head. But I still need to go to school, I know. I enjoy concessions but probably don't want to make a life out of them.') Because he didn't want her to think he was too scared to, he asked her how the pregnancy was going.

aimhigh: Good, mostly. I was really sick in the beginning, but then I got better and felt great. Now something weird is going on.

mstheword: What's happening now?

aimhigh: I feel sicker, which isn't how it's supposed to go. You're meant to feel more energetic in your second trimester.

mstheword: Sick how?

aimhigh: Weird headache. Blurry vision. My shoulders and arms really ache but they're not doing anything.

Hearing this kicked his heart into double time.

mstheword: You've got a doctor there, right?

aimhigh: Yes.

mstheword: Cos it sounds like maybe you should go to the doctor.

aimhigh: Don't worry. Here's the thing I've learned about pregnancy. Everything feels like a crisis and everything turns out to be heartburn.

mstheword: But you'll go if you need to. Tell me you have someone to take you to the hospital.

Funny, he thought. Here he was again, with Amy back in his life, and here he was again, needing reassurance. They talked until he had to leave for an appointment with Beth. Before he got off, he asked Amy to tell him where she was staying. She couldn't tell him, she said. Not yet. He asked what happened at school, but she couldn't tell him that yet, either. 'It's complicated,' she said. Everything was complicated.

At his appointment, he told Beth, 'It's great. It's wonderful. I'm so happy to be talking to her, but I also feel anxious again like I haven't been in months.'

'That's not necessarily bad,' Beth said. 'Sometimes feeling nervous just means you're having a lot of feelings all at once.' That was certainly true. 'Feeling a lot is confusing, but it's not a bad thing.'

But feeling what? he wanted to say. *What am I* feeling? Instead he went home, got back online, and asked Amy more questions. Had she done a sonogram? Did she know the sex of the baby?

aimhigh: Yes, and it's a girl. She's fine so far.

mstheword: Does Sanjay know?

aimhigh: Yes, now he does.

mstheword: What did he say?

aimhigh: That he supported a woman's right to choose. Or not choose. He said he'd sign papers but he didn't have the money to fly home for this. He's sorry but he's barely getting by as it is.

mstheword: Jerk.

aimhigh: I thought that for a while but then I thought – I really don't want him to be part of it anyway.

Matthew hesitated before he asked the next question:

mstheword: Do you want me to be part of it?

aimhigh: I didn't know I was pregnant this summer. I just knew I felt great. Alive and happy because of you.

He was grateful to be alone in his room so she couldn't see that he was crying.

mstheword: I felt the same way.
aimhigh: When I think of this baby, I think of you. You're not the father, I know. But in a way, you are.

He couldn't answer.

aimhigh: It doesn't have to be anything official. I just wanted to say that. Do you want to be part of this?

Finally his body calmed down enough for him to type:

mstheword: I want to see you. I don't want that unless I can be there and help you.

For a while she didn't answer.

mstheword: Please, Aim.
aimhigh: I look terrible.
mstheword: I have to be at work by four. I'll only stay an hour. I'll keep my eyes closed the whole time, I promise.
aimhigh: Fine. I mean, it's a terrible idea. I really do look bad. But fine.

She told him where she was.

★

As it turned out, it wasn't a terrible idea. They had a wonderful time.

Matthew looked great and was kind enough to only mention her few features that had improved with pregnancy. 'Your hair has never looked better,' he said. Which was true: gloriously thick and curly in a way that wasn't too wild. Her chest was also huge now. 'You're full-figured!' he said, a bit breathlessly, which made her laugh.

After he said these two things he dropped the subject and thankfully said nothing about her swollen face and hands. Nothing about the red eczema patches growing on her legs, or the downy blonde hair covering her arms.

She tried to explain how it felt: 'IT'S VERY WEIRD. LIKE MY BODY ISN'T MY OWN.'

He nodded. 'It's not, I guess, right? You're growing someone else.'

This was how Amy thought of it too. It helped her believe in the idea without getting too attached to the actual baby. A subtle distinction. *This isn't my baby; it's a person I'm growing who I'll hopefully meet again someday*. Matthew got that.

'YES,' she said. 'THAT'S RIGHT.'

They kept the visit light. He brought out his work smock to show her how unflattering it was. 'I try to keep it clean,' he sighed. 'But real-butter product is a tough stain to get out.'

He smiled as he said this and she passingly thought: *I wish he didn't look so good*. Still tanned and healthy from riding his bike to work. It made her nervous. 'I BET EVERYONE LIKES YOU THERE.'

'If by "likes" you mean "laughs at", then, yes, you'd be

right. I'm sort of the group joke. The guy who cleans too much. Sometimes they stick a roll of paper towels and Windex in my backpack when I'm not looking. Ha-ha.'

'DO YOU GO OUT WITH THEM? ARE YOU FRIENDS LIKE THAT?'

She saw him look down nervously, unsure how to answer. 'Go out? No. I mean, we're friends, but, no, I don't go out anywhere with them. I haven't changed *that* much.'

He only stayed forty-five minutes, which was fine, given how tired she was these days. As happy as she was to see him, she could hardly keep her eyes open.

And then, right before he left, something strange happened with her eyes. The same thing that had happened twice before. Her vision went blurry. Matthew fractured into two images, then four, coming towards her. It didn't clear when she blinked, but only got foggier, the world a blur of colours. When he leaned in to kiss her cheek, she couldn't see him at all.

She didn't say anything because she didn't want to wreck the nice time they'd just had. She let him disappear, and when he was gone she felt a stabbing pain that started in the back of her neck roll over her.

CHAPTER THIRTY

Matthew worked late that night with Sue and Carlton, who knew enough of the story to ask what was up with his missing friend.

'We found her! I saw her – just now, as a matter of fact.' He was sweaty from his bike ride, but so happy he laughed. 'She's fine! Everything's fine. She just didn't like school all that much.' He was glad this group knew a little about Amy, but he wasn't going to tell them all her secrets.

Sue looked up from her inventory clipboard. 'So, I guess – what? You and Hannah aren't going to happen?'

Matthew's smile faded quickly.

He remembered Hannah's email in the middle of Amy's crisis, which he had pretty much ignored. Everything with Amy had happened so quickly he hadn't thought much about it until now. Fortunately Hannah wasn't on the schedule, so he didn't have to worry about seeing her. Instead he worked, more distracted than usual, especially when a couple came in with a newborn baby sleeping in a car seat. 'We'll leave if he cries,' the dad said. 'We just had to get out of the house.'

Instead of cleaning after that, Matthew texted Amy with a new thought:

Do you have a labour coach? Not saying it should be me, but I'm pretty sure u should have one.

By ten thirty he was surprised. He still hadn't heard back from her. He tried again.

If you want me, I'd do it. No problem. Weirdly, doesn't make me nervous. Don't know why.

It didn't. He imagined himself in a practical mode. Fetching ice chips and washcloths. Making mixed CDs of Amy's favourite music, which was mostly not very good. They could laugh about that in between contractions. Of course there would be mess, but he'd prepare himself for that. Rubber gloves wouldn't be unheard of in a delivery room, he was pretty sure.

It would be fine. Better than fine. It would bond them more than any of the struggles they'd endured to date. They could forget about prom and the bad way he acted on their last night of summer. All that could fall away now that they had a real challenge to face. It put him in a surprisingly optimistic mood – whistling as he made change from the cash drawer, bumping it shut afterwards with his hip.

I can do this, he thought every time he did something. *No problem.*

I can help Amy with whatever she needs. I've done it before.

It was like the voice was back. Only this time it was whispering positive things.

And then at the end of the night he checked his phone. No messages. No texts. Nothing.

Something's wrong, the voice said. *Something's horribly wrong.*

★

265

It turned out the voice was right. Amy had been in the hospital for sixteen hours when Matthew called Mr Heffernan the next morning and found out what was going on. Amy collapsed yesterday, about an hour after he'd left. When they got her to the emergency room, her blood pressure was sky-high and there was protein in her urine. 'All signs of pre-eclampsia, so they admitted her right away,' Mr Heffernan explained to him over the phone. 'This can hit very suddenly like this, without too much warning. The blood pressure is fine one day and it skyrockets the next.'

In the process of getting her admitted to the hospital, Mr Heffernan had to call her parents and tell them what was going on.

'What did they say?' Matthew asked.

'Well, they're happy she's alive. A brush with death usually makes parents forgive other transgressions.'

But this was a big one. Never mind the sex and the baby it had produced. There was also the matter of leaving school without telling her parents. Of staying with an old teacher her mother hated.

Later that morning, he met Mr Heffernan in the lobby of the hospital. Together they walked to the floor where Amy was staying and saw her parents in the hall, talking to a doctor. Nicole was listening, her brow furrowed, nodding. Matthew felt a stab of panic. *She'll blame me for all this. She'll say it's all my fault.*

Nicole didn't look away from the doctor's face, but her father did. When he saw Matthew, he smiled. 'Go on in,' he mouthed, and pointed to the door.

Though Matthew hated to say it, he couldn't believe how terrible Amy looked – swollen and blotchy and ghostly pale. Then her mouth dropped open when she saw him and he felt relieved. This was her smile. Smiling like this, she looked like her old self. She lifted one hand. 'Hii-i-i-ah,' she said.

'Hi, Aim.' He looked around for her Pathway, which was on the table. 'Can I give you this?' He placed it on the bed next to her hand and waited for a minute. She didn't make a move to type anything.

'So I talked with Mr Heffernan down in the lobby. He told me what was going on. Sounds like it was scary, but you're okay now?'

She closed her eyes and nodded.

He wasn't sure what else to say. 'It also turns out he gave me a *conditional* B–plus in his class. Apparently I still owe him a lab write-up.'

Amy smiled but didn't laugh.

'I saw your mom and dad. They're talking to the doctor. Mr Heffernan said the doctors still aren't sure what's going on –'

'I KNOW.'

'You do?'

She nodded.

'What is it?'

He realized then that her eyes weren't closed from exhaustion. She turned her head away. She was trying not to cry. Her hand pushed the computer away, across the bed, on to the floor. Matthew understood. She didn't want to talk or answer questions.

'I'm here, Aim. That's all,' he said, pulling a chair from the far wall next to her bed. 'I'm just here, if that's okay.'

He sat down and squeezed her good hand. 'Is that okay?'

Her hand felt different. Tight and swollen. She couldn't squeeze back. That's when he noticed her whole left side was swollen. Her leg, her hand, even her face and neck were puffed up on one side.

By the afternoon, he'd filled in enough details to know why Amy didn't want to talk about it. Pre-eclampsia was essentially a pregnant woman's bad reaction to the baby she's carrying. For now they would keep Amy in the hospital. If it was pre-eclampsia, they would do everything they could to bring her blood pressure down, but ultimately it would only be a temporary solution, because the only cure for preeclampsia was delivery of the baby. At twenty-seven weeks, that would mean a preterm baby – less than three pounds, probably – who would almost certainly have medical complications. Though the doctor didn't say this, everyone recognized the cruel irony: delivering the baby to save Amy's life could leave the baby as disabled as the mother whose life was being saved. Whose life was worth more? Which risk was worth taking?

After a day, there were decisions to be made. Sanjay called once and talked to Nicole long enough to make it clear: he wanted no part of making this decision.

'IT'S JUST AS WELL,' Amy said. 'IT MAKES THIS EASIER.'

'It makes him a jerk,' Matthew said.

'MAYBE. SOME PEOPLE CAN'T DEAL WITH SOMETHING LIKE THIS.'

Matthew liked what this implied: he *could* deal with it. He *was* dealing with it.

And he was. All day he surprised himself with something new he was doing, no problem at all. Help a nurse lift Amy on to a gurney by holding her bag of pee: no problem, apparently. He washed his hands afterwards, but only once.

As often as possible, he held Amy's hand. Sometimes that meant sitting for an hour, not talking at all. Sometimes it meant holding her bad hand so her good one was free to type.

One afternoon, Amy slept so soundly that he picked up her Pathway, thinking he might check his messages. He switched it over to wireless mode and the desktop appeared with a file that caught his eye: *Notes to Matthew – Unsent*. He opened it and read through everything she hadn't told him about her time at school.

That night, he went home and tried to write back to her:

Aims,

I probably shouldn't tell you this, but I read the file Notes to Matthew *on your computer. I wish we hadn't wasted so much time being mad at each other. I wish it were easier to say certain things. Like now, for instance. I want to say that I don't think this whole business of our not speaking for three months was completely my fault. You could have sent some of those letters you wrote. That would have been a pretty good start. If I hide behind my OCD sometimes, maybe you do the same thing. Suddenly you turn into Ms I Can't Talk At All! No One Will Stick Around To Listen*

To My Speech Device! Which makes me want to say, Of course they don't! No one sticks around to listen to anyone. *You might not be able to talk, but you make your points better than anyone else I know.*

My point is: you know what you want to say.

A lot of people don't. You might not even realize this. A lot of us are still trying to figure out what we want to say.

He stopped writing there, because for some reason writing this down had made him start to cry.

'I WISH I COULD PUT YOU AS THE DAD,' Amy typed the next day when they were alone.

He knew the focus of these visits was to do everything possible to keep Amy calm and keep her blood pressure down. 'Me too,' he said softly.

'A FRAGILE BABY NEEDS THE RIGHT PARENTS.'

'That's true.' He wished he could say: *I'll do this with you. If we have to, we will.*

'I PICKED SOME PEOPLE. THEIR NAMES ARE SUE AND JIM MALLON. THERE'S A BOX IN MR H'S HOUSE WITH THEIR PROFILE IN IT. WILL YOU READ IT AND TELL ME WHAT YOU THINK?'

So far they hadn't talked about Nicole or how she was handling all of this. She hadn't been particularly friendly to Matthew, but she hadn't been openly hostile, either. 'Do you want your mom to talk to them?' he asked.

She was very clear. 'NO. I WANT YOU TO.'

He understood that she asked him to do this because she

wanted it to happen. With her parents, it might not.

That afternoon, he went home with Mr H and found their profile in one of Amy's boxes. The woman was blonde like Amy and was a website designer with a degree in music composition. The man was an environmental lawyer. Their pictures looked unposed and happy. In most of them, they looked like they were talking or sharing a joke. They had a nice house with a fenced yard, and grandparents nearby. Matthew read through everything until he finally sat back in surprise. Both parents had written long letters to prospective birth moms. Sue's was longer than Jim's; in the middle, he found this: 'My husband suffered from a mild anxiety disorder in college, which made it harder for him to make friends. He's much better now, but the journey we shared together bonded us in ways that I feel sure will make us better parents. We have learned that no one is perfect.'

Surely Amy couldn't have predicted the situation he was in now, but maybe this was what drew her to them in the first place. 'YOU'LL KNOW IF THEY'RE HESITANT,' Amy had told him. 'YOU'LL FEEL IT. I THINK WE JUST HAVE TO TRUST OUR INSTINCTS.'

He called them up and explained the whole situation.

Sue listened as he described Amy's condition and the pre-eclampsia that was unrelated to her CP. 'They've stabilized her for now but it won't last long — maybe a week at best. It's enough time to give her steroid injections to strengthen the baby's lungs, but the baby is going to be premature. She'll weigh around three pounds, if we're lucky. She'll probably have complications as a result of that. There's no telling how severe they will be. Amy picked you as her first choice of parents for her baby and now she'd like to know if you'd still be interested in this situation.'

It hadn't been an easy speech to make, but he understood why Amy couldn't make it herself. How could she ask: *If my baby turns out like me, would you still want her?*

Sue answered without any hesitation: 'Of course we're still interested. We've talked over all these possibilities and yes. Yes, we're still interested.'

CHAPTER THIRTY-ONE

The medicine they gave Amy fogged her brain and made it hard to tell the difference between night and day. She had no idea how long she'd been in the hospital. When she opened her eyes, she saw Matthew as often as she saw her mother, which was a relief. She didn't have the strength to fight with her mother. Her good hand was too swollen to type out the things she needed to say: *I don't want to be friends with someone like Brooks. I don't care if he's smart, and you and Dad decided I should be. I know what I want and it's Matthew.*

She'd been here for at least two days, maybe longer, and hadn't been able to say any of that. Instead she drifted in and out of a sleepy/dreamy state, hearing her mother's voice, which carried her back through time and memories of being with her mother in hospitals and doctor's offices. The hours of therapy, of rolling balls between their outstretched legs and blowing feathers across the dining-room table. All of it hard, some of it impossible. (She could never blow, though they kept trying for years.) She remembered being six years old and sitting in her mother's lap with her arms locked behind her, the pain so intense she couldn't breathe. She remembered the day she took her first steps without her walker. She was eight by then, and their house had been furnished with this goal in mind, every chair and sofa placed a step and a half apart so she could lurch like a cruising toddler from one handhold to the next. It happened just before dinner. Usually Amy wasn't hungry at night, but this time she was starving and there was hummus and tzatziki, her favourites. Her mother must have seen the hunger on her face and recognized an opportunity. She put the food on the table and said, 'Come to the table, Amy. If you want to eat, come to the table.'

There were six steps between her and the table. She'd never taken more than three without falling. Amy launched across the divide and veered towards the table. She made it three, then four, then five steps without falling. On the last step, she pivoted too quickly and went down, narrowly missing the edge of the table with her head.

'There,' Nicole said, pulling her back up. 'See? You did it. You walked five steps by yourself.'

How could she hate someone who'd spent her whole life ensuring that Amy had one? But how could she help choosing a person like Matthew, who loved her in a different, gentler way than her mother ever had? She wondered if there was a way to say this without words.

She listened and waited and began to hope: maybe she already had. Having this baby was the first truly independent decision Amy had ever made. Maybe they looked at this and saw how she was moving away. Maybe they understood what she was saying in a whisper so soft only the people who knew her best could hear: *This body, with its needs and its laundry list of problems, is mine.*

Matthew couldn't get over the surprising shift in dynamics. It had gone undiscussed, at least with him. By the time Sue and Jim had driven down from Menlo Park to meet the family and await the birth, it didn't matter who was the father; Matthew

274

had become Amy's partner in negotiating all this. Nicole stood in the background, Max behind her, as Matthew brought the couple into the room and introduced them to Amy. 'Amy, this is Sue. And, Jim, meet Amy.' They each stepped forward and shook Amy's hand. Afterwards he introduced her parents, almost as an afterthought: 'And the grandparents, of course. Nicole and Max.'

Had Amy made this happen by putting him in charge? He didn't know.

That first visit only lasted ten minutes. The magnesium sulphate Amy was getting to lower her blood pressure made her so tired that she often fell asleep in the middle of a visit.

After they left, Matthew kept talking. As long as Amy's head moved in response to a joke, he knew she was listening. He bent over her pillow and asked her what she thought. 'Goo–' she said.

Because her typing was so limited with her swollen hands, he'd begun to understand her speech better. He smiled. 'I liked them too.'

For five days, they kept up a rotating vigil at her bedside – her parents, himself, Mr Heffernan and a random assortment of others. Chloe stopped by, as did some old teachers. Matthew called in sick to work but kept up his appointments with Beth. He needed that anchor to make sense of everything that was happening to them.

With Beth, he surprised himself. When he got to her office, he didn't talk about Amy or the baby for whom he was helping to arrange a life. He talked about what happened with Hannah. That night behind the screen when she leaned over and kissed him. For a long time he hadn't let himself remember it, and now he couldn't seem to forget it. It got bigger in his mind, and worse. What if the bad things that were happening now were proof that the voice was right all along? *See? I told you. If you aren't careful, Amy might get sick and almost lose her baby. If you aren't careful, anything can happen.* Logically, of course, it didn't make sense. His voice didn't care about girls trying to kiss him.

But he couldn't get his brain to understand the difference. Being scared of kissing felt as big and panicky as being scared of germs and death.

'Well,' Beth said when he tried to explain this. 'They both mean something dies. The person you once were – the boy too afraid to kiss a girl – dies when you do it.'

He almost reminded her that he *had* kissed girls, back when he was fine, but that wasn't the point. Beth was right. Something did die every time you changed. Amy wasn't the same person she used to be. Neither was he. Maybe it had already happened.

CHAPTER THIRTY-TWO

One morning Matthew arrived at the hospital to the news that Amy's blood pressure had skyrocketed and the baby needed to be delivered at once. Jim and Sue were in the room, talking to the doctors. Nicole stood on the far side. Matthew wasn't sure if there was time for him to speak to Amy before she went into surgery. Then he heard someone call his name.

'Matthew, we need you to suit up.' It was Max, Amy's father.

'Excuse me?' he said.

He saw Nicole over in the corner by the window, red-faced and weeping. She and Amy had had their fight, apparently. The one he kept expecting that hadn't happened yet.

'Amy wants you to go in with her,' Max said. 'They'll hang a sheet so you don't have to see what they do. She stays awake through the procedure. You'll sit by her head and keep her company.'

Matthew couldn't get over it. Amy decided this? And told her mother?

'You have to wear a sterile outfit. Go on – hurry up – they'll be taking her into surgery soon.'

It happened so quickly Matthew worried about getting his brain to catch up. Maybe it wouldn't. Maybe he'd walk into the operating room, shell-shocked and empty, his mind back in the bathroom, tapping out patterns to keep Amy alive and the baby healthy. Which was more important? In a harrowing, black tunnel of uncertainty – a baby with a fifty-fifty chance of survival – was it better to stay with Amy or follow his body's old instincts to draw up bargains with the fates who could never really be appeased? That was the real lesson he'd finally been learning. The voice in his head was never happy, even when he slavishly followed its whims. It was never happy the way Amy was happy when he finally walked back into the room wearing his sky-blue doctor's outfit. She smiled one of her open-mouth smiles.

'I'll actually be performing the surgery,' Matthew said, bending down to whisper in her ear. 'So that should make you feel better. Turns out you don't need a medical degree at all. Just one of these outfits. I never realized that but the nurse said, yeah, that's about right.'

The epidural drugs must have already been making their way through her system because Amy laughed in a flutter voice he'd never heard before.

'What was that?' he smiled. 'A chipmunk? Is there a chipmunk in the room?'

Her mouth closed and he saw her eyes go serious. A nurse rolled a blue screen of the same material he was wearing across Amy's chest, leaving them strangely alone in the crowded room. 'So maybe your mom is coming around,' he whispered. 'I don't mean to get ahead of myself but I'm a little surprised that it's me sitting here, not her.'

Amy looked at him so he understood: *My decision. Not hers.*

'Right, right. I understand. Probably she's a little funny about blood and operating rooms too. See – me, I have no problem with that.'

He saw her face change: *Stop joking.*

278

'Fine, I'll be quiet.'

But that wasn't it. He bent closer, so his paper-covered forehead touched hers. 'She'll be okay,' he whispered. 'Or not okay, maybe. But no worse than us. She'll live. You did it, Aim.'

He didn't know how he knew it, but he did.

Then he kept his eyes on Amy's. He heard what the doctors near him were doing, but he didn't look. He held her hand and he tried to smile so she knew there was nothing to worry about until he heard a nurse gasp, 'Oh my,' and his stomach knotted. He looked over and saw a flash of red and something too small to be a baby. Too still to be alive.

He looked away and closed his eyes.

Please, he whispered. Please . . .

And then he heard it: a tiny shrieking cry.

And he was right – Amy had done it.

The baby was okay. Two pounds, six ounces, but she was alive.

Her parents named her Taylor, which Matthew and Amy privately rolled their eyes at, but what name would they have liked, he wondered.

'Maybe they're Taylor Swift fans,' he told Amy later, sitting in her room, flipping through an old issue of *Family Circle*. 'There's nothing wrong with that. If I was a girl, my parents were going to name me Tennille, after Captain and Tennille. Then it turned out her name was technically *Toni* Tennille, which they weren't crazy about, so they passed.'

For three days after the birth, Amy ran a fever and had to

stay in the hospital, sweating out the thirty pounds of water she'd retained at the end of her pregnancy. Her hospital gowns were always either damp or drenched depending on how recently a nurse had visited and suggested a new one. They'd been to see the baby – Matthew many times, Amy once. That time they stood together and Sue lifted her off the warming pad and held her in her arms. Because Amy still had a temperature, she couldn't get any closer than the glass window in the hallway.

'IT'S OKAY,' she said when they got back to the room. 'I SHOULDN'T HOLD HER. I'D PROBABLY HURT HER.'

'No, you wouldn't. When they take her out, they wrap her in about five pounds of blankets.'

So far, he'd been amazed at what *was* allowed with such a small, fragile baby – toys in her incubator, cards drawn in crayon. (*Crayon*, Matthew thought. *Doesn't that flake off into her tiny lungs?*) Most surprising of all was Jim and Sue's strange penchant for photographing Taylor beside ordinary objects to show just how tiny she was. Her foot smaller than the first joint of her father's thumb, her body smaller than a ruler.

On Matthew's most recent visit to the window (he never went in; he wasn't going to hold her if Amy couldn't) Jim showed him his new 'discovery': his wedding band fitted round her wrist.

Matthew smiled and gave a thumbs-up because he couldn't think what else to do, but privately he was disturbed. Wasn't it a little cruel to find ways to point out how small she was?

As he neared Amy's room, he saw Nicole outside, sitting

in a plastic chair with her eyes closed. 'I'm not asleep,' she said when he tried to walk by. 'You can sit here if you'd like. They're giving Amy a sponge bath, so you might as well wait.'

He sat. He hadn't talked alone with her since Amy had been found. Now was her chance to tell him flat out what was wrong with him and why he was wrong for Amy. Instead she said nothing for a long time. Finally she sighed and said, 'Have you seen the baby today?'

He nodded, surprised. Nicole didn't go and look at the baby the way the rest of them did. 'Too close to home,' she'd said the first day. Meaning: *Too much like Amy's infancy. No need to relive that.*

'They're doing this funny thing,' Matthew started, instantly regretting what he was about to say. It would only prove the shortsightedness of this whole plan. They'd picked bad parents, or ones with a demented sense of humour, at least. 'Jim has his wedding ring round her *wrist*.'

'I'm not surprised.' Nicole sighed. 'That's what you *do* when your baby's three pounds. You don't see her as three pounds. You see her spirit and she seems so much bigger than that. You have to take pictures so you remember – no, she really was this tiny thing who could sleep in your palm.' She turned and looked at him. 'Have they taken one of those pictures? With her asleep in their hands?'

He didn't know, but probably.

Nicole shook her head. 'You can't get over how something that is three pounds can change the whole world.' Her eyes were closed again. She wasn't talking about this baby, he knew.

'But it does. And in some part of your mind she'll always be three pounds.'

'You did it, though,' he whispered. 'She grew up.'

Her eyes snapped open, the moment gone. 'I suppose that's right. It never feels over, though. I wish it did. For sixteen years, I slept with a monitor beside my bed. When she went away to school, I got a machine to make the sound of her breathing. I couldn't sleep without it. Couldn't sleep a wink.'

Maybe this was how parenting worked. In a few days they'd have to walk away from Taylor. He tried to imagine not tracking the permutations of her fragile life, not knowing her weight or her bilirubin score. How he'd wonder and wonder and want to just call them and ask.

CHAPTER THIRTY-THREE

Inside Amy's hospital room, soft hands lifted her poor, crampy legs and wiped them down. For four days Amy had ricocheted through every emotion imaginable. One minute she was sobbing in self-pity; the next she was weepy with gratitude to Matthew for his unwavering constancy.

'IT'S LIKE YOU'RE FINE,' she told him. '*ARE* YOU FINE?'

She saw no signs of his old nervous finger twitching. His lips didn't move any more with silent incantations. For four days he hadn't lined up a to-do list of places that needed to be tapped. Instead he lined up her water bottle, her nurse call button, her TV remote and her Pathway.

'Have you got everything?' he said every time he left the room.

For his sake, she tried to keep up a front of good cheer. She didn't sob in front of him or type what she really felt: 'I'M A FAILURE! MY BODY FAILED ME! IT ALWAYS DOES!' She suspected he knew that she mostly cried anytime he wasn't in the room.

Once, he'd brought in fresh Kleenex without saying a word; another time, an eight-by-ten glossy of their prom picture, which she'd never seen before. They looked about twelve. His smile was huge; hers was mostly a mouth open so wide it was possible to see the fillings in their teeth.

'NICE CUTAWAY JACKET,' she said.

'I *told* you it was good.'

He looked like a waiter. She looked like she was falling into his chest. Strange, she thought later, that he would bring a memento from one bad memory to mitigate this one. So much about prom seemed distant and small now. Except for Taylor, of course, nothing from that night mattered now. As enormous as it had been in their minds, they'd weathered the blow of its disappointment. Maybe that was the reason he'd brought the picture. *Look, we lived through that too.*

And they had.

She'd so wanted to stun the world by emerging with a perfect baby she'd not only produced but was giving away. She even had a quote she was going to give the newspaper if anyone called to do a story: 'I have been the beneficiary of other people's kindness. I wanted to give back.' If anyone pushed the matter and asked why she hadn't told anyone what she was doing, she planned to say: 'I wanted a little time alone with the baby. I knew I couldn't have it after she was born. So I did it this way.'

It sounded nice and maybe it was even true, but no one wanted her story or was calling for a quote now. It was a failed symbolic gesture, the most embarrassing kind of all.

The nurse wiped under her arms, down the inside of her arm, and into her palm. The water was cool enough to tingle wherever it travelled. She closed her eyes, and tears leaked down her face. *Will I ever stop crying?* she wondered.

The nurse, a middle-aged black woman, tall and pretty, with hair pulled back in a tight ponytail, said out of the blue, 'I did this too. Gave away a baby. You think you'll never get over it, but you do. It gets better. You'll see.'

Amy had noticed something. This whole time in the hospital, people talked very little about her disability. No one marvelled at her Pathway or asked silly questions about whether it had opinions of its own. It was like she'd moved on from the subject. The main topic of her life. The essay that required no research at all. Doing this, she'd moved on. New problems, new challenges. A whole new world.

A three-pound baby had arrived and changed the world.

CHAPTER THIRTY-FOUR

Amy had to stay in the hospital another three days to finish off the final round of IV antibiotics. The medicine made her groggy, but also made it harder for her to sleep at night, which meant she spent the day too tired to type much or respond to visitors. Matthew brought in books to read aloud, which seemed to help. First he brought his copy of *The Awakening*, which produced a smile and then an excited croak of laughter when he started to read. As he worked his way through it, she sighed and lifted her hand as if she were thinking of what she might say.

'"The beginning of things, of a world especially,"' he read, '"is necessarily vague, tangled, chaotic and exceedingly disturbing. How few of us ever emerge from such a beginning! How many souls perish in the tumult!"'

When he'd finished that (it wasn't a long book), she asked if he would go back home with her mother and find one of her old favourite books.

Behind her Nicole sighed. 'Oh, Amy, please no.'

'MOM MAKES FUN OF IT. SHE THINKS I'VE READ IT TOO MANY TIMES.'

'I'll get it, Aim,' Matthew said. 'I don't mind. What is it?'

'TELL ME –' Her hand slipped and accidentally pushed her Pathway on to the floor. It clattered noisily. Matthew bent to retrieve it. He tried to make it a point not to finish Amy's sentences or seem impatient when it was taking her a while to type out what she wanted to say. But now she was so weak he wondered if she'd appreciate the help. Nicole must have thought the same thing.

'*Tell Me You Love Me, Junie Moon,*' Nicole said.

Matthew laughed inadvertently. 'That's the name of it?'

Nicole nodded and suddenly he couldn't get over the surprise of it. Mother and daughter, staring at each other, blinking back tears. 'It's a love story,' Nicole said. 'Between three people who meet in a hospital. They're all disabled. The woman is burned with acid over her face and hands. One of the men is paralysed; the other one . . .' She looked at Amy. 'What was wrong with Arthur?' She nodded, though Amy hadn't indicated anything. 'That's right: he has a degenerative disease. But they've got high spirits and a plucky attitude and they decide to move out of the hospital and set up a little home for themselves.' She looked at Amy and remembered something else. 'Oh, and they get a dog.'

Why the tears? Matthew wondered, thinking this was the nicest conversation he'd ever had with Amy and Nicole together. Like something had changed between all of them. Nicole had stopped worrying that Matthew wasn't good enough.

The next day he started reading the book. Every time he stopped, Amy lifted her hand and rolled it in the air for him to keep going. Her head on the pillow, her eyes closed, she might have been asleep except for these protests if he stopped reading. Eventually he neared the end and understood what the tears had been about the day before. The trio of misfits had taken a vacation together where two of them, Arthur and Junie Moon, look at each other and realize, after a year of living side by side, that they love each other. As Matthew read, his voice grew thicker: '"Arthur thought: I wished I had loved her right from the beginning. Now so many days are lost and gone."' Matthew's voice wavered but he kept going. '"Looking at Junie Moon across the room, Arthur was overcome by such a passionate shyness that he had to turn his head. Calm your heart first, he thought, or it may have its own private fit and die. Then he thought: If I touch her we will both be blown to kingdom come."'

It was the end of a chapter, so he stopped reading. Instead of her hand lifting in protest, it reached over and found his. They sat like for a while, hands intertwined on top of the book. If he spoke, he knew his voice would betray him. It would crack and break and he'd start to cry. So they stayed just like that, as the light through the window drained from the sky.

Later that night, when her parents were in the cafeteria getting dinner, Amy surprised him. He thought she was asleep, and he was reading a book. He didn't see her typing until her Pathway began to speak.

'I WISH YOU COULD BE MY BOYFRIEND,' she said.

He raised his eyebrows in surprise. He wanted to say, *Aren't I already — well,* more *than that?* His name wasn't listed on Taylor's birth certificate, but in every other way, he was her birth father.

'Amy —' he said, and then she spoke again.

'I WISH I COULD FEEL YOUR BODY ON TOP OF

ME.' Her hand wasn't moving, nor were her eyes open, giving him the strange sensation that her computer was speaking with a mind of its own. But of course that wasn't possible.

She must have typed this in earlier and waited for the right moment to say it. He got up and stood next her bed. He took her bad hand in his so her good one was free to type. 'I'm not sure what you're saying.'

'I JUST SAID IT.'

'I know, but –' He turned and looked at the door. 'Now? You want me to do this now?'

'YES.'

'Your parents are coming back any minute. They just went to dinner.'

'I ASKED THEM TO STAY AWAY. FOR AN HOUR.' Her eyes opened. 'I WANTED TO BE ALONE WITH YOU.'

His heart began to hammer against his chest. 'Maybe I should sit down there.' He pointed to the bed beside her legs. 'I'm feeling a little dizzy.'

Her legs were easier to control lying down. She didn't have the spasms she used to. He remembered the time he once held her foot to look at a scrape and she kicked him in the shoulder. He wasn't worried about that now, though maybe that was a bad sign. Her body wasn't strong enough for its old flinchy battles. He hadn't seen her walk at all since the birth. He wondered if she still could.

'Amy, you know I –' He leaned closer to whisper. 'I *feel* like your boyfriend. I feel like *more* than that, actually.'

He waited for a long time. Finally she typed, 'GOOD.'

'But here's the important part, Amy. I feel like I want to always be here, with you. Helping. Like that should be my job or something. This is where I belong.' He couldn't help it. He started to cry as he said this. 'I'm not sure if I'll be good at very many things, but I'm good at this. I'm good when I'm with you.'

'YOU ARE.'

'And you're good with me.'

'I AM.'

As he spoke, he bent down, close to her face. He let his head drop, so his forehead rested on her shoulder. She typed while he caught his breath.

'ALL THIS AND WE'VE NEVER KISSED.'

He didn't lift his head. 'I know,' he said into her shoulder. 'I'm a little scared. But I will if you want to. Do you want to?'

'NOT AS MUCH AS I WANT TO FEEL YOU LYING ON TOP OF ME.'

He lifted his head up and looked at her, surprised. '*Really?*'

'YES. REALLY.'

'We couldn't – I mean, I couldn't take off my clothes.'

'NO. I WANT YOUR WEIGHT. I WANT TO FEEL YOU ON TOP OF ME. I DON'T KNOW WHY BUT I DO.' She started to cry.

'It's okay, Aim. I understand. I want that too.' He bent down so he could take his shoes off quickly without making a sound.

'I don't want to mess up any of your tubes,' he said.

'YOU WON'T.'

'Or the nurse call button. Let's not accidentally lie on top of *that*.'

'WE WON'T.'

They were smiling at each other now – their cheeks wet with tears. He took off his sweatshirt. 'Are you ready?'

She nodded and laughed. Her funny, barking laugh. He bent over, put his hands on either side of her shoulders, and looked her carefully in the eyes. 'You're *really sure* about this?'

She nodded again, not laughing this time. Dead serious.

It was strange then. The way his heart and brain raced at the same time as he lifted his legs on to the bed and gently lowered himself on top of her. He wondered if this was how it had been with Sanjay. If she was trying to erase one memory by creating another. He wondered what he would do if anything broke or collapsed beneath him – the bed, or Amy. He held himself up a little until she whispered in his ear. 'I fi–'

He understood and let himself relax down to his elbows.

'You're sure this is okay?' He didn't hear her breathing.

He held his own breath as if that might somehow help.

Then she surprised him: he felt her good hand on his back grasp his shirt and pull down. He relaxed down completely and let himself bury his face in her neck. She smelled surprisingly good. Fresh like spearmint.

'You smell great,' he whispered.

'Jack wa d ma hai–' she whispered.

He understood: *Jackie washed my hair.* Jackie was their favourite nurse. The one who'd given a baby away too. The one who'd said the main thing they both wanted to hear: *It's hardest in the beginning. It gets easier.*

'Fo you.'

She must have been planning this for a while, because hair washing was a production. Lying like this meant they couldn't look at each other. It gave him the courage to say something he'd been too shy to say so far. 'Thank you for sharing all this with me.' He lifted his head again so he could look at her. 'Thank you for letting me be here.'

Her eyes dropped away so it was impossible to tell what she was thinking. It was never easy with her limited range of facial expressions, but if he looked in her eyes, usually he could tell. Maybe he sounded too selfish. As if he were only thinking about how this affected him. He wasn't. He wanted her to know that he wasn't here to be nice or because he felt sorry for her. He wanted her to know it was much more than that. There weren't words, really, to explain it.

Her hand squeezed his shirt and pressed harder.

'Do you want me to do something else?' What else could he do? She was attached to machines. She'd just had a baby.

And then he thought of something. He lifted himself off her and raised the sheet. She wore a hospital gown and a strange pair of underwear – white mesh with a pad. 'How about if I get under this with you?'

She nodded. He was less tentative this time. He lay down beside her so he could touch her face and stroke her hair. He'd done all these things before, but never all at once like this. Lying side by side on the pillow, smiling like this, grinning foolishly; he didn't understand why he hadn't done this yet. The simplest thing of all – he leaned across the pillow and kissed her.

CHAPTER THIRTY-FIVE

That night Matthew went home and cooked dinner for a strange pairing: his mother and Mr Heffernan.

What's up with that? Sarah texted him. *Matchmaking much?*

It had been Amy's idea. After they'd finished laughing about it, they'd agreed it wasn't a terrible one. Mr Heffernan was very sweet, but socially awkward in ways that would cross him off many women's lists. But his mother didn't keep lists. She hadn't dated in years. Instead of dating, she watched TV and told Matthew she was fine.

Maybe she was. The first time he'd seen her cry in months was three nights before Taylor's birth, when no one knew what would happen and everyone was still so worried.

'I'm so proud of you,' she said as she blew her nose. 'I'm just so proud of you, that's all.'

The dinner went surprisingly well. As he told Amy the next day, 'Maybe Mr H talked a little too much about his fascination with photosynthesis, but, hey, he's a science teacher, right?'

Amy smiled, though she didn't respond.

'Afterwards they watched TV, which might sound a little depressing, but I don't think it was. She talked the whole time, filling him in on the story lines of her favourite shows.' Matthew hadn't stayed with them through that part. Instead he sat in the kitchen, surprised by how much his mother made Mr Heffernan laugh.

Now he looked down at Amy, whose head was turned

away from him. 'Is everything all right?' Matthew asked.

'NO TEMP,' she typed. 'MEANS I CAN GO. TODAY OR TOMORROW.'

He sat down on her bed. He knew this news was a mixed blessing and was happening sooner than they expected. Leaving the hospital meant leaving Taylor. It also meant Amy had to go somewhere. Mr Heffernan's house no longer made any sense. She would have to go home, and – she didn't need to tell him – that wasn't what she wanted.

For a few days now, he'd been thinking of a plan, though he hadn't readied any speech to go with it.

'Listen, Aim,' he said. His heart began to hammer in his chest. 'I've been thinking. Carlton, this guy I work with at the theatre, has his own apartment. Granted, he's twenty-six, which makes him a little pathetic to be working at a movie theatre, but he's a musician so whatever. But I keep thinking if he can do it with this movie-theatre job, maybe we could too. Maybe if I got a few extra shifts, we could afford an apartment. I know that sounds crazy, but maybe it's not crazy. That's what people do, right?' He was talking too quickly. Not giving her a chance to say anything. 'If they don't want to live with their parents for whatever reason, they move out. They live with their friends or their boyfriends. Right?'

'NO,' she finally said, over him.

He stopped talking. He waited for her to say something more. When she didn't, he stood up. 'Well, that's nice, Aim. Just no. That's it?'

'DON'T BE STUPID.'

Stupid? Is that what she just called him? He held up one

hand and moved towards the door. 'Okay, I'll see you later.'

'DON'T LEAVE.'

He stopped at the door and spun round, furious now. 'I make a nice offer. Not an easy offer, not one most people would expect, and you don't even say thanks. You call me stupid.'

'I'M GOING BACK TO SCHOOL.'

What? For two weeks she'd done nothing but tell him horror stories from school. 'No, Amy. Don't do that. That's a terrible idea –'

'NOT STANFORD. UC BERKELEY. SARAH'S HELPING ME ARRANGE IT.'

He sat down in a chair across the room. Another secret she hadn't told him.

'DID YOU KNOW UCB WAS THE FIRST ACCESSIBLE CAMPUS IN THE US? FIRST WITH A DISABILITY STUDIES PROGRAMME. THE ADA MOVEMENT STARTED THERE. IT'S GOOD. IT'S WHERE I BELONG.'

It took him a minute to remember what the ADA movement was – Americans with Disabilities Act. Amy spent last summer reading a book about the history of it. When he asked her about it once, she touched the cover and said, 'MY PEOPLE,' which silenced him at the time. What he could say? In the span of five minutes she'd made him feel small and ridiculous. Hatching his little plan of impoverished domesticity. Thinking he would make them dinners while they waited for new pictures of Taylor in the mail. Assuming Amy would settle for the small life that sounded appealing to him. 'Okay. Well, great. That sounds good.'

'I KNOW YOU'RE MAD.'

'I'm not mad. I'm happy for you.'

'NO, YOU'RE NOT.'

'You're right, I'm not. Look at what you're saying. It would be stupid to limit yourself to my pathetic prospects. I butter popcorn for a living. You're better than that.'

'I AM. SO ARE YOU.'

Suddenly he realized what this really was. Enraging. It was beyond enraging. 'You know what this feels like? I'm a great friend to get you through this little crisis. Where it was kind of about having Taylor and mostly about this face-off you needed to have with your mother. Because she didn't really let you go and do college the way you wanted to, so you had to make this big statement, right? The baby is the statement, right?' His voice was shaking. He thought of Taylor's little face in the bassinet and he hated what he was saying.

'NO –'

'Only you got sad and lonely and you needed me so you could feel better about yourself because all of this made you feel pretty terrible about yourself, right? You needed me so you could feel better about going back and trying again at a different school. I'm right, aren't I? You've been planning this for a while, only you haven't said anything.'

'YES – BUT –'

'And you didn't tell me any of this because I'm so pathetic, I can't deal with this idea of college. It's all I can do to keep my shit together and show up for a four o'clock shift selling candy to fat people.'

'THAT'S NOT WHAT I THINK.'

'Yes, it is. Just say it.' He was talking too loud now. Pacing around the end of her bed.

'ALL RIGHT. IT IS. A LITTLE.'

'Well, screw you, Amy!' he screamed. 'Have you even wondered why I haven't left here at four o'clock since you've been here? Are you curious why you haven't seen my greasy polyester smock at all? I had to quit! I had to be here! I didn't have a choice! So there you have it. I'm not even your sad friend with the loser job. I'm just your sad friend.'

He didn't walk straight out of the hospital from there. He couldn't bring himself to. Instead he went to the bathroom beside the NICU (neonatal intensive care unit). He washed his hands and his face and he suited up with everything he needed to put on: paper booties, face mask, hair cap, smock. Then he shuffled over to the bassinet and asked to hold Taylor.

He hadn't let himself hold her yet. He'd only stood outside the nursery and stared at others doing it. He was waiting for Amy's fever to break so they could be together the first time they both held her. Never mind all that now. He showed the nurse the ID he'd got right after her birth. She nodded and said, 'She's right over here. Now's a good time because she's just about to try a little feeding . . .' So far Sue and Jim had done all the bottle feeding, but, surprisingly, now they weren't around. 'Why don't you settle into the rocking chair and I'll bring her to you.'

It only took a few minutes and suddenly Taylor was there, in his arms. She felt like a weightless bundle of blankets, hardly anything except for a tiny face peeking out of the swaddle and wide-open eyes, staring right at him. He didn't panic or wait to hear the voice in his head. He just stared back and memorized the face he knew he might only see in photographs after this.

CHAPTER THIRTY-SIX

Matthew was right about a lot of things, except for this: Amy *had* thought about staying here with him. She had even thought about living together. They could do it, she knew. If they'd got through the prom debacle and Taylor's birth, they might be able to live together someday. The problem was this: she didn't want a marriage like her parents had, with her mother so fixated on one thing she hardly looked up and noticed the man across the table making it happen. Amy didn't want to become her mother, who quit her law practice the day Amy was born. She didn't want to give up everything for a love that became too all-consuming. 'You are my job,' her mother used to say. 'You are my life's work.' It always made Amy want to say, *You can't turn a person into a job, Mom. People don't pay enough . . .* Then Matthew said something similar, and it scared her. *I feel like this is where I belong, and what I'm meant to be doing. Taking care of you.*

This was where Matthew was wrong. She *had* thought about all of this, and she knew the problems that lay ahead. Her body's needs were boring; no one should have to take care of them exclusively. He could do so much more. So could she.

Amy knew what she'd wanted to say to him. She'd thought about it this whole week. It was the most important conversation they would ever have, and when the time came to have it she'd said virtually nothing. She'd let Matthew walk out. She'd gone backwards to the non-verbal girl she'd once been, the same one who got to college and never figured out how to speak in public.

She couldn't remember having ever failed so badly at something. And then she thought of a letter Mr Heffernan wrote to her mother, back in seventh grade.

I worry what will happen if she doesn't learn what it feels like to not succeed. *Has Amy ever failed at something? If not, she should learn how. It's an important lesson.*

Maybe he was right. She had to learn this. So did Matthew. Maybe it would mean they'd never find their way back to each other. Never be as close as they had been this week. Maybe she'd never feel the glorious comfort of him lying on top of her. She'd loved that moment so much. If it never happened again, it was hard to imagine feeling the same way with anyone else.

But she couldn't stay here.

The best she could say was: If all this was a test of her ability to articulate herself clearly when it mattered most, then she was following Mr Heffernan's suggestion five years ago. She was learning how to fail.

For two weeks, Matthew didn't leave the house. He couldn't bear to. There were too many babies everywhere, which created a new fear – that if he looked at all of them he'd forget Taylor's face. It wasn't a completely irrational fear. Newborn babies had more in common with one another than they did with the parents pushing them around in their elaborate car-seat strollers. They all had the same quizzical expressions on their face; they all had little hands curled into fists. It made no *sense* to feel the loss of one more than any other, so he felt it every time he passed any baby.

'It makes me *mad*,' he told Beth during his next session with her. 'I wish I didn't feel it. I don't even get it. I only spent a week with her. I only knew about her for two weeks.'

'How do you think Amy's dealing with all this?' Beth asked.

He wouldn't know. She'd written to him once, but he'd deleted the message without reading it. If he read it, he feared he would lose the resolve of his anger, which was important to hold on to. He wanted to make his point: that Amy couldn't use him whenever she needed a friend. This was the problem with the way their friendship had started. There was an imbalance from the beginning. He loved being needed in some of the surprising ways she needed someone. He liked taking care of her, and later, after she started giving him 'assignments', he liked being her project. He tried to explain it to his mother once. 'Our weaknesses aligned pretty well. We filled each other's gaps.'

Then he discovered saying things like this didn't help him hold on to his anger. Saying things like this made him cry for an embarrassing twenty minutes straight.

Days bled into one another without him doing much of anything. He didn't go into work or try to get his job back. He didn't say much when his mother asked what he was thinking about for next year. 'Should we get some college applications? See what they look like?' she said once.

'I know what they look like, Mom. They look like forms online that you have to fill out.'

Christmas came and went and he remembered nothing that happened except a fleeting feeling of victory that he'd got through the day, made ten times worse by Jana, his father's new wife, explaining to her sister and parents, 'Matthew's just had a falling out with a very good friend, so he's feeling sad today.'

Nothing was a conversation stopper quite like that.

He got through it, and January rolled in with its white-grey skies and endless rain. On TV, he and his mom watched the news, which had footage of mudslides around Southern California, carrying houses down rocky embankments. It startled him, watching that. Houses could move these days and he couldn't.

Or at least he hadn't, in almost a month.

It made him feel terrible. Like if he wasn't careful this really could become the rest of his life. He'd be one of those strange sons who lives with his mother until they both become so old they look like a couple shopping once a week and bickering in the grocery story about their purchases.

That could happen, he knew. She'd gone out to dinner once with Mr Heffernan. When she came home, she said they'd had a lovely time but were probably better off thinking of each other as friends. 'Good friends,' she said, which made Matthew think about Amy. He and Amy had never really been anything more than that, and look at how that much had destroyed him. *Good friends?* he wanted to say. *You'd better be careful.*

His mother wanted him to move on with his life, but not so desperately that she'd force him. If he was still here five years from now, she would probably pass him the remote control and ask him what kind of soup he'd like for dinner. She didn't want that for him, but, if it happened, so be it. She wouldn't push him out of this house or this life.

He'd have to do it for himself.

Finally in late January he rode his bike to the La Tierra movie theatre. It was four o'clock when he got there. Mr Ilson stood outside wearing one of his stupid suits, holding his janitorial ring of keys.

'Hi!' Matthew said, too loud.

It had been a few days since he talked to anyone beside his mother. They often talked too loud, because the TV was always on.

'Well, look who it is.' Mr Ilson held a hand up to block the sun in his eyes. 'Nice to see you again.' He didn't step forward to shake Matthew's hand (because Mr Ilson never shook hands), but Matthew could tell he was happy to see him. 'So we've missed you a little bit. I forgot how bad the nacho machine could get. Everyone else is pretty much a surface cleaner.'

'Not me.' Matthew nodded.

'Not you, Matthew. That's right.' He unlocked the door and held it open. 'You want to come in?'

Matthew assumed his job had been filled. He didn't even have a job, really; he had a few shifts that anyone else could have done as well as he did. He'd come back to say hi to whoever was working. To see if anything had changed, to 'visit' like he remembered other ex-employees doing over the summer when they were home from college. You knew they'd once worked there by the way they reached round and helped themselves to popcorn.

'You looking for some shifts again?' Mr Ilson said. 'I can go back to my office and see what I've got.'

Matthew wasn't sure if he was saying this out of pity or not. Surely he knew if he had open shifts. Probably he would go back and say he was sorry; he had nothing open. He was just pretending to be nice.

'Sure, thanks,' Matthew said. Standing alone in the lobby was strange. One of the last times he was here, he'd stayed late and played truth or dare with Hannah in the beanbag chairs behind the screen. It wasn't a bad memory; it just felt like it had happened a long time ago to a different person.

'Oh my God! Matthew!' It was Hannah, in the doorway, wearing a bike helmet. She looked good – friendly and sweaty and happy to see him.

'Hi, Hannah.'

'Are you back or just visiting?'

'Just visiting, I think. But we'll see – he's checking the schedule.'

She walked towards the employee changing room. 'That means he wants you back!' She flashed a thumbs-up and disappeared. He remembered the rules and looked at his watch. They weren't allowed to clock in before they had their smock on and their hair up. If they took too long changing, they got docked for being late. 'Rules are rules,' Mr Ilson always said. 'I didn't make them up.'

It would be nice to come back here. To have someone else make up rules that everyone was following, not just him.

No jeans. No open sandals. White shirts only under smocks. No smoking. No eating. Some rules were 'soft rules', which meant no one paid attention to them, like the no-eating rule. Everyone ate. And the 'no hanging around after work hours' could have been rewritten slightly to say 'no hanging around after work hours unless these people are your friends and you feel like it'.

Hannah came back out, dressed in her unflattering smock, hair pulled back. 'Let me punch in,' she said. When she returned, she surprised him. She didn't go behind the counter to start her shift inventory on drink cups and candy. She came over and hugged him. The longest hug he'd had in a while.

'I'm sorry about everything you've gone through. We've all been thinking about you and hoping you'd come back.' Finally it occurred to him: *Chloe must have told everyone. That's why they're all being so nice.*

He smiled into Hannah's hair. It was nice of her to say, though it couldn't possibly be true. Unless they missed making fun of him behind his back.

'Carlton wrote a song about you,' Hannah said. 'His band really likes it and they're going to play it at their next gig. It's called "Mr Careful". The chorus goes, "Mr Careful takes care/Wherever he goes/He doesn't leave traces/So nobody knows/What's in his head or in his heart/He lives in this world and lives apart. But if you look close/There it is, you can see/His heart. His heart".'

She had a pretty voice, much nicer than he expected. She must have practised a little, waiting to sing it to him.

'Wow,' he said. 'That's nice. I like it.'

'He wants everyone to know he's not gay or anything. It's not a love song.'

'Right, no.'

'It's a story song. He made up some parts.'

'That's fine. Do you want me to help you start inventory?'

'I guess. Sure.'

After they'd made six stacks of twenty cups, Mr Ilson appeared. 'Good news!' he said. 'I can put you on two shifts a week to start. Not tonight, though. Renalda's coming in tonight. She's new. No comments, Hannah. We're still not too sure about Renalda.' He held up a flat stop-sign hand. 'Don't push me on this, Hannah. I've got Matthew on Friday night with you, and Wednesday afternoon with Carlton. That's the best I can do.'

For the first time in months, Matthew felt like he could understand what wasn't being said directly. Hannah had pushed for this.

Maybe Carlton too.

If he comes back, you have to give him another chance, they must have said.

And why would they have done that unless they liked him a little? He didn't want to start crying, so he forced himself not to think of something Amy had said in the hospital: *People like you, Matthew. They do. You have to start seeing that, sooner or later. It's a waste if you don't.*

He wouldn't waste this. Any of it.

He didn't want to any more. He wanted to help Hannah count her cups and her candy, and ask if she was closing tonight. If she was, he'd offer to give her a ride home. Midnight was too late for anyone to take a bus home in the dark, he was almost sure. He wasn't being Mr Crazy-Careful to offer to come back and give her a ride. He was being thoughtful. He was being a friend. And, if she wanted to kiss him after he dropped her off, so be it.

CHAPTER THIRTY-SEVEN

For almost two months, Amy spent most of her days sleeping in her room. When her mother finally came in, sat down on her bed and said, 'We're taking you to a doctor to treat this depression,' Amy didn't protest.

At the doctor's office she didn't say much. Talking required energy, and she didn't have much. When he asked how often she thought about her baby, she managed to type, 'ALL THE TIME,' which was true. At least she dreamed about her all the time, and since she slept so much it seemed like the same thing. Every night she imagined nursing Taylor; every morning she woke up, her breasts soft and empty and aching.

She'd never felt so unmoored by anything in her life.

Finally Amy told the doctor the truth: 'I WISH I'D KEPT MY BABY. I KNOW IT'S TOO LATE NOW, BUT I STILL WISH I'D DONE IT.'

In the end, the doctor wrote her a prescription that didn't do much except help her sleep without dreams haunted by babies. She couldn't bear to think about Matthew, because she vaguely understood that she'd done something terrible to him. She'd talked about moving on, and starting school again as if everything they'd gone through together – having this baby, giving her up – would be nothing from which to recover. She'd been wrong about that. She'd also been wrong to diminish everything he'd done on her behalf – coming to the hospital, sitting at her bedside.

Christmas came and went. Her grandmother visited, and

her aunt from Boise, Idaho. Someone cooked a duck. Other people made bread pudding that Amy tried to eat but couldn't.

In the first week of January, a package arrived from UC Berkeley, welcoming Amy as a transfer student. The semester started at the end of January, meaning Amy had been home for almost two months and on medication for one. She didn't know if she could survive starting a new school, but she was fairly sure she wouldn't survive her only other option: staying home all semester.

None of it was easy. Packing up and driving six hours north. Registering for classes at a huge university. Navigating a campus that was five times the size of Stanford. It helped that this time she was in a real dorm, the handicapped-accessible one with two wheelchair users on her floor. Compared to them, her motorized scooter manoeuvred like a dream and went twice as fast. She felt like a show-off every time she passed one of them coming or going to class, but they didn't seem to mind. They always waved, and she beeped her horn to say hi.

She was surprised to discover that her favourite class by far was playwriting, which met once a week for three hours. There were fifteen students enrolled and an ensemble of student actors there to perform the scenes the writers brought in. From the very first class, Amy couldn't get over the miracle of hearing her words read aloud by real people. The wonder of inflection! Of a real person delivering one of her jokes with comic timing!

She loved watching actors play with her lines – deliver them one way, then change their minds and try another. It was almost like the thrill she felt in fourth grade when she got a DynaVox, her first talking computer, and then again with the Pathway, her first computer that sounded (more or less) human. But this was even better – her words being spoken by real people.

Unfortunately none of her early playwriting efforts were very successful. Her comic monologue had some good lines, but overall fell flat; her two-character confrontation – old people fighting over a bench – was overwritten and screechy. The teacher didn't soft-pedal his critiques for Amy. ('A comedy should never look like it's trying too hard . . . The conflict was compelling but I'm not sure these *characters* were . . .') Amy hated the fact that she wasn't good at this right away. With every failure she flew back to her room and started a new play.

By March, she was writing all the time, at the expense of all her other classes. Some nights, she stayed up until one or two o'clock in the morning writing. She could say this much: for the first time since she'd had her, Amy went a whole night, and then two, without dreaming of Taylor. Instead she dreamed about writing bad plays that everyone she'd ever known showed up to watch. She also dreamed about failing every other class she was taking.

That dream almost became a reality as she got more obsessed with her theatre class. She couldn't help it. She couldn't get over the fascination and frustration of writing scenes that were almost good, but not quite. She spent one weekend reading the entire textbook (*Scenes for Student Playwrights*) and another weekend buying and reading more plays online. She'd never heard of Mamet until she fell in love with him over the course of a long Sunday spent happily holed up in her dorm room.

By the following week, she'd produced her own Mamet homage, abounding with expletives and unfinished sentences. 'THE SWEARING IS ESSENTIAL,' she told her classmates the next week because she felt that it was.

'Amy's finding her own voice,' the teacher said afterwards. 'This is part of that process.'

Amy interpreted his remarks to mean, *Another failure but closer.* Then he added this: 'I'd be curious what would happen if Amy wrote her final one-act on a subject closer to home. It wouldn't necessarily need to be true, just something inspired by her own experience. For some people that produces weaker, self-conscious writing. For others, it produces by far their best. Everyone should try it at least once and see.'

A boy in the back who wrote exclusively science-fiction vignettes that read like video games without special effects groaned in protest, but Amy went home that night and started something new.

She wrote a ten-minute play about an agoraphobic boy who hadn't left his house in over six months, and his old friend, a girl, who tries to talk him into going out to dinner with her. When she read it over the next morning, something happened that she never expected. She found herself crying.

A week later, hearing it read aloud in class, she almost cried again. After the scene ended, no one spoke for a few minutes.

Finally the teacher said, 'Lovely work, Amy. Just lovely.'

The short-play festival for which it was selected was meant to showcase the work of theatre majors, which Amy wasn't yet.

'I'LL DECLARE TODAY,' she said to the teacher when he told her she'd been selected.

'Only if you're sure this is what you want to do.'

'YES,' she typed quickly. 'I'M SURE.'

She didn't know many drama majors, but she liked the ones she'd met. They filled a room in ways that took her out of her own head. Around them, with all their many eccentricities, she didn't feel disabled so much as eccentric in a different way. *You talk with your hands flying around your body and I talk with this computer.*

The three weeks of rehearsal were intense and overwhelming and some nights she hardly slept at all. Working so intensely with such a small group of people made her think of Matthew and the group he'd found working at the movie theatre. A week before opening, she wrote him a note:

To: mstheword@gmail.com
From: aimhigh@comcast.net
Re: what I'm doing . . .

I'm a playwright now! It's only a twenty-minute one-act, but I made it into the Shorts Festival, which means it's getting a full production with a director and actors and a set design too! Objectively speaking, it's not the best play of the evening, but it's not the worst one, either! And I'm the only freshman writer included, which might mean something? I know you can't come up and see it, but part of me wishes you could. Part of me wishes we'd ended things differently so I could say, 'Matthew, I'd love you to see this so I could see you.'

She sent it before she could think about it too much. Who could be sure if he'd even open it and read it? She'd sent him messages before and hadn't heard back.

Probably he wouldn't.

Which was fine, she told herself. Even if it wasn't fine. Even if none of it would seem real unless he came and saw it. Because she'd written it for him. To say what she'd been trying to tell him all along.

CHAPTER THIRTY-EIGHT

It wasn't really an invitation, Matthew thought. It didn't include dates or times or anything like that. It was typical Amy – full of feeling without too much in the way of practical logistics. Still, he was curious. He looked up UC Berkeley Shorts Festival online and discovered it was running the same weekend that Hannah would be away at her cousin's wedding. 'They said I could bring you,' she'd told him. 'But I'm not sure I should. Considering everything. Then years from now people in my family will keep asking me about you. I'm just not sure that's a good idea.'

Matthew wasn't sure what Hannah meant by this; he only knew that in the few months they'd been semi-dating he'd mostly been a disappointment to her. He didn't call when she expected him to; he bowed out of most of the group activities. The one time he went with everyone to see one of Carlton's shows, he had a mini panic attack on the mosh-pit dance floor. She found him outside, sitting on a kerb still trying to calm down.

He took it as a sign that Amy's play was running the same weekend Hannah wasn't taking him to a wedding. *Maybe you're meant to go*, his old voice told him. These days it was interesting: sometimes his voice told him to do things he wanted to do. *You probably owe her at least that much.*

His first surprise: Nicole offered him a ride when he called them to find out the times of the play. He'd been researching buses, which took between eight and twelve hours depending on which schedule you looked at. Then there was the matter of navigating a strange city once he got off the bus. It was all a little harrowing, like the old challenges Amy gave him last year. This felt like one of those, only Amy didn't even realize she'd given him a challenge.

'We'd be happy to have you ride with us,' Nicole said. 'We could even keep it a secret and surprise Amy when we get there.'

Is she serious? his voice asked, and then it answered itself: *Yes, she might not like you that much but she appreciates everything you did last winter. You shouldn't say no just because it sounds awkward to sit in a car with her.*

'Thank you so much,' he heard himself say. 'That would be great.'

As it turned out, the car ride was pretty awkward. They were classical-music fans, which he thought meant it was okay to talk as they listened to music, but apparently not. Finally Nicole said, 'We've been looking forward to listening to this sonata, Matthew, if you don't mind.'

As they got closer (and the music ended) they talked a little more. Nicole told him that Amy had really thrown herself into the drama programme at Berkeley. 'She's already saying this is what she wants to major in . . .'

Matthew couldn't tell how Nicole felt about this. Probably not all that happy.

'We worry of course about whether she'll ever find a career in this. Or even get paid.' She was trying to smile, he could see.

'I think she could,' Matthew said. 'People are fascinated by Amy. Look at all the newspapers and TV stations that did a story on her getting into college. I bet the same thing will happen when she writes a play. People want to know what she thinks.'

He was surprised at how certain he sounded.

Nicole smiled from the front seat. 'I hope you're right, Matthew.'

The theatre lobby was crowded, but it wasn't hard to find Amy, sitting in a scooter with a small basket on the front that already had a bouquet of roses in it. Matthew felt nervous and a little stupid. He hadn't even thought about bringing flowers.

Amy looked beautiful. Older, and draped in a theatrical, fringed scarf that looked great on her. They'd got there a little late, though. The show was starting so quickly that Amy could only wave in surprise before they went in to get their seats.

They were in the fifth row, across the aisle and behind the cut-out space where Amy parked her scooter. Before her play started, he spent almost as much time watching her face as he did watching the actors. He had no idea what she was thinking or if she was happy that he'd come.

Amy's play was the second to last one. It was called *Alone Together*, and was about a boy with agoraphobia, and his friend – a wildly dressed, bubbly, sort of hyperactive girl – trying to convince him to go out to dinner with her. For a while, it was funny. He kept saying, 'No, thank you, I'd prefer not to,' and she kept calling him Bartleby the Scrivener, a story he read over the summer at Amy's recommendation.

Apparently the whole audience had read it as well, because everyone around him laughed at the joke.

Matthew felt self-conscious sitting there next to Nicole. He dreaded where the scene was headed – the boy hasn't walked outside in six months; the girl keeps trying to talk him into doing it. There was even a doorway built into the set that the girl kept pointing to. 'Let's just try it,' she says. 'Let's walk into the hallway.'

Of course it made Matthew nervous. Everyone watching a jokey version of his own terrible struggles a year ago. That panic attack in yearbook. And later at prom. Then it was interesting – the actor didn't play the panicky part. He didn't sweat or shake. He simply sat on the sofa and refused to move. 'I'm not ready,' he said. 'I'll let you know when I am.'

The more the girl pleaded, the more she seemed like the crazy one.

'This is my life, not yours,' he said. 'I'm allowed to make the choices I want to make.'

She stood in the hallway and pleaded. She dangled money and food. She promised him all sorts of favours and rewards if he'd walk outside with her and eat dinner in a restaurant.

'No, thank you,' he said. 'I'd prefer to stay here.'

Finally she got mad and stormed out. She cried in the hallway and screamed at him for almost four solid minutes. By that point, Matthew had to admit it was an effective piece of theatre: watching the actor register the drama taking place offstage. A slow smile spread over his face, as if he knew what was coming: finally the screaming stopped and the girl came back in, carrying a bag of food. 'Move over,' she said, sitting down on the sofa beside him. Then – this was the part he liked best – they moved on to other topics. She had a story to tell him; he had one to tell her.

It was about acceptance, he thought. About realizing no one is perfect and no one can expect to change someone else. Which was a nice message, but also – he had to admit – sort of a confusing one. Did she really think he hadn't changed at all? What about everything that happened in the hospital? This was a play about friends, and hadn't they been more than that?

After it was over, Matthew waited in a small line in front of Amy's scooter. 'It was a great play, Aim,' he said when it was finally his turn to talk to her. He hugged her, though it meant bending over, which was awkward.

'NOT REALLY.'

'It *was*. It reminded me a little bit of that book I read you.'

'JUNIE MOON? REALLY?'

'You know. Oddballs finding each other.'

'IT'S A THEME I ENJOY.'

'You do it well.' He smiled and then looked away. There was more to say, but he didn't want to do it here. Other people were lining up behind him. 'I can't believe you wrote this thing and took three classes. How did you sleep?'

She made a funny gesture with her hand, something he'd never seen before. He realized she was telling him to lean closer so she could say something softly. 'I GOT TERRIBLE GRADES THIS TERM. DON'T TELL MY PARENTS.'

He laughed because he knew: 'terrible' for her probably meant Bs.

'MOSTLY I JUST WROTE THIS THING. THAT'S ALL I'VE DONE THIS YEAR.'

He looked at her. 'Not *all*.' He wanted to ask if she kept Taylor's picture next to her bed the way he did. The latest one had a big, toothless smile. She looked so happy it was hard not to smile when he saw it.

'NO. YOU'RE RIGHT. NOT ALL.'

He couldn't say Taylor's name here. It might make one or both of them cry, and he didn't want that. 'Are you thinking about coming home this summer?' He tried to make it sound like a casual question, even if it wasn't. 'You know, just for a visit.'

'YES. I'LL BE HOME FOR THE WHOLE SUMMER. I HAVE ANOTHER PLAY I WANT TO WORK ON.'

'That's great, Aim.' He was happy to hear this, but he was also aware of the line forming behind him. 'I should probably go. I'll talk to you maybe, when you get home.' He held up a hand in one of his horribly awkward windshield–wiper waves. He felt like a cartoon character miming, *See ya!*

Then she did something else he'd never seen before: her bad hand shot out and caught his shirt. 'WAIT,' she typed. She kept holding his shirt. 'JUST WAIT.'

She couldn't let him just leave. Not after four months of waiting.

She nodded to the people standing around him. With one hand still clinging to his shirt, she typed, 'WILL YOU EXCUSE ME? I NEED TO TALK TO MY FRIEND.'

He blushed, but it worked. The other people walked away.

She steered her scooter over to a corner of the greenroom with an empty chair on which Matthew could sit. 'I DIDN'T KNOW YOU WERE COMING. I HAVE THINGS I WANT TO SAY BUT THEY'RE NOT TYPED IN –'

'I know. I'm sorry. Your mom wanted to make it a surprise. Which sort of surprised me, obviously.' While she typed, he kept talking. 'We drove up together and I have to say, it wasn't as bad as I thought it would be. Only about a six on a scale of ten for uncomfortable. Maybe a seven in the middle there . . .'

Amy stopped typing for a moment and pressed Play. 'BEFORE I LEFT THE HOSPITAL, YOU WERE RIGHT WHEN YOU SAID I HAD TAYLOR AS A WAY TO PROVE SOMETHING TO MY MOM. BUT I ALSO WANTED TO TELL YOU SOMETHING. I WAS TRYING TO SAY IT ALL YEAR.'

'What?'

'THAT I LOVE YOU.'

He smiled. And then he looked away and laughed. 'You got pregnant with someone else's child as a way of telling me you loved me?'

'IT WAS BYZANTINE, I'LL ADMIT. NOT THE CLEAREST WAY TO DELIVER MY MESSAGE.'

'Maybe not.'

'BEING FRIENDS WITH YOU MADE ME FEEL LIKE I COULD DO MORE THAN I EVER REALIZED.' Did he understand what she was saying? She was typing as fast as possible, but the room was crowded and this was hard. 'I NEED TO BE HERE FOR SCHOOL, BUT I KNOW

320

I'LL NEVER LOVE ANYONE ELSE THE WAY I LOVE YOU.'

For a long time he didn't say anything. He still smiled a little, like he didn't mind hearing this, so she kept going:

'I DON'T THINK I'LL EVER TRY TO DATE. I DON'T SEE THE POINT.'

'Well, I'm trying it,' he said, and then laughed a little. But this obviously wasn't funny.

She hadn't expected this. 'YOU'RE DATING SOMEONE?'

'A little,' he said, and drew a deep breath. 'And there isn't really much of a point. What I've learned is that I have certain qualities that are annoying to other people.'

She typed without looking away from him. 'SO DO I.'

'Like, really annoying. I had a soda thrown at me.'

'OH, MATTHEW.'

'I know, right? One time she told me I wasn't over you or something like that.'

'WHAT DO YOU THINK SHE MEANT BY THAT?'

'That I wasn't over you, I guess. Or that maybe I loved you, I don't know.'

He was really smiling now. They both looked away. It was too much to look at each other, with everything they were saying.

He took her good hand and squeezed it, then bent down so his mouth was close to her ear. 'You're going to be a great playwright someday,' he whispered. 'You're going to think of all the right things to say.' He had her hand so she couldn't say anything back. She turned so her cheek touched his lips. They stayed like that. Him breathing next to her cheek, pressing his nose to her hair. She felt his touch all through her body.

'Let's have a nice summer,' he whispered. 'Let's start with that.'

ACKNOWLEDGEMENTS

Countless thanks to my dearest early readers: Mike Floquet, Melinda Reid, Monty McGovern, Elizabeth McGovern, Valle Dwight, Carrie McGee, Katie and Bill McGovern, Charlie Floquet and Matilda Curtis. All of them have contributed invaluable comments.

Thanks to Eric Simonoff, who read too many early drafts of stories with this character and, even so, remained enthusiastic. Thanks to Margaret Riley King, who found a home for the final draft and has done such a wonderful job ushering me into this world of young-adult publishing.

A million thanks to Tara Weikum, who has edited this book with astonishing care and has made HarperCollins feel like a wonderful new home filled with bright people like Christina Colangelo, Chris Hernandez, Susan Katz and Kate Jackson.

Across the seas, many thanks to Rachel Petty at Macmillan Children's Books for her enthusiastic support of this book and for providing such careful notes and a home away from home.

I am very grateful to you all.

FANGIRL

Cath and Wren are identical twins and until recently they did absolutely everything together. Now they're off to university and Wren's decided she doesn't want to be one half of a pair any more – she wants to dance, meet boys, go to parties and let loose. It's not so easy for Cath. She would rather bury herself in the fanfiction she writes where there's romance far more intense than anything she's experienced in real life.

Now Cath has to decide whether she's ready to open her heart to new people and new experiences, and she's realizing that there's more to learn about love than she ever thought possible . . .

A tale of fanfiction, family and first love

RAINBOW ROWELL

Stella

HELEN EVE

Seventeen-year-old Stella Hamilton is the star blazing at the heart of Temperley High School. Leader of a maliciously exclusive elite, she is surrounded by adulation – envied and lusted after in equal measure. And she is in the final stage of a five-year campaign to achieve her destiny: love with her equally popular male equivalent, and triumph as Head Girl on election night.

By contrast, new girl Caitlin Clarke has until now lived a quietly conformist life in New York. With the collapse of her parents' marriage, she has been sent across the Atlantic for an English boarding school education, only to discover that at Temperley the only important rules are the unwritten ones. It's a world of the beautiful and the dangerous, and acceptance means staying on the right side of Stella Hamilton, the most beautiful and dangerous of them all.

Not everyone is happy to be under the Hamilton rule. But fighting the system means treading the same dark path as Stella – and if Caitlin puts a foot wrong, it's a long way to fall.